GORILLAZ IN THE BAY 2

De'Kari

Lock Down Publications and Ca$h Presents
Gorillaz in the Bay 2
A Novel by De'Kari

De'Kari

Lock Down Publications
P.O. Box 870494
Mesquite, Tx 75187

Visit our website
www.lockdownpublications.com

Lock Down Publications
Like our page on Facebook: Lock Down Publications @
www.facebook.com/lockdownpublications.ldp
Cover design and layout by: **Dynasty Cover Me**
Book interior design by: **Shawn Walker**
Edited by: **Tammy Jernigan**

Stay Connected with Us!

Text **LOCKDOWN** to 22828 to stay up-to-date with new releases, sneak peeks, contests and more…

De'Kari

Gorillaz in the Bay 2

PROLOGUE
2012

The sounds of Dem Hoodstarz newest release "How I Really Feel", blasted through the ultra-sonic Bose audio system.

/If you don't know you probably neva will / I'm just saying though I could show you how a youngsta feel /

/I'm drinking death and I'm smoking kill / I'm just saying though I can show you how I really feel /

Voorheeze sat low with the driver's seat leaned back. A bottle of Remy Martin XO in one hand, a 45 Dragoon Colt resting on his lap and tears running down his face. How the fuck did shit get this crazy, he wondered. Everything was all good at first, Niggaz were on top of the world. The next thing a nigga knew, the bodies started dropping.

This wasn't how it was supposed to be. He didn't have any misconception about this shit like most of these fake niggaz. They had life and bullshit fucked up. With their backward ass thoughts that the game was all glamour, money, cars and bitches. He knew that this shit was full of ups and downs, wins and losses! Because of that he always expected a loss or two, hell he even accepted them.

It was as if the "Game God or the forces that Be" had to spank you every now and then if niggaz couldn't. That's how shit stayed balanced. It's almost like for every few wins you had to take a loss. If niggaz couldn't dish out your losses, then the Game God would. It's that simple, pluses and minuses! That was life's way of keeping the scales balanced. But that wasn't what the fuck had happened. It actually played out completely different. That's what was fucking with his head.

He tilted the bottle and took another long guzzle. The hot brown liquid no longer burned his throat. He was working on his second bottle already. But no matter how much he drank, it did not ease his pain like he was hoping. He had lost too many of the people he loved! As he sat in his 1970 Chevy SS in front of the church at another funeral, nostalgia of Deja-vu hit him.

Just a few years ago he sat right in the same exact spot getting ready to attend the funeral for T'Rida. Today he was here to bury another brother. As the rain drops splashed and bounced off his windshield, Scoots verse began...

/half empty Remy Martin bottle, smoking kill / rain drops on my windshield, I clutch steel / Let me tell you how I really feel.... / when the stage lights go off, and the red carpet disappear...

De'Kari

It felt like it was Voorheeze's soul that was spitting the hurtful and heart-felt lyrics. Involuntarily he gripped the handle of the Dragoon. The pain was too real. As he sat and reminisced, rage burned in his heart and his blood began to boil. He was ready to kill whatever, who-ever, whenever and however!

/Tonight, I aint fucking wit no champagne / I got Patron problems. Remy Martin issues nigga dis real pain!"/

He took another swig. He just didn't give a fuck anymore! Voor-heeze was truly the epitome of death right at that moment. He took another gulp of his misery tamer. He thought to himself how true the words were "Nigga dis real pain". Too many members of his family had died. Members of a family that was supposed to be untouchable.

Everyone was already in the church waiting on him. They all knew how hard the young killa was taking the loss of his brother, no one dared to interrupt him! His mood was too fucked up.

This shit would be answered in the worst way possible, he vowed. The Summer of Blood was nothing compared to the shit that Jason Voorheeze was about to unleash on mothafuckas! He wasn't about to let anybody breathe! It was murking season. And when the smoke cleared, for the first time in his life he didn't care if he was still stand-ing!

/A week ago, my Uncle Chucky lost his wife / the same week my Uncle Melvin lost his life / Den Man Man got murdered, one-week later G-Boi got tortured / ...."

Fuck what bitch niggaz talk about, real niggaz cry. It's an unspo-ken fact that gangsta's cry too. Most don't know this but it's true. The only difference is when Gangsta's cry, mothafuckas die. Voorheeze couldn't remember the last time he cried, but he was crying now. After this funeral a whole lot of mothafuckas were going to cry.

"Man fuck it! Let's get this shit over with", he said to himself. Then he took one last gulp.

As he reached for the cap to the bottle he thought he caught move-ment in his rearview mirror. The distraction caused him to knock the cap onto the floor. He stared intently into the rearview but didn't see anyone. So, he leaned down to pick up the bottle cap. That one move saved his life!

BOCCA!

In one split second the passenger window shattered, he heard the blast of the gun as a hollow-tip flew past his head, missing him by inches. With no hesitation he palmed the big revolver.

BOOM! BOOM! BOOM!

Gorillaz in the Bay 2

He let out three rapid shots through the passenger side glassless window. Before the third shot entered the would-be killa's body, Voorheeze's free hand was gripping the handle of the driver's side door.

He dove out of the would-be coffin!

"These punk mothafuckas really must think this shit is a game", he thought to himself as he rolled on the street just in case there was more than one shooter. A moving target is harder to hit than a stationary one. As he rolled, he grabbed his second Dragoon from its shoulder rig. He came up both arms raised ready for whatever.

He scanned the streets; he didn't see anyone other threats. So, he made his way around to the front of the car looking for the nigga that shot at him. He was on the sidewalk desperately trying to crawl to his banger that fell three feet away from him.

"You o'le bitch-nigga! You thought you would just walk up and knock me down!"

BOOM!

Voorheeze shot the nigga again, this time in his back!

"Bitch I don't get knocked down, I knock niggaz down!" At that point the Remy started having a slight effect, he felt woozy.

BOCA! BOCA! BOCA! BOCA! The sounds of a 40-caliber erupted.

That old familiar burning sensation shot through his upper right chest as one of the bullets found its mark. The other three missed. The bullet that struck his chest caused him to stumble backward.

BOOM! BOOM!

Voorheeze returned fire not letting the pain in his chest distract him.

"How many of you faggot ass niggaz wanna die today, huh?" He was way past the point of reasoning.

Instead of crouching down and taking cover, he struggled his way toward the middle of the street, so he could get a better aim at the bitch ass nigga that shot him. He was hiding behind the back of a Malibu.

"Come on fuck nigga! What the fuck you hiding foe! Nigga, dis what you want? Come get it!" He taunted his assailant.

At the sound of Voorheeze's voice coming from the front drivers' side, the second shooter thought he could get the drop on him. He raised half way up to send a slug at Voorheeze.

BOOM!

That mistake proved to be fatal!

Voorheeze wasn't a new booty to this pistol playing shit. He'd been sending hot shit at niggaz for years. So, his aim, although slightly off from the Remy, was still on point.

De'Kari

"If they sent two, they might've sent three", he thought to himself as he used the moment to eject the empty speed-reloader out of his first Dragoon and slap in another one.

This little nigga Sutton had proven to be more of a fucking problem than anyone could've ever expected. When the beef initially started, Voorheeze took the click of young niggaz as just that, young niggaz! He neva would have thought that the little nigga Sutton was a real life hitta! And not just a hitta but a mothafuck'n hitta with the mind of a war strategist.

As he begun to spin around Voorheeze already knew that he'd fucked up. Although he didn't hear any sound at all, he sensed someone behind him. He knew his thoughts had distracted him. His head and eyes made it fully around before the rest of his body did. So, the recognition of who was behind him registered before his body was able to react.

Tattat! Tattat! Tattat! Tattat!

Gorillaz in the Bay 2
CHAPTER I
2008
Open Bible Baptist Church

As the lyrics blared out of the speakers Jason Voorheeze sat behind the wheel of his Lamborghini with a look on his face, full of anger and grief. He sat in front of the Church with a bottle of Remy Martin in his hand trying to numb himself enough to brave the fact that he had to bury his brother.

He still found it hard to fathom the fact that T'Rida was gone. The guilt of not being there to save his brotha when safety and security was all Voorheeze preached was eating away at his soul steadily. Voorheeze was far from what anybody would call a soft nigga, but as he sat in the Lambo his emotions were way out of sync. In his mind he replayed the last time he saw T'Rida.

Voorheeze had pushed the Lambo so fast it literally hugged the corners as he raced through the streets to get to Tanya's house. As he made his way up the stairs, he tried to picture his brother smoked out like some base-head. The broad had to be mistaken. That thought went away when he entered her apartment. When Voorheeze saw T'Rida, he couldn't believe his eyes. T'Rida was smoked out, up for days and on one. He had locked himself in Tanya's bathroom and spent days getting high. Finally, Tanya was so worried for him that she was forced to call Voorheeze to come over and see if he could talk to him.

He lifted the bottle to his lips and took a long guzzling gulp. The Remy Martin XO burned a fire of bliss as it made its way down his throat and into his belly. He looked up and into his rearview mirror. His older brother Clarkola, who was his first lieutenant, sat behind his Lambo in his Dodge Daytona Charger. All their goons sat in cars back to back to back as far as he could see. Tommy Gunz sat across the street in his Aston Martin with a line of soldiers parked behind him. Neva Die was out in full force to pay their respects to their Boss and fallen comrade killed by the police.

Only T'Rida's immediate family and Neva Die were allowed to come to the Church to pay their respects which would make the viewing of the body small and intimate. Every member of Dragon Gang had already been in and said their goodbyes. They were waiting on Monique and the children to come out of the Church. Then they were heading to Skylawn Cemetery where everybody who was somebody would be to pay their respects.

Monique came out of the Church with the children and climbed into the stretched, black, Mercedes limo. They all headed out as one unit. As Voorheeze led the procession, he thought about that fateful day while he lit a Newport 100.

He was downstairs in the den with Gunz at T'Rida's and Monique's place when he heard the Breaking News Special Report playing on the television. Reporting that the Milpitas Police were involved in an intense stand-off and shoot-out and seeing the War Room on the screen. He and Gunz rushed out the house to get to T'Rida.

Voorheeze couldn't keep his mind from flashing back to that day. As they drove to Skylawn Cemetery he continued to think about it.

When they pulled up to the cemetery there were so many cars and people assembled together it looked like it was a funeral for the president of the United States. There were E.P.A. niggaz, Oakland niggaz, Berkeley niggaz, Frisco and San Jose niggaz, mothafuckas even came from Vallejo to show their love for the deceased Boss.

Because of the publicity behind the shootout with the police, various media sources were present at the funeral to cover the story of the man who was named the most notorious gangster to ever exist. One man that was responsible for killing seventeen police officers and injuring eleven more! Even the police were out in full force to attend the funeral in hopes of learning T'Ridas known associates. Since he was dead they were looking for someone else to pay for his sins.

There were dark, black and gray storm clouds overhead. However, there was not a drop of moisture in the air, only gloom!

Some would later look back at that day and swear that the weather was a premonition of what was to come. An omen of deadly proportions. But for now, one of the Bay Area's greatest Kings was being celebrated and remembered. The streets had definitely lost one of its elite! A rare breed indeed!

Although T'Rida had his flaws, the mere fact remained that even with his flaws, T'Rida had done something that most people could not fathom doing but wished they could. The fact that T'Rida had achieved the level of success that he did all while he was fighting a cocaine addiction was beyond impressive. Hell, the shit was downright mind blowing. Some of the heavy players, when discussing it amongst themselves, often wondered just how much more he could have done, had T'Rida been functioning at 100% capacity. They thought about it, not on some backdoor disrespectful shit but on some jaw-dropping "I wonder" shit.

Voorheeze walked in front of Monique and the children escorting them to their seats in the front row. He and Monique had already talked and gone over the course of action if anything was to jump off. If anybody thought they were going to do something, he had something for that ass. He wished a mothafucka would bust a move. Voorheeze would put anybody down who showed the least bit of disrespect.

As they walked down the aisle he thought of his grandma and her death. She was buried at the same cemetery. Involuntarily his hand moved towards one of the two Dragoons that rested inside his double shoulder rig. When they made it to the front row Voorheeze stepped to the left allowing her eight-year-old son, Titas' and her nine-year-old, Na'Shay to take their seats.

And he stood with his left hand covering his right wrist down in front of him. Voorheeze scanned the entire grounds taking it all in. When his eyes came to rest on a group of police officers who were gathered in the back off to the side, he clenched his fist and jaw! If it wasn't for the children and Ms. Veronica being present, he would've opened up and let missiles fly at the faggot ass cops. Even though they were not the Milpitas Police Department, the officers responsible for T'Rida death, to Voorheeze they were all the same, "A Pig was a Pig" straight the fuck up!

He leaned forward and placed a kiss on Monique's cheek, "I'm right here lil sis, right here."

She nodded her head up and down in response as tears cascaded down her chocolate cheeks. Next, he leaned down and gave Ms. Veronica a hug and whispered "thank you" in her ears. Ms. Veronica was Monique's mother, who he thought didn't care much for T'Rida in the first place. She was there, Voorheeze assumed, to be a source of strength for her daughter who was going through it.

What Voorheeze couldn't have known, hell T'Rida himself hadn't even known, was the fact that Ms. Veronica did love T'Rida. He had been with her daughter since they were in junior high school. She loved the way he treated her. Ms. Veronica was just hurt and disappointed in the lifestyle that T'Rida had chosen to live. All of his younger years had been spent in and out of jail. She just wanted the little skinny boy to make something of himself. As Voorheeze turned away, he didn't see the tear that slid down her face. But she saw the pain and hurt that was scrawled all across his face.

Leonard "Tommy Gunz" Johnson was an entirely different story. He leaned up against his black and red Aston Martin with a bottle of Patron Platinum in one hand and a blunt in the other. He had the jacket to his silk Armani suit in the driver's seat of the car so his double shoulder rig that held twin 44 Desert Eagles were open for any and everybody to see. He also had a Glock 41 in his waistline.

If for some reason you missed the bottle of alcohol, the smell of purple Kush or the three cannon's, the look on Gunz face spoke volumes without making a sound, "*Leave me the fuck alone*". A blind man could see the warning. Big Roc and A.J. stood to his immediate right and left, even though their weapons were completely concealed, they too were strapped for war.

DeeDee and DJ were leaning up against DJ's black and red Daytona with identical looks on their faces. Between the two vehicles stood twenty war-tested, pistol totting, ex-convicts all wearing R.I.P. T'Rida shirts. They looked like twenty niggaz you would want to leave alone. Especially since the R.I.P. on the T-shirts didn't stand for rest in peace. The shirts read "REVENGE IS PROMISED!!!" The exclamation marks were actually 7.62 bullets.

Tupac's "*I Aint Mad at You*" was playing on the Bose speakers of the Aston Martin and as Pac rapped Gunz heart cried. No-one besides Monique was taking the shit hard as Gunz.

For Gunz, it wasn't the loss of T'Rida as an individual that was fucking with him, it was the loss itself. It seemed that all Gunz knew was loss and heart ache. Everybody Gunz had ever loved had died or was murdered. Gunz literally didn't have anyone but his Neva Die family. And he thought he and his Family would grow old together. But the faggott ass police stole his brother. Reality smacked him right in the face! They were not invincible! So, fuck it!

Gunz decided that day in Milpitas when they pulled over and heard T'Rida die, that he would take them before they took him! These thoughts went through Gunz' mind as he glared at the rookie cop who kept looking over in his direction. Gunz took a long slow drag on the blunt, then took a swig of the Patron before he blew his smoke out. The whole time he was glaring at the rookie like he'd raped his mother.

"Fuck is you looking at pussy boy?" The pure venom in which Gunz spit the question out should've told the rookie to leave well enough alone, but not Officer Hedgecock. Officer Hedgecock was determined to make a name for himself inside of the department.

"Ex-Excuse me, sir?" You could hear the fear in Hedgecock's voice.

"You heard me, mothafucka! I said what da fuck yo bitch ass over there looking at?" Gunz could smell the fear coming off the rookie like a shark smells blood and he wasn't going to let up, not today!

"Umm. Sir, do you have a license for those firearms that you are carrying?" Officer Hedgecock didn't want a confrontation with the young thug but the captain was nearby and Hedgecock wanted to impress him.

He started walking towards the group. Officer Hedgecock repeated his question "do you have a license for those fire arms that you are carrying?"

Gorillaz in the Bay 2

Gunz looked at the white boy like he just saw him suck on a log of shit. "I'm carrying them aint I?"

"Sir I'm going to have to ask you to put your hands in the air!" Officer Hedgecock told Gunz as he brought his hand to rest on the top of his service weapon.

That was the wrong thing to do at that moment.

**** N. D. ****

When Captain Sweeney looked over and saw his dumb ass rookie looking over at Leonard Johnson and the group that was with him, he knew there was going to be a problem. After nearly 30 years on the force, he's both seen and done it all. Enough that he could spot a problem before it arose.

Personally, he liked the rookie. Hedgecock was eager to prove himself worthy, he loved his job and was a stickler for detail. The problem was, he was hands down a complete moron! He didn't possess the ability to use common sense. Because of this, the young rookie had already been at the center of quite a few shit storms and he hasn't even been on the force for a year.

Sweeney began to make his way over to Hedgecock. He wanted to stop him before he did something stupid, but it was too late. Hedgecock had already said something to Leonard.

Capt. Sweeney told Lieutenants Urena and Boots to follow him. There were about twenty-five San Mateo County Sheriff Deputies that attended the funeral. If needed, he could make a call and have an additional thirty or so on their way. If they locked down the Maguire Facility, that would be another twenty at his disposal. That was somewhere around seventy-five to eighty Sheriff Deputies.

Sweeney knew that there was well over two hundred armed and deadly killers at the funeral. Even a fool wouldn't buck against those odds. It didn't matter that they were the law. These were not the type of people that would run from the law. They killed the law and anybody else that they wanted. Plus, there was a shit load of media around. The last thing that his department needed was more bad publicity. With all the complaints of police brutality and corruption, the department had a bad image in the eye of the public. He didn't need anything adding fuel to the already raging fire.

As Sweeney was getting closer to the group, he saw Hedgecock put his hand on the butt of his service weapon. He knew all hell was about to break loose.

De'Kari

Sweeney opened his mouth to tell the fucking moron to stand down but before he could utter a word, so many guns were pointed at Hedgecock that Sweeney instantly feared for the rookie's life.

"Fuck you gone do Cracker?" DeeDee spit out as fire burned inside his pupils.

Staring from the wrong end of the long Desert Eagle, Officer Hedgecock really thought that he was looking in the eyes of the Devil himself. He had neva seen so many guns drawn so fast, all at the same time in his life. To make it even worse, all the guns were pointed at him.

"Hey! Hey! Hey! Fellas whoa whoa!" Captain Sweeney cautiously walked through the group trying to defuse the situation.

"Fellas! We don't need to do this. Not right here, in front of all of these cameras!" Sweeney thought mentioning the cameras would detour them.

"Nobody asked yo fucking ass for yo advice!" The captain bars on Sweeney's collar didn't mean shit to DeeDee. To him a pig was a pig and DeeDee just wanted a reason.

"Put the guns down!" Gunz spoke low but with authority. He walked up to Hedgecock getting directly in his face. He was so close to that when he spoke Hedgecock could feel Gunz breath on his face.

"Let me tell you something, bitch, I hate cops, so I hate you! This is my fucking Family right here!" He turned motioning to all the killaz surrounding them. "Now we're trynna say goodbye to our brotha and you wanna bring yo disrespectful ass over here and fuck with me. I should knock yo bitch ass down. I don't give a fuck bout them cameras. Understand the only reason yo bitch ass aint laid out right now is on the strength of yo Captain and out of respect for my brotha. But if you don't get yo bitch ass out of here and let me say goodbye to my brotha, yo brotha's gone be saying goodbye to you."

Hedgecock was so scared he didn't know what to do. He was embarrassed to be talked to like that by a common thug especially in front of the Captain! But he was too scared to even consider saying something back to Gunz. From the look in all their eyes Hedgecock knew that if he said or did anything besides leave the cemetery, he would lose his life.

When Gunz turned away from Hedgecock he made eye contact with Capt. Sweeney and gave him a head nod in acknowledgment. Lieutenant Boots and Urena stood by ready for action during the entire exchange. Although they knew that the odds were very much against them, they were trained and seasoned vets ready for combat. They've been through the fire numerous times and was ready to go through it again if need be!

Gorillaz in the Bay 2

Chapter II
(East Palo Alto)

The steam that was coming off of Gunz could easily be seen if someone was there to look at him, Rarely did Gunz find himself in a fit of rage. He was seething.

In his heart, the fact was that he couldn't deal with the loss of his brother. The disrespect of the fuckin white boy was stuck in his mind. He couldn't believe that mothafucka had the nerve to step to him.

In his mind, Gunz was following Officer Hedgecock so that he could teach him a lesson about stepping to a mothafucka like him. As he took a hit off the blunt he was smoking, his head nodded to the sounds of C-Bo "Til My Casket Drops." The more he listened to the song talk about killing cops, the greater his rage became. He didn't realize that he was angry at the fact that he didn't know how to process T'Rida's death.

The Granddaddy Purple wasn't helping the situation any. He was a few cars back from Officer Hedgecock. Gunz mind was set, the moment this son of a bitch stopped he was going to air his mothafuck'n ass out.

The sound of his phone ringing came over the speakers. Without looking at the display on the ten-inch screen he pressed the button on the steering wheel to answer the call.

"Yeah?"

"Yeah? Oh, excuse me! I must have the wrong number, because that is not how the man I love answers the phone when I call." Natasia's voice was like an instant warm front over his ice-covered heart.

To him even the way she said that sounded sweet. Catching himself he said, "Sorry about that Babe. I didn't look to see who was calling."

"What's up with you Beautiful?" Even though he tried to mask it, she could hear the anger in his voice.

"I was just calling to check on you. To see how things went today. Babe, I'm sorry I couldn't come back and be there for you." She used her soft, innocent voice.

"It's okay Babe. How's things going out there?" Natasia could hear the strain in his voice. He was trying to change the subject to avoid dealing with the issue, but she wasn't letting him off that easy.

"So, since when do we do that?" She asked.

"Watcha mean, Babe?"

"Leonard, no matter what is going on. You and I have neva kept our feelings from one another. Nor do we just sweep things under the rug and ignore them. Babe, if I am your better half, you have to trust me enough to let me in, even when you don't want anyone in".

The more that he listened to Natasia talk, the further he came out of that dark place he had gone. His gangsta still screamed "Murda" but reason screamed "A Future". She didn't know it, but he had plans to propose to her the moment he gets back to her.

"Leonard!" She called into the phone bringing his attention back to the conversation.

"Huh? Oh, Babe excuse me I was paying attention to the cop behind me." He expressed, lying to her.

"You're right though, Babe, it's just right now I have to process all of this before I can even begin to talk about it."

Hedgecock's blinker came on as he turned right onto Kavanaugh Street. Gunz slowed down so he wouldn't be so close behind him.

"I promise you Babe, once I process things, we'll discuss it, okay?"

"Okay Babe!" She responded feeling that she'd won.

"I'll call you in the morning."

"I heard that, I'll call you in an hour and your butt better be home." She joked but was serious.

"Love you Babe."

"Love you, too."

Then he heard Natasia's voice talking to him inside his head and his heart, begging him not to do this. He wasn't that man any more. The more he wanted to get out of the car, the louder he could hear her voice.

"Fuck!" He mumbled as he dropped the gun back on his lap. Then he pulled off.

Hedgecock thought he was going to have a heart attack. The moment his eyes saw the Aston Martin creeping past his house. His service weapon was under the driver's seat locked in the car. He couldn't see past the tinted windows, so he didn't know who the driver was. Being that it looked like the exact same car from earlier, he had an idea.

He was frozen still with fear, looking like a deer in the headlights. As the car drove past he didn't' know if he was just being paranoid or if he should be saying a silent prayer of thanks.

When he was finally able to move, his damp pants leg pissed him off past the point of prayer. Ego bruised and feeling ashamed, he made his way into the house.

**** **N. D.** ****

Gorillaz in the Bay 2

Everything about the brothers were completely opposite. They were indeed blood brothers but still the two couldn't be more different. Voorheeze was a people person. He was outgoing, yet calculative and analytical, but when called for he was ferocious and deadly. But, for the most part he was a gentle giant. Clark on the other hand was calm and quiet. Yet, he was quick-tempered and ill-mannered.

Voorheeze would do his best to avoid violence as much as possible. Whereas, Clarkola was always ready to pop off! Clark was the eldest and he was a true thug. He was a street nigga through and through. You would usually find him in some designer jeans with a white tee and some top of line sneakers.

Voorheeze was a true gangsta, his designer suits and Mauri gators would attest to that.

Because of his temper and antics, the entire city knew about the shit Clark had done. He was a Hot Boy who stayed blazin his gun, but if the truth was revealed, Voorheeze had a body count that would make Ted Bundy shiver. He just didn't advertise his shit. He didn't see the need in all that "ra ra" shit. Too many niggaz went down behind niggaz running their mouth. But a nigga couldn't run his mouth, if he didn't know shit! So Voorheeze didn't do shit for show.

Their little sister was a by-product of both of them. French Tip was hot and ready like her oldest brother, analytical and calculating like her younger brother. Though she had a temper like Clark she would hold her emotions in check like Voorheeze until the time came for her to be pernicious. She may not have had as many bodies as Voorheeze but hands down she was the most lethal. If the Boogey Man was real, he'd be scared of her.

Only two women ever could be classified as more dangerous or deadlier than French Tip. The first was Anne whom some called Chiba. She was a young lady the late T'Rida himself had brung into the folds of the Family. She was a quick study and progressed quickly. T'Rida saw her potential and hooked her up with French Tip and Cantelope. She would become a member of the infamous She-Wolves. After months of teaching and training by Cantelope and French Tip, Anne became something that both women were proud of.

Anne's murder game was second to none; living that is! The shit legends and hood myths were made of. Which brings up the second person deadlier than French Tip or even Anne for that matter, the "Black Widow". She was an older Mexican chick that ran with a team of killaz out of Redwood City. They were murder for hire. Their loyalty was only to each other and the contract they were hired for. They were good, they were efficient, but they weren't cheap

De'Kari

Back, before the war in East Palo Alto, when niggaz still traveled to Lil Mexico to buy their dope, her team put it down. They were the deadliest team around.

The Black Widow was the scariest of them all. She took the jobs no one else wanted and she touched people that were supposed to be untouchable. The thing is, it didn't matter the level of security a person had. If the Black Widow was hired, you were going to die.

"I ain't heard from you since the funeral big brah. You been alright?" French Tip asked Voorheeze with genuine concern in her voice.

"I ain't gone even lie to you sis, this shit got me fucked up." The pain in Voorheeze voice spoke volumes.

"It's like me, 'Rida and Gunz were the perfect ingredients to this shit. Not too much this, not too much that but the perfect combination! Now without 'Rida it just doesn't feel the same. Like me and Gunz don't fit." She didn't interrupt him. She knew he needed to get it off his chest.

Voorheeze looked like hell! He hadn't been eating or sleeping much. He was still massive, but he'd lost considerable weight and it showed. He would sit around drinking all day blaming himself for not being there for T'Rida. His conscious was telling him that when he first learned of T'Rida's drug usage, he should have taken it more seriously and done more to help him.

"I wasn't there when my nigga needed me the most! What kind of brotha am I? I was too busy worrying about money to see that my brotha was crying out for help! I should've seen that something was wrong!" The guilt was eating Voorheeze alive.

He'd always been big on loyalty and was questioning if he was loyal to his brotha. In his mind, not helping T'Rida meant that he wasn't loyal.

"Brah, you can't beat yourself up over that shit. You couldn't have been there for him if you didn't know that he was getting high", Clarkola spoke for the first time. Hearing his little brother profess his love and loyalty to another nigga was starting to get to him. Fuck that other nigga! He was his blood.

"Fuck you know bout it nigga? You aint neva been there for nobody when they needed yo ass! So, what the fuck can you tell a nigga bout beating himself up?" Rage flashed in Voorheeze's eyes.

Brother or not, Voorheeze was hoping that Clark acted stupid. He wouldn't hesitate to let his older brother feel a little bit of the pain that he was feeling. After all, Voorheeze's need to be there for his people stem from a lack of his older brother and family being there for him when he needed them growing up. He vowed he would neva treat the people that he loved the way his family had treated him.

Gorillaz in the Bay 2

French Tip knew that if she didn't jump in things were about to get very explosive. So, she spoke up.

"Look, no matter what we Family! And us, we're Family twice!" She said pointing her finger to the three of them. "Now Voorheeze I know that you are hurting. Baby, I can see pain all over you. But "T" wouldn't want you to carry on like this." She pointed out his appearance to emphasize what she was talking about then she continued. "And he damn sure wouldn't want us at each other's throat! Yeah! None of us knew T'Rida like you did, but I knew him enough to know that he would be on you tough right now for what you are doing to yourself. This ain't the answer, baby. You gotta find another way." It killed her to see him like that.

Voorheeze knew that French Tip was right. Hell, she was always right. Even when she wasn't he would still listen to her. He loved her more than life itself. But, being around his brother was only opening old wounds making him think of his inner pain. He needed to get away from the restaurant before shit got real ugly.

He stood up, "look it's good Booger you're right. I love both of y'all but I gotta get up outta here before I Beni somebody's Hana." Clark knew his brother well enough to know that the comment didn't have anything to do with him. He knew his brother didn't send subliminals, so he didn't say shit.

Even though Clark would neva admit it to anybody he knew that he hadn't been a good big brother. He was too busy running the streets with his two cousins trying to make a name for himself.

"V rogue I'm here if ever you need me, lil brah", Clark declared as he stood up. The two embraced.

"I know rogue, it's good."

French Tip stood and hugged her brother tight as hell.

"I love you brother."

"I love you too, sis."

Love, vows and promises were non-verbally spoken as the brother and sister shared an intimate hug. Voorheeze turned away to leave. He thought about something for a minute, then turned around and said, "I'mma see y'all at The War Room this week. Clark, Friday is on you. Don't pick no more bootsie ass restaurants."

"Nigga what you talking bout, nigga Nation's is the shit.

Clark would spend lots of money on clothes, cars, jewelry and everything else but he was cheap as hell when it came to food. Since coming back together in each other's lives as adults, the three of them made a pact to always hang out on Fridays no matter what. It was their way of making up for so much lost time as children. Voorheeze and French Tip always chose something extravagant like Benihana's.

Fucking around with Clark they'd be eating at Nations or Jack in the Box next week.

When Voorheeze left Benihana's he drove to a liquor store and got himself a bottle of Remy Martin. He knew everything that his sister just told him was true, but it still didn't take away his pain or guilt.

If it wasn't for T'Rida they neva would have gone out jack'n that night and came up on that lick that started it all so long ago. After killing Bamma in West Oakland, it was T'Rida that came up with the idea of putting things together and building some shit. They all worked their asses off to make it happen. But it was T'Rida that had the vision.

Voorheeze took a long gulp of the sweet poison, screwing his face up as it burned going down his throat, then drove off. As he was driving his mind continued to fuck with him and so did his guilt. It's like his mind and his guilt played tug-of-war over what could make him feel more like shit! Because the truth of the matter was, if it wasn't for T'Rida, Voorheeze wouldn't be alive!

Voorheeze turned 19 when he was incarcerated at Duel Vocational Institution in Tracy, CA. Also known as DVI. Though he was in prison nearly a year by the time he got to DVI, he was serving a three-year sentence for a dope case. Not too long after arriving at DVI it was decided by classification that Voorheeze could no longer be housed in dorms due to all the violence he was involved in.

He was sent to J-wing to serve the remainder of his time in cells. They put him in the cell with a big-time gang banger nigga named Dawoo. He was a lifer who had been down already for almost twenty years. Dawoo was known for bringing most of the dope into the prison and messing around with the homosexuals. He also had a thirst for raping young niggaz.

He was a huge dude. He stood six feet three and weighed almost three-hundred and fifty pounds. The first night Voorheeze moved in, they didn't have any problems.

At lights out, while Voorheeze slept on the top bunk Dawoo laid on the bottom bunk and jacked off thinking about what he was going to do to Voorheeze. In his sick and twisted mind Voorheeze was his new woman.

The second night Dawoo came in from night yard drunk off pruno (jail-made alcohol). After lights out Dawoo attacked Voorheeze! At first Voorheeze didn't know what was going on, he thought it was a normal fight. But being the sadistic, sick twisted fuck, he was, Dawoo was talking to Voorheeze while trying to overpower him. He made his intentions very clear. Voorheeze fought like a man possessed. He wasn't big at the time, so it took all he had not to become a victim. The other cells could hear what was going on but were used to it. Dawoo's sick habits were well- known.

After what seemed like forever, Dawoo grew tired and let out a mighty roar-like laugh, finding amusement in the fact that Voorheeze held him off. He's neva been challenged physically, most of his prey simply folded. For the rest of the night he taunted and tormented Voorheeze telling him tomorrow night he wouldn't go easy on him. Tomorrow, Dawoo declared, Voorheeze would be his bitch!

Voorheeze didn't know what to do. He was skinnier than a toothpick. He couldn't tell the police or else he would be labeled a snitch. But he wasn't about to let the faggott take his manhood! He refused to go to sleep or even lay down for that matter. He had to figure something out. The next morning all eyes were on their cell when the doors were opened for breakfast. This was the first-time convicts saw a bruise on Dawoo's face. Silently everybody's respect level for the youngsta elevated, no-one had ever stood up to the rapist before. But fuck respect, Voorheeze needed a solution. It came in the form of a childhood friend he hadn't seen in years.

T'Rida like everybody else in J-wing knew all about Dawoo's activities.

T'Rida was sleep when Voorheeze moved into the cell that night. Then the next day, he was at work. He didn't know that it was Voorheeze that was fighting for his life that night.

That morning when T'Rida saw Voorheeze come out of Dawoo's cell he knew he had to do something, the two embraced like brothers. After they embraced, T'Rida went back into his cell and grabbed one of his many knives. The 9-inch piece of metal was sharpened to a very sharp point. The handle consisted of a piece of cloth wrapped and black electrical tape wrapped around it. Grabbing the knife, Voorheeze felt a surge of confidence. What had happened the night before was something new and unusual to him. He heard about weird mothafuckas like Dawoo but had neva encountered one, but a young Voorheeze was no stranger to murder. Instead of going to breakfast he and T'Rida stayed back and discussed what Voorheeze was going to do. T'Rida was willing to lend Voorheeze a hand but Voorheeze knew that it was something that he had to take care of on his own. Dawoo was so big, he really wanted help, but he couldn't look like no bitch in niggaz eyes. Knowing this, he declined the help.

It was a good thing that T'Rida had given him the knife because Dawoo didn't wait until night time. As soon as he came back from breakfast, he attacked Voorheeze again. Voorheeze decided at that point that it was kill or be killed, because he wasn't about to be fucked. He pulled out the knife during the tussle and managed to stab Dawoo

De'Kari

seven times. Still Dawoo didn't go down! The knife had gotten so slippery from the amount of blood that leaked out each time he stabbed Dawoo. He couldn't risk taking the time to wipe the knife or his hand off, so he just did his best to keep a tight grip on it. He swung his arm in preparation to stab Dawoo some more but Dawoo had timed the blow and deflected it when it came.

The knife dropped out of Voorheeze's hand and fell on the floor. After pushing Voorheeze out of the way Dawoo picked up the knife and let out a sinister laugh. Voorheeze knew his life was over but at least he had put up a damn good fight. Dawoo was humongous but still Voorheeze gave it all he had. Dawoo rushed at Voorheeze and brought his hand back to stab him.

Neither Dawoo nor Voorheeze saw or heard the door to the cell fly open! T'Rida stormed into the cell with a knife as long as his forearm. He stabbed Dawoo under his left arm as he was in mid swing. Dawoo went down, instantly dropping the knife. Voorheeze rushed to pick it up and stabbed Dawoo seven more times! It wasn't until T'Rida called him that he stopped. Voorheeze was in a fit of rage. His body was overcome with adrenaline from fear of being victimized.

Both exited the cell and went to the back of the building where one of T'Ridas homeboys gave both of them some new clothes. Next, they rushed to the third floor and took a shower. Washing away any and all evidence. Voorheeze was still visibly shaken but he tried to conceal it. He didn't want T'Rida thinking that he was a pussy or something. When they left out of the shower the last of the evidence was the bloody clothes which were now soaking in a bucket of industrial strength bleach and water.

It was yard release when they exited the shower, so they went straight to the yard. Even though he didn't have anybody to call, Voorheeze made sure to sign up for the phone three times.

The phone logs would be hard evidence that he was on the yard. The two of them made sure that they passed in front of a few cameras' multiple times and as final insurance they made sure to ask a few of the correctional officers a bunch of questions so they would remember them.

They stayed on the yard the entire time until the alarm sounded, and the officers laid the yard down when they found Dawoo's body. The second time the police laid the yard down it was to come get Voorheeze.

After questioning him for nearly three hours they threw Voorheeze in the hole and charged him with murder. The police knew the sick shit that Dawoo did to young boys, but they didn't give a shit. To them they were all criminals and niggers, which meant they were all animals!

Gorillaz in the Bay 2

The guards knew that Voorheeze killed Dawoo they just couldn't prove it. The time of death was estimated to be the exact time Voorheeze signed up for the phone and was on camera at the phones. He sat in K-wing for six months waiting to see if the D.A. was going to pick up the case but with the amount of evidence they had (none) the D.A. wouldn't go near the case. Voorheeze was released from the hole and he and T'Rida became cellies. By then everyone knew what happened and the two youngsta's respect level went through the roof!

Voorheeze continued to hit the bottle as a single tear slid down his face. He was far from a bitch nigga or a soft nigga so shedding a few tears didn't bother him the least bit. Nobody but the two of them had known what was really real! Had it not been for T'Rida, Voorheeze would have surely died that day back in that cell in Tracy. Along with, only God knows what, other sick humiliation he would have faced before he died.

The fact of knowing his brotha was there for him when he really needed him, but when the shoe was on the other foot Voorheeze wasn't there for him! This was fuckin with him! He wanted to pick up his phone and call his brother so bad, but he couldn't. His brother was gone! Instead, he did the next best thing.

"Hello?" She answered after the third ring.

"What's up sis?" Even if he didn't slur his words, Monique knew Voorheeze was drunk and that he was hurting behind T'Rida's death.

"Hey Jason, how are you honey?" She did her best to mask her own grief.

"Shit sis, you know aint no need asking a nigga that." He told her truthfully.

"Jason, I know you loved him, but baby you got to let him go. You have to stop blaming yourself! It was not your fault. My husband had demons that nobody knew about. Those demons eventually would have gotten to Tommy whether you were there with him or not". Voorheeze didn't know just how true Monique's words were. As far as he was concerned, he broke his oath. He'd faltered at his comrade's side.

"Sis check me out! I know that you only trynna help a mothafucka out and believe me I love you for it, I do. But my job is safety and security period, point blank! From sun up to sun down I push safety and security and I push that shit to the fullest. Now if I would have really been on my shit, this would not have happened, because I would've saw my brotha falling".

"Instead I forgot about safety and security and was focused solely on money. So, it is my fault"! He hit the steering wheel as he spoke.

"Now I aint gone let this shit kill me or even allow it to break me. What I am gonna do though, is let it do what it do! And right now, that's kick my mothafuck'n ass! I gotta let it kick my ass so that I can absorb some of this pain. If I don't, then believe me, the pain is going to kill me!" Monique heard the sincerity in Voorheeze voice and she understood the rationality behind what he had just told her.

Voorheeze was T'Rida's brother, but over the years she had come to see him as a big brother also. She didn't want her big brother hurting. Voorheeze was always the strong one! She could only pray that after he went through, whatever he was going through, that he would be back to his normal self.

They talked for a little longer on the phone before hanging up. By then Voorheeze was completely drunk and damn near out of it. Monique was completely worried about him. She was so worried that she called Gunz after they had gotten off the phone. Gunz assured her that he had everything under control. Which he did and would keep an eye on Voorheeze.

Monique felt a whole lot better after she got off the phone with Gunz. T'Rida used to always tell her when he was alive, that he trusted Gunz instinct and judgment, hands down! Because he was always thinking and calculating, Gunz rarely made a mistake. He took this Neva Die shit way too seriously for him not to be on his square. And he'd be damned if he let anybody knock him off his pivot. Not even his other brother! After getting off the phone with Gunz. She grabbed a bottle of wine and cried herself to sleep.

CHAPTER III
(Meanwhile)

As the pink rim's road along with the jet-black run flats road along the asphalt, the illusion was that of melting starburst against the pavement. The big engine of the black and pink Camaro was so quiet it could barely be heard as it purred down the city street. It was a good distance behind the car it was following. Inside of the Camaro its occupants rode silently with chrome hammers on each of their laps ready for whatever.

"You gonna lose him if you don't speed up." The passenger's attitude was evident.

"How will I lose him when the car is in front of us?" The driver scolded.

Nina just hated when people drove slow. "Man, we should've used my car! Your car is too slow", Nina told her sister as she picked up the cannon off of her lap and caressed it involuntarily.

"What? Nina, we got the exact same car!" Trina began cracking up, she knew that her sister was just getting bored.

Nina was tired of following this mothafucka around. She was ready to get it poppin! Nina was like that, she was always ready to let her hammer speak for her. She believed deep in her soul that there were too many suckas in the world, and it was her job to exterminate them one bullet at a time.

Club Carsjanaes was jumping! Tonight, was the night of nights! It was T'Rida's birthday party and everybody who was anybody showed up to show out. Everybody in the building was having the time of their lives. The entire Neva Die family had pulled up in full force and shut the mothafucka down. T'Rida was currently on the middle of the center stage and was proposing to Monique.

All eyes in the building were on them. People were either looking directly at the couple or watching them on one of the many flat screens that were located throughout the club. It was a memorable moment for all that were in attendance. But for Nina, the importance of that night was something totally different altogether while everybody else was on some "party bullshit", she stayed on point. No drinking, no nothing. So, when she peeped a nigga eyeballing T'Rida she decided to make it her business to keep an eye on the nigga and see what was what.

The She-Wolves would come to realize the best decision they ever made was recruiting Nina and her sister. The twins had been laying there murder game down for a long time by the time French Tip had reached out to them. They were so low key about their shit, that almost half of the bodies that they were responsible for were credited to other people. But those who knew, knew better.

First chance she got, Nina told her sister about the nigga and together they watched him all night. When T'Rida and Monique got ready to leave, T'Rida assured his family that he didn't need any security. Niggaz didn't feel that shit but respected it. He and Monique left and so did the nigga! The twins were right on his ass. No matter how hard they searched their memories, the twins could not place his face.

The entire time they followed the mothafucka, they debated over what to do. Nina's plan was to follow whoever the mothafucka was and the first chance they got leave his ass slumped, no questions asked, no regrets! Trina on the other hand was down to put her murder game on without question, but she wanted to follow protocol.

Their debate was interrupted by a phone call from French Tip who noticed that the t wins were missing. She figured knowing them and their attraction to violence, something was up. The twins put in work together as a unit and they were damn good. So, when they were both missing that usually meant something was up, and somebody was about to die.

After they put her up on what was popping off, she alerted Gunz who immediately jumped up ready to run right into some shit. After learning from French Tip that it was only one nigga Gunz fell back. He told French Tip to send a back-up unit just in case and to inform the twins to look, but do not touch.

Nina was pissed off when the order came for them to just stay on the nigga and learn what they could about him, unless he posed a threat. Gunz figured that was the call Voorheeze would have made. "Learn as much about a possible threat as you possibly can and then eliminate it once it served its purpose!" Voorheeze believed you neva move on a threat without fully understanding it because you may move too early and lose out on some important detail. "Fuck around and think you've eliminated a threat and all you've really done was exposed your hand", is what he would always say. The twins did as they were instructed, they followed the nigga that night and the next day.

That fateful day in Milpitas they were parked on the corner of Vienna Drive a few houses down from The War Room. They sat in a rented, charcoal grey, V6 Honda Accord watching the mothafucka that was following T'Rida. He had been still following T'Rida since he left Carsjanaes the night before. He was two houses up in front of the twins. Nina didn't like just sitting there watching the nigga one bit.

She lost track of how many times she brought it up to her sister, the idea of just getting on the niggaz helmet. Fuck all this waiting shit, they could knock the nigga down and come up with a reason of why they had to do it, later, that was Nina's reasoning. Trina hated when her sister got like that, but she was so used to it that she didn't trip.

As they sat and watched Wendell talk on his cell phone all hell broke loose! What the twins didn't know was all this time Wendell had been on the phone with the Milpitas Police Department. He'd called in an anonymous tip about two men dragging little girls out of a van tied up and blind folded into a house.

Trina's heart skipped about three beats. She had neva seen so many police cars come flying around the corner at one time. She didn't know what was going on, but she didn't like it! Nina cocked both of her pistols getting ready for the show down. She would be damned if she didn't take a bunch of them bitches with her.

Thinking quickly, Trina picked up her phone and called French Tip. After hearing what Trina was telling her and analyzing the situation French Tip told the twins to stand down. She figured it was just a raid. If T'Rida got locked up they could easily bail him out. Wasn't no sense in the twins getting snatched up too.

Nina told her sister that she knew the nigga in the car was responsible for calling the police, she could feel it in her gut. The proof came when he got out of his Cadillac and started talking to the cops pointing and gesturing with his hands.

Nina was squeezing the handles of her pistols so hard her knuckles were turning white and hurting. She hated snitches! All she could think of was she should have killed the fuckin maggot last night. Now because she didn't, she would have to watch T'Rida go to jail. At least that's what she thought.

"BOCCA! BOCCA! BOCCA! BOCCA!

Somebody inside of the house opened fire on the cops. Before the twins had a chance to make sense out of what was playing out. Shit got real as fuck.

During the commotion of the shoot out the twins lost track of Wendell, but it didn't matter because they knew where he lived and planned on making shit right! He neva returned home, Nina had sat on his house 24/7 waiting. Finally, the day of the funeral, they spotted him. He was sitting in the same Cadillac in the parking lot eyeing the funeral. Determined not to let his punk ass get away, Nina dipped off and retrieved a can of florescent, invisible, glow in the dark paint from her car and tagged both sides of his bumper.

Now they were following him and ready to fill him with some hot shit.

Wendell drove at a nice respectable distance away from Voorheeze. His mind was all over the place. The inside of the car smelled of sweat, ass and crack. The crack that he continued to saturate his system with only added to the problem. As he thought about his losses, tears continued to slide down his face.

Wendell didn't know how things had gotten so out of hand. He had put his cousin Melvin up on a nice little lick. All the mothafucka had to do was keep his fucking mouth shut. Instead of doing that, the stupid mothafucka ran his mouth, ninety going north! Now everybody that he loved was dead.

Melvin's dumb ass brought it on himself for running his mouth and choosing the wrong tramp to make his woman. But Jack, Dollar and Lynch didn't have to die because of Melvin's mistake, especially Lynch.

Wendell's heart dropped at the thought of Lynch. Wendell had been in the closet for the last five years. He wished he could go back in time just to be able to tell Lynch that he loved him. Hell, right now he didn't care who knew. Wendell wouldn't be in the closet any more. He would rather deal with the embarrassment of people knowing than to be without the love of his life. If only he could bring Lynch back. The two of them had been sneaking around behind Dollar's back for a year and a half and Wendell had fallen in love with him.

He thought about the day he made it to his mother's house and watched the fire department fight the flames. Wendell's problems began with T'Rida, but Voorheeze took things to another level when he and his bitch ass boy killed Wendell's mom and sister!

Wendell picked up his pipe and took another hit off it. He didn't even feel the enjoyment of getting high any longer. He continued to smoke, chasing the high. Placing the pipe inside of his cup holder, Wendell picked up the old 9 mm Beretta and held it in his lap.

"Yeah lil bitch! Let's see how tough you are when I hit you with some hot shit. Mothafuckas can pick on little o'le ladies well just wait until I start choppin at you." Wendell was yelling out as he was following the car Voorheeze was driving. White foam flew from his mouth.

Tonight, would be the night he would finally get his revenge for what was done to his mother and sister. Pink's body had laid in the trunk of her car for three weeks. The smell of her rotten corpse finally prompted someone to investigate, was the only reason she was found. Fuck that! All these mothafuckas were going to pay for what was done to his people.

Voorheeze was making it as easy as pie as he rolled around getting drunk as hell. Wendell decided he would kill him the next time he pulled over. Although Wendell didn't have a snowball's chance in hell going up against Voorheeze. The crack cocaine told him a different story.

Gorillaz in the Bay 2
**** N. D. ****

Officer Peters didn't know exactly what he'd stumbled across when he spotted the three cars, but he knew something was up. As far as the officer could tell one car was following another car which was being followed by another one! He was following them all. His instincts told him to radio in for some kind of backup, but Peters didn't listen to reason. He neva did. Peters believed you had to take the risk to catch the Big Fish. Besides, what would he say? He had three cars following each other? Peters didn't want to get his ass chewed out or get humiliated. He'd been through the ringer way too many times to count. His "Lone Ranger" antics kept him in trouble, but he believed one day they would put him ahead of the game. He had big dreams, so he knew that he had to take big risks. What was the saying of the young black guys? "Scared money don't make money!"

As he was thinking this, Peters watched the lead car pull into the parking lot of Garden Supermarket. Only one man in the Bay Area drove a Lamborghini Vereno and that was Voorheeze. Whatever was going on, Peters was ready. He knew who drove that car. He pulled into the lot and parked off to the side of the building out of sight, a few seconds after the Cadillac pulled in.

The Cadillac pulled in the lot from the opposite end. The Camaro that was following the Cadillac, pulled in behind him. The driver of the Cadillac was so preoccupied with something. He neva saw the Camaro pull in and kill its engine. Officer Peters decided not to pull into the crowded parking lot, instead he pulled up to the curb and watched.

Wendell parked the Cadillac and grabbed his pipe. He took one last hit off of it and was ready. Voorheeze was about to die. He exited the Cadillac, gun in his hand and crept towards the Lamborghini with only one thing in mind: Killing Jason Voorheeze.

When he reached the Lamborghini Wendell crouched down by the driver's side and waited. The passenger side of the car faced the entrance of the store.

"Oh, hell naw! Trina he bout to try to ambush Big Brah when he comes out of the store!" Nina said as she was double checking her pistols, making sure they were cocked and loaded. "It's time to lay my murda game down, fuck talking!"

"Fuck protocol let's go", was all Trina said when she opened the door and slid out of the car feeling the same way her sister did!

At six-foot-two, two-hundred and fifteen pounds, Trina was an Amazon, but she had all the agility of an Olympic gymnast.

The twins were nineteen years old, both beautiful and lethal. Every man that laid eyes on them wanted to get with them. Unless someone had the ability to tame a wild animal, they wouldn't dare approach them. They were that feisty.

As they reached their target, the sisters split up. Trina came from the passenger side. She didn't have to look up, she already knew where her sister was. She could sense it, they moved in sync like that. As she rounded the front of the Lambo Trina could see Wendell stooping down waiting. He was a bald, fat, brown skinned nigga. He resembled Carl Winslow from Family Matters.

He was sweating profusely from the crack cocaine and from fear, he wasn't a killer. When he saw Trina, his eyes lit up. He'd neva in his life seen something so beautiful. Just as he opened his mouth to speak *Pop! Pop! Pop! Pop!* Nina had walked directly up to him from behind while he was distracted staring at her sister. When she was a foot away from him she shot him twice in the back of the head. When Wendell's body fell to the ground, she shot him twice more.

Nina didn't come here to talk or play games. When she lifted her head to look at her sister, her heart froze. Some mothafucka was pointing a gun at the back of her sister's head. Trina saw the look in her sister's face and instantly knew something was wrong. She spun around bringing her arm and gun up, ready to fire. "Freeze!"

Peters couldn't believe what had happened, it had all happened so quick. When he saw the crackhead get out of the car with the gun and hide by the Lambo he got ready to call it in. He had to use his phone because he was in his personal vehicle. Just as he was dialing, two fine ass sistah's climbed out of the Camaro with guns in their hands. The way they carried their guns, the way they moved, his experience told Peters that they weren't about to do any talking. These two were the real deal.

Forgetting about backup, Peters got out of his car and drew his weapon. He saw the smaller female walk right up to the crackhead and blow his head off like it was nothing. She was colder than the freezing black night. The look that he saw in her eyes as she pointed the 9mm at him had him ready to piss his pants.

"Stop pointing that fucking gun at my sister!" The venom that flew off Nina's lips was more poisonous than any snake.

"M-mam I need you to drop your weapon and put your hands up", Peters couldn't conceal his fear or hide his shaky hands. There was just something about the woman in front of him. "Nina, shoot this mothafucka! Whatcha waiting on?" Trina was livid as she stared down the barrel of his service weapon without flinching.

"Drop your weapon and put your hands up!" The cop repeated. This time with a little authority.

Gorillaz in the Bay 2

To Trina's horror and shock her sister hesitated and lowered her gun. Trina knew her sister loved her hands down. But she would've neva guessed that love would cause her to bitch up one day.

"Nina what the F..." was all she got out of her mouth.....

De'Kari

CHAPTER IV
(Meanwhile)

You don't get a name like Jason Voorheeze by being soft or by being a dumb nigga. Voorheeze is a name that LaMont worked hard to receive an even harder to live up to, just ask anybody that did time with him.

Especially in DVI, that's where he really honed his skills and terrorized niggaz.

Even though he was fucked up over T'Ridas death Voorheeze stayed on point, especially when it came to safety and security. Somebody should've told the mothafucka in the Cadillac that was following him that shit! Voorheeze saw the nigga a long time ago. He purposely kept riding around going from place to place waiting for the sun to go down. It was still day time when he left his brother and sister. When he felt it was dark enough, he headed towards a liquor store that was ducked off in the cut, so he could see what was up.

Making sure that both Dragoons were in place he got out of the Lambo and walked into the store. He was wondering about the second set of headlights that he kept seeing while he was watching the Cadillac, but he couldn't worry too much about that, he had to focus on one thing at a time. Voorheeze knew one thing, *Anybody Could Get It!*

The clerk in the store was a young brotha who looked like he would rather be anywhere else in the world, than at the store and at work that night.

Grabbing a stack of bills out of his pocket, Voorheeze placed them on the counter. "Brah this ain't a joke and you ain't got all day to make your decision. That's about $5000 right there, it's yours if you give me the videotape that's recording on the store cameras and don't put another one in."

The little nigga working behind the register knew something was about to pop off, he wasn't stupid. He was only making $8.50 an hour to work at the store. A stack of hundred-dollar bills made his mind up for him fast. "Aint no tape, shit on a DVD but just taking the disc ain't no good you gotta take the whole DVR or else they can just reprint the disc." He honestly told Voorheeze.

Shit, the little nigga was from the hood too. He was working at the store cause his mom got sick. He was paying the bills. He wasn't about to take the money and not keep it real.

Voorheeze liked the little nigga's get down and respected the little game he just kicked to him. "I tell you what take that and head to the back", he told him as he pointed at the stack of money. "Disconnect everything and when I'm done I'll come tighten you up. Oh yeah you might wanna stay low rogue." Both Dragoons came out of their resting place, ready to breathe fire.

The clerk took one look at the two cannons and got Lil like Wayne. As soon as he got to the back he started counting the money.

Pop! Pop! Pop! Pop!

Voorheeze crouched down low instinctively when he heard the shots. He wondered what was going on. Instantly, he thought of the second set of headlights. Just when he was about to check it out he saw a figure run right by the front of the store. What the fuck is going on, he wondered again. Though he killed two full bottles of Remy he was sober now. That little buzz was gone the moment he sensed a threat, now his mind was racing to access what was going on.

"Freeze!" When he heard those words he thought to himself, that must have been a cop that just ran by, but who the fuck was the shooter?

"Stop pointing that fuckin gun at my sister?" Voorheeze couldn't believe his ears! It was one of the twins. It sounded like the little feisty one they called Nina.

"M-mam I need you to drop your weapon and put your hands up!" Voorheeze rose up the moment he heard the twin's voice. He was out the door by the time the cop finished talking. Fuck hiding, she was one of his family.

"Nina shoot this mothafucka! Whatcha waiting on?" Trina was livid! You could hear it in her voice.

The cop had his back towards Voorheeze. His attention was so focused on Nina, he neva sensed anything wrong. He was pointing his gun at Trina's head. Her back was towards Voorheeze as well. The only person facing him was Nina. She gave no sign that she saw him.

"Drop your weapon and put your hands up!" First Nina lowered her pistol and then she bent over and placed the gun on the ground. She stood up with her arms in the air. When she did this, the cop took his gun off Trina and then pointed it at Nina.

"Nina what the F…"

BOOM!

The sound of the loud Dragoon filled the night. Voorheeze blew Peters mothafuck'n head off the moment the gun wasn't pointed at Trina. His entire face was gone. Trina spun around ready to get active, when she saw Voorheeze, she smiled.

Pop! Pop! Pop! Pop! Pop!

Nina walked up to the already dead cop and shot him five more times in the head or what was left of a head. She wished she could bring him back to life, so she could kill him for pointing a gun at her sister!

Gorillaz in the Bay 2

"Look we gotta move. Trina find his keys and search his car. Make sure there is no surveillance shit in there, if it is we gone take the car. Nina shoot them cameras out and follow me!" Voorheeze neva wasted time or panicked, this violence shit is what he lived for.

He walked to the trunk of the Lambo and retrieved a black Gucci bag. When he made it back to the front of the store Nina was right by his side with a new clip in her pistol.

He entered the store, he looked around and then called out "Youngsta where you at?" After a few seconds they heard a rustling from the back of the store. A few seconds after that the youngsta call back out "Brah that's you?"

"Yeah Rogue it's me" Voorheeze assured him.

The young clerk came out of the back holding an old beat up rifle shaking in his hands, he was scared but he would do what he had to if needed. At age 16, life had already taught him many lessons. When he saw the man that handed him the money he started to lower the rifle.

Seeing the youngsta's hesitation Voorheeze spoke, "you don't need that, you and me good unless you changed your mind and wanna be a hero then that little shit aint gone help you." The two Dragoons in Voorheeze's hands solidified his statement.

"Naw big Homie, I ain't no hero. I just ain't no dumb nigga either! I done seen your face, Lil Mama face", he nodded his head towards Nina. "How I know y'all aint gone just kill me?" The fear evident in the young man's voice and what he said was true. It told Voorheeze that the kid was smart.

Voorheeze took the Gucci bag off his shoulder and tossed it to the youngsta. Fuck the chit chat, they had to get out of there before the place was swarming with police. "I like your style youngsta but it aint no time foe conversation. That's a hundred racks up in that bag. That's yours if you stick to our agreement. Now if you don't want it, Lil Mama as you called her, gone knock yo dick in the dirt. I aint into killing kids but I aint into going to prison either."

"A hundred racks! Shit Big Homie hold up let me get that for you." He ran to the back so fast and retrieved the bag wit everything in it that Voorheeze and Nina barely had time to exchange glances.

Grabbing the bag the kid brought, Voorheeze checked it. He then told Nina to check the back and make sure the youngsta didn't forget anything. Then he instructed the youngsta to put the money in the trunk of his car. It would be hard to explain a bag with $100,000 inside of it to the police.

Trina didn't find anything in the car but a cell phone. She took it for good measures and turned it off before stuffing it in her pocket.

De'Kari

After giving the kid an airtight story for the shooting, they got the fuck up outta of there.

CHAPTER V
(Oakland, CA)

The Koffee Shop was hardly ever quiet. 24/7 it ran a pretty smooth, detailed and accurate ship. Tonight, happened to be one of them rare moments that some quietness was found, 1:15 in the morning. Gunz was thankful for the peace and quiet. He had too much shit on his mind. The death of T'Rida not only hit Gunz hard. It happened to come at the wrong fucking time. Gunz loved T'Rida like a blood brother. T'Rida had helped them all bring out their "A" game and be the best that they could be.

A couple of years back Gunz played around with the idea of branching out to Philly. He had some cousins who kept telling him how good it was out there. Gunz took a trip out there at the suggestion of his cousin. He liked what he saw out there enough to bring the idea to the round table. When his plane landed back in Cali from his visit, T'Rida had been shot before he had a chance to go over the plan with his brothas. Gunz put his idea on the back burner and answered Voorheeze call to arms.

Gunz neva forgot about Philly, he was just waiting for the right time. He started reconnecting dots to make the move happen, when T'Rida was killed. Gunz knew the Philly move would be a good look for the family but even a better look for himself since Natasia was staying out in Philly.

Natasia was this sistah he had met at the airport years back. She was the definition of elegance, beauty and grace. While shit was hot he neva once contacted her ever, though he thought of her all the time. But when he finally did reach out to her she grabbed on. They stayed in constant communications and whenever time would permit Gunz would go see her or Natasia would come and see him.

As he sat in his back office with his drink in his hand, Gunz knew T'Ridas death was about to send Voorheeze over the edge which would only fuck everything up. Everyone always calls Gunz the loose cannon but Gunz simply believed that you "get off where you get mad at". So, he would bust on sight, middle of the night or broad daylight! That's just how he was.

Voorheeze on the other hand, it took more to set him off, especially with him always pushing safety and security. But once you successfully got him to go off his square, he was an animal of a completely different breed.

Gunz' cell phone rang, bringing him from his thoughts.

"Yeah, what's good?" He answered seeing Trina's number in his caller I.D. "Brah look, I know its late, but I'm guessing that you might wanna meet up?" She spoke first.

"Is something wrong?" Gunz already knew the answer to the question. Trina wouldn't be calling that time of the night unless there was something wrong.

"Naa, I just wanted you to know that we couldn't wait any longer. We were too hungry, so we already eating. Oh, big brah saw us at the restaurant and stopped by and ate with us. He complained about the food afterward". The phone was silent for a moment…

"Where you at"? He asked her.

"W.R." was all Trina needed to say.

"I'm on my way." Gunz hung up the phone and smiled to himself.

He shook his head from side to side and downed the glass of Remy XO he had before making the call. Still shaking his head, he stood up and grabbed his two 40s. Placing both on his waist band he spoke out loud, "That's what the fuck I get for thinking negatively about shit. If there was a possibility for some shit to go wrong, that shit gone go wrong as fuck" he chuckled to himself. Referring to her telling him that they killed Wendell and somehow Voorheeze was there. Gunz knew he was going to be pissed.

Even though Trina was talking code, Gunz knew exactly what she told him. Their method of talking in code was something Voorheeze came up with. You could use the exact same sentences for different meanings. Deciphering the statement depended solely on what the topic was. They called it "spit talk". They've been using the system for so long that they could hold a full-on conversation about the 49ers football game and be talking about a new shipment or some funk or even how the blocks were maintaining.

Wendell was dead, that was inevitable. What he hadn't expected was for Voorheeze to get involved in the shit. Gunz grabbed his keys and locked up the shop, double-checking that everything was on point. Then he jumped into his Aston Martin and drove to the War Room ready to meet the confrontation that was guaranteed to be waiting for him from Voorheeze. No doubt he was going to be hot about the situation, but Gunz had to make a decision and figured he made the best one given the situation.

Gunz pulled up to the house on Santa Elena Way. He couldn't help but to think that this was the type of neighborhood where a nigga could raise a family. Nina answered the door when he knocked. Without saying a word, she stepped aside, let him in and locked the door after closing it. Gunz was used to Nina's quiet persona and stand-offish attitude. The shit didn't bother him one bit. She didn't know it, but Gunz was the one person who understood her, they were just alike in a lot of ways.

Trina was her usual cheery self and greeted him in the living room with a hug.

"Where he at?" Gunz asked referring to Voorheeze.

"In the living room", she replied as she let him go.

Gunz smiled at Trina and winked his eyes before turning to Nina and asked, "What Nina, I can't get a hug?"

"Boy please you better go somewhere!" The roll of her eyes and snap of her neck when she said it, made both Gunz and Trina laugh.

"Naa for real. Y'all ok?" Gunz demeanor turned serious.

"We good! Hell, we always gone be good. I don't know about him though. He over there with an attitude like we didn't just save his life or something. Ugh!"

Although Nina stayed with an attitude 24/7. She couldn't 'stand it when someone showed attitude to her. It really drove her crazy. Big brah or not, Nina wouldn't hesitate to get off on Voorheeze's ass if he didn't turn shit down.

"What he know?" He asked Nina, who was fuming. "He don't know nothing! That's why he got that little funky ass attitude! We told him we weren't going to break the chain of command. Protocol was protocol. If he wanted answers, he had to get them from you."

"Aight bet. Y'all hang out and let me go deal with brah." He turned to go to the other room but paused and then turned back around. "I thank both of you from the bottom of my heart. Bullshit is bullshit, but real shit is real shit and I couldn't have lost my otha brotha", Gunz revealed a small window of vulnerability.

To him, death was death, but a loss was everything and he was losing it all. Voorheeze was all he had left from the beginning.

"Don't mention it big brah! That's what family is for to be there for each other and have each other's back!" Trina meant every word she spoke, her grandma, Mama Butler instilled in all of them, the importance of family and the love of family when they were little kids. Nina was shocked at the rare display of emotion from Gunz. Granted it was a small show of emotion, she had neva seen or heard of him showing a single iota of emotion before.

Voorheeze had blown a punk ass cops head off, only to find out that the twins had been following both he and the nigga the entire time and Gunz knew. Now he was out there in the front room playing "family reunion" instead of having his ass in the den and giving him a full report.

De'Kari

"I mean god dam nigga", its bout time you brought yo ass in here! For a minute I thought y'all was having a fucking picnic or something up in dis bitch. You wanna tell a nigga what's going on?" Voorheeze told Gunz as they embrace.

"What's going on is, everybody's been playing their positions making sure we don't take no losses, while we're all trynna get thru dis shit to da best of our abilities". Gunz told him as he walked over to the bar and poured himself a double shot of Hennessey.

"I see that, but don't act like you don't know what da fuck I'm talking bout! What' sup wit dat shit tonight! I'm talking bout, why I spot dis bitch ass nigga following me, then find out the Twins been following me or him or both of us, the entire time! When I stepped to dem after the shit popped off dey tell me some shit about protocol! But when Trina picked up the phone she didn't call French Tip or Cantelope, she called you nigga! You not a She-Wolf, so where the hell is protocol?"

By now Voorheeze's voice began elevating. It was beyond rare for him to lose his cool, but he was losing it.

"First of all, big brah, I think you need to lower yo voice some. Sit down, relax and let me break it down to you". Gunz wasn't worried about the neighbors hearing the yelling. The house had been sound proofed after they had bought it. He was just getting tired of being yelled at and spoken to disrespectfully. Brother or not, he would only allow so much.

He expected Voorheeze to be hot behind the situation, but blood was still doing the most and Gunz wasn't about taking no bull shit.

"Lower my tone…. Mothafucka who the fuck you think you talking to, nigga?"

Voorheeze jumped up from the leather sofa spilling his drink in the process. He was working with emotions because he still couldn't deal with the pain of losing T'Rida, so his anger was misplaced.

Before Gunz realized what he was doing or could even stop himself, his instincts kicked into gear. He shot off the bar stool, drew one of his pistols from his waist and had crossed the living room in two big strides. He was now directly in Voorheeze's face, breathing like a mad animal.

Gunz was so close they could each smell the alcohol on the others breathe.

"Nigga you got me fucked up, V! Blood I know you going through some shit right now! My nigga, we all going thru some shit! But, nigga don't ever forget who the fuck I am, nigga, straight up! I ain't yo bitch and you aint bout to talk to me like I am!" Spit was flying from his lips, he was so furious.

Gorillaz in the Bay 2

"Like I said nigga, lower your mothafuck'n voice when you speaking to me!" Gunz was beyond pissed off. He loved Voorheeze but if he had to remind Voorheeze about how his gangsta was, then so be it.

"Or what nigga? Fuck you gone do with that?" Voorheeze knew that he had gone too far and crossed the line out of anger. But he wasn't about to bow down like a bitch to nobody.

The Twins couldn't believe what they were hearing as they waited.

Fuck it! If this was how Voorheeze wanted to play it, Gunz was ready to play! He cocked the 40 back putting one in the head.

Voorheeze stared deep into Gunz eyes, neva blinking as he pulled one of his dragoons slowly out of its holster. It didn't' matter to him that Gunz had 30 shots and he only had six. This close to each other, neither was going to miss!

"This nigga got me fucked up", Voorheeze thought as he pulled the dragoon out.

"Nigga, you brought it to some gangsta shit! Bust a mothafuck'n move!" Voorheeze challenged Gunz.

BOOM!

The bullet smacked hard into its intended target.

The sound of the gun going off continued to echo inside of the sound proof house. Neither one of the gangsta's flinched, nor looked at the hole in the wall just above their head where the bullet landed.

"What's the hell wrong with y'all?!" Trina yelled at both of them as Nina stood by with her smoking pistol in her hand.

When neither one of them answered, Trina shouted again. "Voorheeze! Gunz! I know y'all hear me. We are supposed to be family and you standing there like two common mothafucka's in the street getting ready to kill each other on some childish shit!

"Where are the bosses that y'all supposed to be? We just buried our brotha! We supposed to be helping each other get thru this shit, instead you mothafucka's trynna give us some more shit to have to get over!" Trina's words were real as fuck.

But it wasn't the realism of what she said that got everyone's attention, it was the fact that she was cursing. Hearing Trina curse is what got their attention.

Voorheeze was the first to react. Still staring into Gunz eyes, he placed his cannon back in its holster. Gunz unclocked his 40 and placed it back on his hip. He walked to the bar then walked back over to Voorheeze and handed him a drink.

"Look big brah…" he began, but Voorheeze cut in.

"Ain't nothing to speak on. I was way out of line, but you my brotha and I love you!" Voorheeze meant just what he said.

De'Kari

He also meant every word that wasn't said too! He wasn't sure what caused him to spazz out, but he knew he was wrong. So, what they followed him. They were protecting him.

The pain he was feeling had him fucked up. All the alcohol and coke that was in his system was fucking with his mind. It didn't matter though, Gunz drew down on him! The moment he did, he became a threat and Voorheeze didn't tolerate threats. Gunz had to go!

"I love you too, big brah." Gunz told him (glad he didn't force him to take his life over some stupid shit). The tension subsided a bit. The twins took up places in the living room. They weren't trynna hear jack-shit about their presence in the room. They were posted-up, to make sure shit else didn't pop off.

Over the next 30 minutes, Gunz let Voorheeze in on everything that had happened from the night of T'Rida's birthday until now. Voorheeze's anger subsided greatly after hearing he had been slipping for so long. Yeah, he knew that Wendell was following him. But he'd only known since leaving Clark and French Tip at the restaurant. Shit, Wendell had been following him since the funeral.

"Fuck!" He thought, "*I was really slippin.*"

Learning that it was Wendell who called the police on T'Rida that day made Voorheeze wish he could go and kill the nigga again. It also explained to him why the twins were reporting to Gunz instead of Cantelope or French Tip. If either of them received wind of this shit, they would've killed Wendell a long time ago. There would not have been any debating whatsoever.

Finding out that Wendell was feeding information back to some little cats from the Village in East Palo Alto was a good thing. Although, Gunz didn't know just what to do with that information, he figured it might be important.

Voorheeze agreed with him one hundred percent on that. At the very least it meant that somebody else was interested in the family. Voorheeze wanted to let the Dragon surface and breathe fire on them niggaz right then, but **safety** and security came first.

They needed to know just what the fuck a Young Nigga Mafia was. Couldn't have been too much because this was the first he'd ever heard of them. But Voorheeze knew it's always better to be safe than to be sorry. With that in mind, he gave the twins their new assignment. They were to find out any and everything they could about these little niggaz. After that, the Twins left.

Gunz and Voorheeze remained at the War Room clear into the next day discussing plans for the future of Neva Die. Gunz told Voorheeze about his plans for Philly and Voorheeze gave him his blessings. Gunz was shocked. He'd expected Voorheeze to argue with him about it.

Gorillaz in the Bay 2

What Gunz didn't know was Voorheeze only agreed with the idea so he wouldn't have to kill him. He was serious about threats and pulling that Cannon was a threat.

They agreed that they would lay everything out for the family in a couple of days at the next meeting.

De'Kari

CHAPTER VI
(A week later)

Clark loved his little brother. He always had. He just didn't know how to show it. All his life he had to fight just to prove himself and make a way. So, it was hard for him to show weakness. Love was a sign of weakness. Clark didn't have time for none of that bullshit! He was always about his money and handling his business, but a mothafucka could get it quick, fast and in a hurry!

He knew that there were a lot of things that he could have done differently but fuck it! It is what it is! He neva cried over spilled milk. Though the brothers were different in a lot of ways, in this area they were both alike. Neither one of them lived with regrets! Regrets were for the weak! Weak niggaz turn soft and soft niggaz got killed. There wasn't anything weak or soft about Clarkola! That's for damn sure!

As he pushed the High-Performance Dodge Charger through the streets of East Palo Alto, aka, "little bitty Baghdad" bumping Young Jeezy, shit was really looking good. Money was flowing like he had neva seen in his life.

The City belonged to him now. Hands down, he was Top Dawg! His little chick was pregnant and expecting a little girl. So soon he was going to have two daughters.

At new War Room, Gunz had brought up the conversation of expanding out to Philly, something that he into before T'Rida's untimely demise. Now he was making things official. They would be opening a chapter of Neva Die out there. Gunz would be expected to oversee building the strongest team possible.

This move would ultimately put Voorheeze at the head of the table, Commander and Chief! The three-branch leadership that everyone was used to, would now be a one-man dictatorship. No one had stepped up to fill T'Rida's seat, because his seat couldn't be filled. So Voorheeze was now running the whole organization. Which was all good with Clark. It would give him the room that he needed to do him fully. Although he played his position to the tee, anybody would feel some kind of way taking orders from their little brother, he was no exception. Not that he held any resentment or anything. He just needed to be able to breathe. Shit, Clarkola *wasn't* a worker he was a Boss!

He pulled up to the spot and hopped out. Seeing Tut Tut, he called out, "What's up rogue? We good?"

"Shit, we good Dad." Tut called back.

De'Kari

Clark walked to the trunk of the Challenger and retrieved a duffle bag. Inside the big bag was this week's shipment. Normally Sam would've handled the pick-up since he handles distribution, but he was on another mission. He could've appointed someone else to do the pickup, but Clark didn't mind getting his hands dirty. He wasn't the type of nigga to look and watch other niggaz work.

Clark and Tut head into the trap house. As they hit the front porch Tut issued out a set of orders to one of his soldiers making sure mothafucka's stayed on point.

Once inside the trap, Clark tossed Tut the bag. Tut caught it then chuckled.

"What nigga, you demoted yourself or something. Cuz nigga if you'll demote yourself, ain't no telling what you'll do to another mothafucka!"

"That's why yo ass better stay on point nigga, you wanna keep a job." Clark joked back at him but was dead serious.

"As long as they make guns, I'mma keep a job Dad."

Even though the package came directly from Clark's hands, Tut walked over to the table and began removing kilos out of the bag, taking his own count. Clark didn't feel disrespected in the least. If anything, he was impressed. Hell, the average nigga would've just taken shit for granted that the count was good. That's how shit get fucked up, taking shit for granted. In Clark's mind, there was no room for errors. It was simple, the cost for a fuck-up was your life.

"What's up with that thang though?" Clark asked Tut once he was done with his count.

"Ten kilos present and accounted for".

"What you talking bout Dad?" Tut asked him as he knocked on the door behind him and handed the dope over to one of his workers.

"That shit wit lil Ju-Ju, nigga."

"Oh, it's good Dad, he got court in the morning. It looks like the judge is gonna give the lil nigga bail. Soon as he does we already all over it. "

"Make sure you are Rogue. This is important to me." Ju-Ju was Clarks little cousin. He was a hot head, but he was loyal and reliable.

"Alright Dad, I got you." Tut already knew how bad Clark wanted to get lil Ju-Ju out. He was thinking of a way to ensure Ju-Ju got bailed out when Clark spoke, bringing him back to reality.

"We bout to make some changes in a minute my nigga. Shit's bout to grow and get better for everybody. Especially for you, so keep yo head in da game." Clark was referring to what was just discussed at the War Room. After the meeting at the War Room a whole lot of shit was about to change.

Gorillaz in the Bay 2

Just when Tut was about to ask him what he was talking about, Tut's phone rang.

"Yeah, what's up Dad?" Tut answered the phone noticing it was one of his block lieutenants. He listened for a few seconds, then he hung up the phone.

"Brah, we got a problem."

"What's up Rogue?" Clark asked not liking the sound in his little cousin's voice.

"Somebody just hit house 2."

Clark barely held his anger, "What?"

Niggaz didn't get much though. I guess while they was hittin da spot, that nigga D-Rocc was on his way to drop some loot off at da house. Dat nigga Dunk say D-Rocc did his thang! But we still lost one of the little niggaz in the house and them niggaz got away." Tut could feel the heat coming off Clark.

"What about all the rest of the shit that was in there?" Clark didn't like taking losses, but it came with the game.

Hearing that he lost a little soldier was unacceptable. Somebody most definitely had to answer for that.

"Everything else is secure. Brah and dem moved everything to house 1 before the police came!"

"Let's go check it out." Clark told him as he headed to the door.

As they made their way to Menlo, Clark was trying to figure out who would be stupid enough to try and knock off one of his spots. Whoever did it, had to know the hell they would bring down on themselves for trying some shit like that! Dragon Gang was coming, there was no doubt about it! East Menlo was Al-Qaeda territory! Everybody knew that, and them little Al-Qaeda niggaz wasn't playing bout shit! They've had the city on lock for the past couple of years and wasn't letting go. Their body count was off the charts!

Clark turned left onto Ivy Drive off of Willow Road, headed towards the spot. When he hit Sevier, he looked towards the 1200 block, but he turned down the 1300. Even from Ivy Drive they could see that Sevier was blocked off halfway down the street. He drove down there any way, as far as he could make it. Four houses away from the actual scene, he couldn't make it any further, so he pulled over.

Menlo Park Police Department was everywhere. They were trying their hardest to keep everyone back and maintain some type of order, but that shit was senseless. Niggaz wanted to know what happened and was there to find out!

"Whatcha thinking, dad?" Tut spoke up, he didn't like sitting in a parked car, he felt trapped.

"Shit let's check it out." Clark told him in response and climbed out of the charger.

As they stepped up to the crowd, the first thing that either of them noticed was the body that was on the sidewalk.

"That's that nigga Jack from the Vill stretched out right there." Tut said just loud enough for Clark to hear him.

Clark didn't respond he just took in the entire scene. There were two more bodies. One was halfway across the front yard and the other body which was much smaller than the other two, lay just inside the doorway. Immediately, he knew that body belonged to the soldier that he lost, Munchie.

A sharp pain shot through his chest at the sight of the little nigga who wasn't old enough to even fuck, let alone be in the streets. Clark used to date his mom Pam, back in the day. He remembered how the little mothafucka would ride his big wheel up and down this same exact street, acting like he was cool while they hustled. Now he was looking at the lifeless body laying helpless in the doorway of the house at 1338 Sevier Avenue.

Cops were placing little red cones all over the place, which were markers for the bullet casings. To Clark's surprise, there were way more bullet casings than he expected to see. From the number of cones that were out in the street. It looked like a war kicked off. The cops were still finding shells.

Knowing that they'd seen all that they were going to see, Clark decided it was time to go. They jumped back into the car, hit an illegal U-turn in the middle of the street and headed towards the 1200 Block to see what was what.

They pulled up and hopped out at J. Clinton and D-Rocc's spot. The crazy thing about Menlo was mothafuckas stuck to the script for the most part. There was a shootout just a block down the street. Yet, there wasn't an onlooker out on the block trying to be nosey.

"WwaWwa what's up y'all." Young Drew bounced off the porch and greeted them.

"What's up, Drew?"

"Ggg ggg gettin' dis money nigga!" Drew was by far the skinniest nigga in Menlo. However, many niggaz lost their lives for underestimating him. Lil Drew was a shooter fa'sho.

They made their way to the backyard, no doubt everyone would be there.

"Man, you know G-Town niggaz don't come across Willow!" D-Rocc jokingly called out when he saw Clark and Tut walk in the yard.

"Shit nigga, if you mothafuckas were out here handling yo business they wouldn't have had to call the Big Dawgs to come lend support." Clark joked back as he embraced D-Rocc. They'd known each other since they were kids.

"Come on Clark, we all know you be trynna take notes on dis murking shit. So, nigga, I know you rolled thru dat little scene down da block already and seen first-hand how the kid do." Rocc spoke with a grin on his face.

Tut looked around the area. Even though he pushed that Neva Die shit, he was still C-Street and to Menlo niggaz, C-Street was the Village plain and simple. The Village was beefing with Menlo niggaz, Al-Qaeda niggaz to be specific. So, Tut kept his hands ready right next to his banger, and his eyes on swivel.

"So, what's da business?" Clark asked as he looked at the group of young killaz.

"Al-Qaeda. business, Clark. We got it. Don't get it twisted, niggaz called you and told you what was what as a courtesy, cause that's yo spot they tried to hit Rogue. But when dem niggaz crossed Willow, they invaded Al-Qaeda. territory. No disrespect Big Homie, I know you got yo City on lock, but you gotta stay out of this one. We got you though." Dunk was soft spoken and at 5'5" he was a lil nigga in size, but he commanded so much respect and authority that even when he talked low, he spoke volumes.

"I hear you nigga, but a mothafucka crossed me so I'm taking that personally. Whoever tried that shit disrespected the Mobb my nigga. Now I aint neva stepped on y'all toes or clashed wit y'all. But you do what you do and I'mma do what I do. One of us will get them." Clearly it wasn't up for discussion.

Dunk didn't give a fuck about no Neva Die shit, in his mind it was Al-Qaeda or nothing, but he knew Clark was right. If it was one of his spots that got hit, he would be out for blood.

Once they came to a mutual understanding about how to proceed, D-Rocc explained to Clark what happened. He was on his way to drop off some loot to the spot when he saw four niggaz hop out a Jeep Commander that was in front of him, with bangers in their hands. Roc's first mind was to stay out of it because it wasn't Al-Qaeda. business. But he realized it was Clark's spot and Al-Qaeda. was getting money with Neva Die so it was his business. Not to mention it was a direct insult to Menlo for niggaz to try anything in Menlo. So, he hopped out his car with both his bangers in his hands. As he was getting out his car he saw one of the niggaz shoot lil Munchie in the face as soon as he opened the door. Roc immediately started bussing with both thangs.

The niggaz that was hitting the spot were caught off guard and confused. They tried to bust back at D-Rocc, but they were unorganized and unprepared, so they panicked. There was a duffle bag right inside the door. The nigga that shot Munchie saw it and snatched it up, he didn't want to leave empty handed. As he raced to the Jeep he barely made it to the sidewalk before he was gunned down. There was a nigga still in the Jeep on the passenger side, he hopped out, grabbed the bag and they sped off. D-Rocc drove to this lil bitch house by the Boys Club in the back of Menlo and switched whips before heading back to the spot.

While Clark was there he took the opportunity to drop them niggaz off some more work. Business was so good, the price was right, he damn near supplied the entire town. The new design he had on how he did things was smooth, but now he had to change it. Everybody assumed that the house on Sevier was a stash spot, but it was simply just a decoy.

Clark also owned the home directly behind the house on Sevier, no one knew but Munchie. After the money was dropped off at Sevier, it was counted and then Munchie would walk out the back door and go through the adjoining gate in the back yard to stash the bag of money at the house on Madera. Every night the nigga in charge of the house would take the money dropped off to the real stash spot. Niggaz were actually trynna to rob an empty house, but they didn't know it.

After they left J. Clinton's spot they decided to head over to Jonathan's Fish & Chips on the other side of the freeway to grab something to eat since they were already out that way. As they were parking the thickest thing Clark had ever seen came walking out of Johnathan's.

"Got Damn!" They called out in unison.

The chick was five-foot-five with high-yellow skin with just a kiss of cinnamon. 38DD chest with an ass that looked like it stood out at least two feet and a half from her back. Her reddish-brown hair ran all the way down her back and rested on her ass. She was almost the perfect specimen!

When they yelled out damn so loud that she heard them, she paused for a second which was a natural response, then she continued on about her business. Clark wasn't going to let her get away. He jumped out the whip while Tut was still parking. "Hey excuse me! Say beautiful!" He called out as he jogged up to her.

"Yesss", she responded as she rolls her eyes, while she continued to walk.

"Look, I know you heard us sounding all juvenile and shit but Damn you're beautiful! I'm not going to apologize for being mesmerized by your beauty!"

He used a line he had heard his little brotha use before when he approached females. Nevertheless, Clark was dead serious when he spoke.

Gorillaz in the Bay 2

"Mesmerized huh?" She replied after giggling at his comment.

"Look Lil Mama, I don't know who you are or who you belong to but if you don't realize that your beauty is beyond breath taking, in fact you're mind blowing and alluring, then somethings wrong! I mean, I'mma real hood nigga so don't get me wrong, I'm what they call rough around the edges. But if I had you, I would let you know every day just how captivating you are." The words rolled off his tongue like butter, real smooth.

"Okay, so I see we have a way with words." She told him as she looked up into his face with a big smile.

"Believe me I really don't, but your aura was calling out to a nigga so tough. My subconscious had to tap in to another plateau mentally and give me some of that Super Fly mouthpiece!"

She laughed so hard, Clark knew he was in.

"They call me Clarkola beautiful, what's your name?" He asked while extending his hand out to seal the deal.

"You better not let that fine man get away girl. Gone and take his hand". Some little old lady threw her two cents in as she walked by smiling.

"Clarence don't act like you don't know me." That caught him completely off guard. Not the fact that she knew his name, shit East Palo Alto was only 2.2 square miles, most people knew him. But she called him by his government, that had him on the defense. People didn't use that name, his real name. They either call him Clarkola or Clark.

"Wow! So now you don't remember me?" She asked him seeing the confused look that came across his face.

"Ma look, I don't know how you know me. Because, if I ever in my life saw someone as gorgeous as you I would remember." The way he bit down on his lip when he said that, turned her on.

"What if I once was your woman, yet you took me for granted, would you still remember?" Hearing those words shocked him. He looked closer and noticed her green eyes. Clark stumbled backwards as the look of recognition slowly crept onto his face.

"Fuck naw!" Clark mumbles to himself and shakes his head in disbelief.

"Yes, it's me Clarence. How have you been?" Tieka was his high school sweetheart.

It had been about fifteen years since he'd seen her. She looked completely different than she used to. But as Clark looked at her more closely, he could see some resemblance. The two of them chatted for a while to catch up and exchange numbers. Then she said good bye and turned to walk away.

De'Kari

As he watched her walk off he silently kicked himself in the ass. He thought to himself; *How did he ever let that go*? That has got to be the biggest, firmest ass he had ever seen on something cute. Niggaz always use the expression ass like a donkey, but watching Tieka walk away, that ass really did look like a donkey or a buffalo.

Inside Jonathan's, Tut informed him that he'd already ordered his favorite for him, the catfish meal, fried oysters on the side with extra tartar sauce.

"Alright now Mr. Mouthpiece. Nigga you need to change your name to Don Juan with them lines." Tut teased him when he walked in.

"Nigga, you know I spit that shit!" Clark joked but beamed with pride.

"Your beauty is mesmerizing and breath-taking." Tut mimics Clark's voice.

"Nigga Ice Berg Slim couldn't write it, better than I spit it."

While they were clowning around their order came up. After checking their food, they headed for the door to go.

As they exited out of Jonathan's, Clark dropped one of his tarter sauces out of his hand. He was going to leave it but considering it didn't burst open, he bent down to pick it up. That change of mind saved his life!

Tat! Tat! Tat! Tat! Tat! Tat! Tat!

The sound of automatic gun fire erupted. The bullets riddled the wall of Jonathan's spreading out in a clear line of holes on the wall behind the area where Clark's head had been.

FOCCA! FOCCA! FOCCA! FOCCA! FOCCA! FOCCA!

At the first sound of gun fire Tut dropped the food and snatched out his bangers, like clock-work. He let both of his bangers, bang out!

FOCCA! FOCCA! FOCCA!

Although he couldn't see where the shots were coming from because of the parked vehicles he was crouched in front of, Clark's instinct was telling him they were coming from behind the Honda to his left.

BOOM! BOOM! BOOM!

The sound of his new .44 Desert Eagles sounded like bombs from Bagdad.

"It's four of em Dad! Niggaz in a blue minivan! Tut called out to Clark.

Tat! Tat! Tat! Tat! Tat! Tat! Tat! Tat!
BOCCA! BOCCA! BOCCA! BOCCA!

It was like a scene out of a gangster movie. Pedestrians screamed as they scrambled to get out of the way.

Gorillaz in the Bay 2

Four niggaz against two aint neva been good odds. But Clark aint neva been the type of nigga to bitch up or turn pussy under no circumstance!

Crouching down right now he was starting to feel embarrassed. He could only imagine how he looked to the people who were hiding in the stores or behind cars and looking at the shoot out! Fuck this nigga! Pride was more important than caution! He wasn't about to look like no sucka!

He noticed there was a brief pause in the gunfire, which could only mean they were reloading. Fuck it! It's all or nothing! He thought to himself. He pulled his second Desert Eagle from his waist and stood clear up!

BOOM! BOOM! BOOM!

With both guns blazing he walked steadily towards the minivan.

BOOM! BOOM!

The niggaz who were shooting at them were caught off guard by the brazen act. They too began to duck and cover.

Tut looked up and couldn't believe this nigga was pulling a Denzel from Training Day. Tut thought he was crazy but watching Clark right then, he knew that nigga had to be crazy hands down!

"Fuck it Dad! What's happening!" Tut yelled out as he jumped up and start bussin. He wasn't about to be outdone! They didn't call him Tut-Tut for nothing. Let them thangs talk!

Tut! Tut! Tut!

The sudden move threw the four shooters off. In a panic, the driver hit the gas pedal. A nigga was on his knees shooting from the sliding side door. He lost his balance and fell out of the van when the driver hit the gas. When he hit the ground, his 9mm fell out of his hand and slid under a parked car. He jumped up as fast as he could.

Fuck his banger, he had to get back in the minivan. He knew if he didn't, he would be dead. Just then, a bullet caught him in the shoulder. The force of the bullet caused his body to spin around. He fell halfway inside the van. His torso landed inside on the seat while his legs were hanging out the open door. He could see Clark steadily advancing. Right then, he wished he had his banger in his hand.

BOOM! BOOM! BOOM!

The sound of the gunfire made the nigga try to jump all the way into the minivan. He was too late! The shit was getting too hot for Roscoe, who was the driver of the van. They'd had the advantage and perfect opportunity in the beginning. Now shit had changed, they'd lost the upper-hand, and it was time to get outta there. Roscoe hit the gas pedal, nearly side-swiping a car as he sped out the parking lot.

De'Kari

As he sped past the car, he heard a loud thump, and someone cry out, but he neva stopped! He didn't care if he ran somebody over, fuck 'em, at least he made it up out of there.

**** **N. D.** ****

Just as the minivan lurched forward the young shooter was trying his hardest to pull the lower half of his body in the minivan using just his upper body. The pain in his shoulder from the gunshot was unbearable. *Almost in,* he thought to himself as he inched closer!

Thump!

As Roscoe sped past the parked car that he'd almost side swiped, he neva realized that it was his niggaz body that collided with the car that made the loud thump. The shit looked sickening. His body was bent and twisted like some type of contortionist. One leg was torn completely off. It was on the ground next to the parked car, the other leg was folded backwards, broken in three places. But the pain from the wounds didn't bother the little nigga, what was killing him the most was the sight of Clark walking up to him looking like the grim reaper himself.

Little Ned's heart was beating so hard, he could hear it beating in his ears.

"I would ask you who you are or who yo boys were, but it don't matter. I'll find out!" Little Ned didn't think he could feel any more fear, but he was wrong.

Hearing what Clark just said, he knew death was here! He wasn't sure if he was pissing his pants, but he knew they were now soaked.

"What you and yo niggaz should've realized is, Nigga dis Neva Die! We get it the "Smack Mobb Way"."

BOOM! BOOM! BOOM! BOOM! BOOM!

Five slugs to his head ended Ned's life. After killing him, Clark walked casually back to the whip. Tut reached the whip at the same time as Clark did with their food from Jonathan's in his hands.

"How can a nigga worry about food in the midst of a shoot-out?" He asked himself.

"Nigga I know you ass ain't that fuck'n hungry!" Clark couldn't believe that Tut had all the food in his hands.

"Come on Dad, fo real? Blood you just bodied that nigga and our fingerprints all over dis shit"! He nodded to all the bags of food in his hands, "no fingerprints, no evidence, Dad! Now get yo Smack Mobb ass in and let's get up outta here". With two shootouts in one day, Menlo Park P.D. was guaranteed to be on shit. As sure as shit, they saw

Gorillaz in the Bay 2

Menlo Park P.D. coming over the ramp as they were hitting 101 heading South.

Across the street, sitting in a car in the parking lot of Baneth's Pharmacy, Tashira Green aka Tieka sat with a smile on her face. She was sitting in her car thinking about the encounter she just had with Clark when the shooting broke out.

As the war broke out in front of her, she was so scared she didn't know what to do. Instincts told her to help, but rationale told her not to do jack shit. So, she watched it all. She was scared and at the same time turned on by Clark's Rambo-like behavior. As a swarm of squad cars screeched to a halt all around the area, Tieka pulled off with a slight smile on her face.

De'Kari

CHAPTER VII
(Later on, that night)

"Fuck you mean you left him! How da fuck you leave 'em brah?" He paced back and forth with his banger in his hand. "Nigga if dat was yo mothafuck'n ass would you have wanted a mothafucka to leave you?" Young Sutton was furious. He couldn't believe what this coward ass nigga had just told him. Sutton was a Village nigga thru and thru! A ride about it or die about it type nigga! So, hearing that Roscoe let lil Ned fall out of the minivan and left him behind to die, he wasn't trynna hear none of that shit!

"Rogue, I didn't know he fell out. One minute he was on the floor blaz'n wit us, then shit got so fuck'n hot, I got up out of there! Like anyone would've done. I thought he was in the back!" Roscoe pleaded his case. The fear in his voice was evident. He glanced around the room hoping to find a sympathetic eye from his comrades. Someone that would take his side, but all he saw was shame and anger on everyone's face.

They'd lost two brothers today and had a taste of blood in their mouths and hatred in their hearts! They all had been together for years. This was the very first time they had taken a loss. So, to hear that Roscoe abandoned Lil Ned had them all silently questioning him and his motives. *If he left Lil Ned in the midst of the funk, he could abandon any of them*, was the thought in all their minds.

"Brah it was four of y'all! Four of y'all!" Sutton shouted and then repeated to himself, not understanding how four niggaz could be out gunned by two.

"Brah it was four of you mothafuckas! How in da fuck did two niggaz make it hot for y'all!"

"Brah w-we had them from t-the jump." Roscoe was fumbling over his words because of fear, trynna get them out.

KeKe didn't have a problem sitting back watching Roscoe get embarrassed. He didn't like Roscoe, so the shit was hilarious to him. But now Sutton was starting to make them all look like some pussies by the way he was talking, so he spoke up.

"Look Blood, I know what that nigga just told you sound like a bunch of bullshit. But, Blood I'm telling you on my dead granny, what just happened out there was some made in Hollywood shit!" Everyone looked at KeKe as he spoke, he commanded that type of respect. That is why he was the second in command.

"Blood we had both them niggaz pinned down behind a car blaz'n and closing in on 'em. When outta nowhere that nigga Clark stands straight the fuck up like da terminator or some shit. Wit bullets flying by him he just starts letting go wit two, big, loud ass Dessert Eagles!"

"Blood I don't give a fuck what nobody says! That shit was so crazy all a nigga could do was stand there shocked, like what the fuck is this? By the time niggaz recovered from the shock of seeing that shit, it was too late. They had the upper hand! Mothafuckas were lucky to get the fuck outta there period Blood! As for Lil Brah, dat shit hurt like a motherfucka. But Blood, I thought the lil Nigga was in da back too. I saw him dive back into the back!" KeKe called it, how he saw it.

"Okay, hold up! Hold the fuck up!" Sutton's patience was below E. All this fucking talking wasn't going to do anything for his two fallen soldiers."

"Roscoe, you was driving?" He looked at Roscoe waiting for confirmation. Roscoe reluctantly nodded his head.

"And KeKe you say you was in the passenger?"

"No doubt blood I'm always shotgun.

Boom! Boom! Boom! Boom!"

Without hesitation, Sutton lifted his five-seven fn herstal and sent four hot slugs through the chest of J.J. knocking him off of his feet and landing on what was left of his back.

While KeKe was explaining shit to them, a little bit of clarity was able to sink in through the many clouds of rage inside of Sutton's head.

Four niggaz meant two in the front and two in the back. From the way they broke it down Lil Ned dove back in the van. So, the niggaz in the front would not have had a clue that the loud thump they heard was Ned's body hitting the parked car. But J.J. would've known, because he was in the back of the van. This whole time he had been sitting there like a little bitch. Neva once saying a word. Guilt was written all over his face before Sutton blew his chest out his back!

"Dem mothafuckas aint gone respect us or fear us if we keep missing. That's 0 for 2! Right now, dem old mothafuckas is laughing at us! How yall expect to take ova and you can't even bust that thang? Huh?" Sutton's frustration was causing his anger to rise again.

He loved everybody in the room like family, they all grew up together. Even when his mom moved them to Oakland, his sister always brought him down to East Palo Alto and dropped him off at his Auntie Rena's house. As him and his friends grew up they watched all the older cats getting their money, mostly Neva Die crew. Flossing like the world was theirs and it was. Neva once did they give back to the same people that they stepped on to get to the top.

Sutton thought about the many nights he watched his friends starve because they had a dope fiend for a mom or a dad, or both parents. Sutton's big sister always made sure he had food, but he would always feel guilty that his friends were going without. Other times he would save his meal in a plastic bag and give it to his peoples the next day to share.

"Have yall forgotten why we decided to do this? Or what we said we were gonna do?" He looked at every face in the room.

"Chanel how old were you when that nigga Lerone told you he would give you twenty dollars to suck his bitch ass dick?" He asked full of rage.

"I was only twelve." Instantly she relived the memory in her mind.

Her mother had been gone for five days, leaving little Chanel with no food. The hunger pains were so severe she cried most of the day, balled up in the corner of the room. Chanel had hit puberty young, at age 9, so by twelve her 38C breast and widening hips made her look years older. She drew a lot of attention from all the neighborhood D-Boys, but she always ignored them. She was so hungry by the time Lerone made the proposition, she didn't hesitate. Even though she was a virgin, in his sick and perverted cocaine filled mind, he was just glad that he had her first.

To add insult to injury, the nigga didn't even pay her. When she asked him for the money, all he did was laugh at her. Even though it happened years ago, the memory still hurt her and brought tears to her eyes. They fell down her face as shame filled her heart.

"Terry!" He looked at another girl in the group.

"Huh?" She looked up at Sutton with a concerned look, but she already knew what he was about to ask her.

"How old were you when that hoe ass nigga took your innocence?" With no remorse in his voice.

"Thirteen." She mumbled, still ashamed even though it wasn't her fault that the hoe ass nigga Rico was a fuck'n pedophile.

"I'm not trynna put nobody on front street! Everybody in this room knows what we've each been through. We all know what we're doing! Mothafuckas got lessons to learn and we the ones to teach em. When we're done they gone know that there's a price to pay foe da shit they did! The-Hate-U-Gave-Little-Infants-fucks-Everybody!" Everyone in the room cheered and hollered. That was Tupac's definition or meaning of "Thug Life" that he quoted, and it was the fuel that fed their fire.

They were all babies, no one in the room was older than seventeen, except Sutton who was nineteen, but they were all forced to grow up way too soon and way too fast. This was the life that they were given. This was the hands they were dealt. And they were gonna to play that hand to the best of their abilities.

Shit this was YOUNG NIGGA MAFIA, how else would they do it!

De'Kari

Voorheeze was addressing Gunz crew as they sat around the table.

"As far as I'm concerned, my brotha trust and respect yall enough to have full faith that you'll run this ship as smooth as he's been running it, when he leaves! And I love and trust my brotha enough to honor and respect his decision, even in his absence." The people in the room looked on intently as he spoke.

Each person knowing the magnitude of what was going on. Their dragon chains let the world know what time it was, while the dragon tattoos under their clothing signified their loyalty to one another.

"This is still Neva Die. Make sure everybody from yo lieutenants down to yo soldiers know that! For all intents and purposes, A.J. is now running the Oakland Chapter. His word is Law! A.J. and I say this in front of you, so there will neva be any misunderstandings... My word supersedes your word, period point blank! I know I ain't gotta say this, but I will. And if Gunz returns, he will retain his position and full authority. However, I aint about fuck'n niggaz over so the pay raises that everybody is receiving will remain in place even if brah returns!

A.J.! You, me and Gunz will get together after this to check some shit out but little brah this yo house, run it as you see fit. Just don't run it in the ground."

"No doubt." A.J. wasn't much for words everyone knew that. He was bout that action.

"Roc, a couple years ago I watched you make an oath to my lil brother. And I've watched you honor yo word and oath without question. Now I gotta ask you, O.G. are you still bound by word?" Voorheeze neva forgot how vicious Big Roc was or how adamant Gunz was about taking him out back in the day he was a threat way back then. Voorheeze wasn't taking no chances. If the wrong thing came out of Big Rocs mouth he would die right here and right now.

"That oath applies as long as my man lives lil homie. But V this aint nothing to do with that oath. We family now and I ride lil homie cause we all we got!" Big Roc meant each and every word.

Yea he was doing his little thang before this Neva Die shit, but it wasn't nowhere near the shit he was doing now. He's grown to love and respect his team, which was one of the things he had always wanted, a team of his own. Voorheeze didn't know it but Big Roc felt the same way about him as he did about Gunz, they were both his nephews. Big Roc was Neva Die till da casket dropped!

Voorheeze made eye contact with each person in the room. He had to admit that Gunz built one solid fucking team. Looking at them he could feel their fierceness. Even DeeDee sat there without a lick of larceny in his heart. Everyone assumed when word first got out about Gunz deciding to head out towards Philly that he would place the reins in DeeDee's hands. DeeDee was as loyal as can be and solid thru and thru.

What the rest of the team didn't know was Gunz was going to put DeeDee in charge. DeeDee came to Gunz a few nights before and told Gunz to put A.J. in charge. DeeDee was a wild child, he knew he needed somebody to tell him when to fall back because he didn't know when himself. He was a goon not a leader. So, if he was in charge his temper would bring the whole ship down.

A.J. knew he couldn't allow that to happen.

Voorheeze picked up his glass and everyone in the room followed suit.

"To our new head of state! And to Neva Die Oakland!" Everyone saluted and paid their respects.

"Oh, Rogue I almost forgot!" Voorheeze said as he dug in to his pocket.

He fumbled around for a minute making a big show like he couldn't find what he's looking for. Finally, he pulled his hand out of his pocket and A.J. a key fob.

"What's this big brah? A.J. asked excitedly. He already knew how Voorheeeze got down.

"That's you Rogue. Nigga, bosses don't ride muscle. Nigga, we drive foreign.

Everyone followed A.J. out to the front of the Koffee Shop to see what Voorheeze was giving him. Right outside the doors sat the brand new 2008 Porche Cayanne with custom black licorice and cherry red paint. Sitting on 24-inch black and red Forgiattos. The interior is an Italian dark almond butter, soft leather with deep, dark Mahogany, wood grain. All sitting behind deep, dark window tints.

A.J. could give a fuck about trynna front and be poised like a boss, he was excited as hell.

"Brah! Brah! Fuck nah! Luv you brah!" Acting like a little kid at Christmas.

Right then Voorheeze's phone rang. He checked the caller I.D. to see who it was, then answered, "What's hood wit it?"

"Brah, I just got done watching the news. Nigga dey just put dis new bitch in da white house. Brah dat bitch bad ass fuck!" The caller said.

"Brah dat bitch old." Voorheeze already knew this shit.

De'Kari

"Naa naa brah, I ain't talking bout that old bitch brah. Don't get me wrong she was cool and all but brah dat bitch done. Niggaz don't wanna see dat bitch no more! Not after they see this new bitch blood!"

"Come on brah you know you putting da ten on the two!" Voorheeze interest was starting to peek.

"Brah dat's on my mama Blood. That bitch so bad I damn near wanna kiss the puss!" Voorheeze had to laugh at that one. The analogy was a double innuendo.

Styles was letting him know that he dropped the new shipment off at the White House and that Samori had given them some new shit. Voorheeze would've had a problem with the sudden change without his prior approval but the way Styles was talking, this shit was better than the normal shit. Hence the double innuendo Styles don't fuck with white chicks and he ain't gone get caught eating the pussy on no female, everybody knew that.

"Brah bring a video copy of the news segment to the WR. and I'll watch it and see what you talking bout." He told him to bring the video to the War Room.

"Aight bet! Gimme like thirty."

"Aight one."

"One."

By the time he hung up the phone, A.J.'s excitement had calmed somewhat. A.J. is only twenty-two years old so his excitement was understood. Hell, his excitement was a good thing to the rest of the team because shit runs downhill. Good shit and bad shit. Maybe his being blessed would cause him to bless them. Right now, let that good shit roll.

"Looks like things just keep getting better." Voorheeze said addressing the group, "Our connect just hit us wit some new shit. Supposedly the shit is even stronger than our normal shit."

Everyone looked at him like he was crazy because their normal shit was shutting shit down. To have something stronger, the fiends were going to go bananas, which meant more money.

Voorheeze turned his attention to A.J.

"When you think you gone be ready for your first drop?" He asked A.J., ready to see how he would perform.

Now that money was being mentioned, everybody got serious. Two things that'll make a Black man serious real fast, money and murder.

"As soon as you can, get it to me big brah!" A.J. told him with full confidence, ready to do his thang.

"Aight bet. And bout that other thang, we'll hook up on the rebound." He said referring to the next meet with Gunz.

Gorillaz in the Bay 2

Again, he trusted Gunz, so he trusted Gunz' judgement. So, finalizing everything wasn't necessary. Voorheeze jumped in the Lambo and pulled off.

**** N. D. ****
(Milpitas, CA, a few hours later)

Voorheeze sat real low in the seat with a half empty bottle of Remy in his hands, listening to the song as it played low through his audio system. The song was a throwback to early ninety's. It made him smile while tears rolled down his face as he reminisced on all the joy and all the pain.

The song he was listening to came out while he and T'Rida were kids. It was dark times in the Bay Area. A war between Oakland and East Palo Alto was raging in full force. Bodies were dropping on both sides every day.

T'Rida was from East Oakland, this tested and strained their friendship with Voorheeze being from East Menlo Park which was considered part of East Palo Alto.

Daily, they were tested and daily they proved their loyalty to one another.

There were so many murders back then that EPA was the murder capital of the United States for the third time. Ever since then Voorheeze and T'Rida would listen to DRS "Gangsta Lean" whenever they lost someone. It was their tradition.

He wasn't drunk. That bullshit with Wendell had taught him a lesson, he wouldn't slip again. Nevertheless, he missed his brotha, so here he sat in his all black on black Yukon across the street from 109 Vienna Drive trynna visually replay in his mind what happened that day.

As he was going over the last conversation he had with 'Rida in his head, a dark blue Crown Victoria pulled up to the house and parked. Voorheeze kept sipping on the Remy as he watched detective Russo got out of the car.

"Fucking pig!" He mumbled under his breath after taking a long gulp. Although the detective could neither see or hear him, Voorheeze was mean mugging him like Ice Cube mugged Dre when N.W.A. split up.

Oblivious to the killer sitting across the street behind tinted windows watching his every move,. Detective Russo was busy at work. Something about the case was rubbing him raw but he can't quite figure it out. Though he couldn't put his finger on it, he believed if he stayed focused and went over every little detail then it would jump out at him.

De'Kari

As Voorheeze watched the white boy he continued to replay that last conversation over in his head. He and T'Rida were arguing

"You know I'm not gone let these mothafuckas put me back in a cage!" Voorheeze knew from the amount of venom in T'Rida's voice that the only thing on his mind was death.

"We Gangstas! You hear me nigga? Gangstas! We came in dis mothafucka wit nuttin ready for everything. We knew the consequences to dis shit, yet we accepted dem when we chose da game...."

The more he thought back to that fatal day when T'Rida died, the more he began gritting his teeth. Voorheeze was fuming. His anger mixed with the Remy and the cocaine he was snorting was a fatal concoction. He emptied a lil mound of coke onto his closed fist and snorted it. He did the same thing up the other nostril.

"You want to help me my nigga? Den my nigga keep it lit. Make dese mothatfuckas regret the day they took a Don. Make this Family stronger than eva!"

Voorheeze kept replaying that one line over and over in his head. Make these mothafuckas regret the day they took a Don.

"I got cha Big Brah." Voorheeze spoke out loud to T'Rida, who was only a memory.

With a sinister smile on his face, Voorheeze took another snort up his nostril and grabbed his banger. He yanked the silencer out of the center console and said a small prayer. "Lord if it aint your will then stop me. But if it's your will then please protect me."

All Voorheeze wanted to do was the right thing. His mind-state was so fucked up he didn't know any longer what the right thing was. His mind was going from reality to what his mind thinks is reality.

Russo grabs his pen light from his shirt pocket and heads to the side of the house. He wanted to check out the backyard again. Hell, every since he was a kid, he could sense things, it's like Russo always had a sixth sense to find things. And something kept telling him that he needed to be here at this house tonight. It was like fate was calling him.

His horoscope this morning said, "Re-visit old places for new clues." He had to be a complete moron not to know that the cosmos was telling him to recheck this crime scene. This was the biggest murder of the century Russo thought to himself, *what if they overlooked something*? That was possible considering how many people from different labs and organizations were involved with the crime scene.

Russo thought he heard something. He spun around and shined the light where the noise was coming from, but .... nothing! He turned back around and continued searching. From time to time he would check behind him due to the noise he'd heard.

Gorillaz in the Bay 2

Once he made it all the way to the backyard he scanned it completely. After a few minutes of looking around, he sat down in a lawn chair, that was off in the corner of the yard to think. Although it was in the darkest part of the yard; Russo wanted to be able to see the entire backyard and from this viewpoint he could. He sat in the lawn chair in deep contemplation. Unaware of anything else, he lost himself into his thoughts, trying to visualize them. This was his way of dealing with a serious case. One of his methods, letting the scene talk to him.

"What am I forgetting?" He finally asked himself out loud.

"That Dragoons are immortal bitch!" At the sound of the voice Russo spun around, only to see the dark night light up as the bullet spit out the barrel into his left eye snapping his head back. The first bullet was followed by two more landing into him before his body even hit the ground. Voorheeze stood over Russo's lifeless body and shot three more times. Afterwards he dragged the bloody body down into the basement. He would worry about what to do with the body later. For now, he would leave the faggott ass cop right in the basement.

Back in his truck and driving down highway 880, Voorheeze felt like a small part of the burden he had been carrying was lifted.

De'Kari

Gorillaz in the Bay 2

CHAPTER V111
(The following morning)

Clark'd only had a few hours of sleep, but he was feeling good. Regardless of how anybody looked at it, Clark knew he was supposed to be dead yesterday. Four niggaz had the drop on him and Tut but somehow, they pulled it off and got through it without getting shot or even a mark.

This was not the first time that Clark escaped death by far. He was accustomed to cheating death ever since the car accident that should've killed him when he was a child. Clark had been riding his bike, drinking a Tahitian Treat soda when out of nowhere a car slammed into him. Since that fateful day so long ago, he had faced death and won countless times. Yet each time he did, Clark knew that it was God's doing. He always would wake up the next day feeling good. Not your normal feeling good, but that *"can't nothing ruin my day,* feeling good"!

At first, he thought about picking up the phone and calling a female. Some good pussy would be a great way to keep the day going good. But he decided his mood was too good for pussy. He picked up the phone and dialed a number. The phone rang so long he thought he was going to get the voicemail.

"Umm hmm…. Hello?"

"What's up blood? Wake up nigga." Clark yells excitedly into the phone.

"Big Brah, umm rogue what time is it?" *Why is this nigga bothering me already today?* Voorheeze loved his big brother but got dammit he was tired.

"Blood, it's like eight o'clock. Get up nigga we got something to do." Clark could hear from his brothers' grogginess that he wasn't feeling his phone call, but he doesn't give a fuck! The early bird gets the worm.

"Clark, Blood, I just went to bed 30 minutes ago." Voorheeze felt like he had a hangover.

"Rogue, that aint my fault. Tell that to whatever trick had you up all night."

Voorheeze thought about correcting him but didn't want to waste his time.

"Blood get up and meet me at mama's in an hour." He didn't even wait for a response, he hung up the phone.

Cark knew that if he waited on the phone Voorheeze would talk his way out of it. So, he hung up before he could say a word. Right after he got off the phone with his little brother Clark immediately

69

dialed French Tip and told her the same thing. Clark may have played his position in the Mob, but aside from that he was still the big brother.

An hour and a half later he was walking up to the front door of their mother's third floor apartment. He tried to tap the door lightly with his foot but no matter how hard you try to kick light, kicking a door is gonna make a thump. The door immediately swung open. Voorheeze was standing there with a Desert Eagle in his hand looking like Satan. French Tip was right behind him with her banger in her hand.

"Why you hittin the door like the mothafuck'n police?" He saw all the bags in his brother's hands but Voorheeze don't care. He didn't budge to grab any. He hated when people bang on the door, that shit wasn't cool.

"Hey!" Watch yo fuck'n mouth!" Mama B. yells from the couch where she is sitting.

"Sorry mama!" All three of them laugh and snicker at their mom. Mama B was a real O.G. she'd seen it all and done it all. Back in her day she'd done both fed and some state time. She cursed like a sailor, but she considered it an act against God himself if you cursed in her presence. And if you corrected her for cursing, her favorite line was, "I'm you Mama!"

"Ooh! What you got brotha?" French Tip finally took notice of the bags in her brother's hands.

"Aww you know just a little sum'n sum'n" Clark told her moving his head like Bill Cosby in a pudding commercial, as he heads to the dining room table.

Fuck what they were thinking, walking enough food for four grown ass people up three flights of stairs was getting heavy ass fuck in his hands. Especially with all the shit he bought.

"Nigga it took you long enough! How you gone call somebody, wake them up and tell them to be somewhere, nigga when you aint there yo' self?" Voorheeze asked.

"Blood, it took them damn near 45 minutes to make all of this shit!" Clark shot back in his defense. He wasn't listening to no complaining after all the time he'd waited fo this shit.

"Hey!!! Watch yo mouth! I'm still you mama got dammit!" Mama B called out.

"Shit! Yall kids gone send me to an early grave", she spat out.

"An early grave? Shit, mama you older than the grave", Voorheeze couldn't help himself he had to throw that part in. His sister and brother laughed.

"Fuck you!" She yelled out.

"Hey, Hey watch yo mouth!" Voorheeze yelled out mimicking her.

Gorillaz in the Bay 2

"Yeah! Watch your mouth drama queen", French Tip chimed in between laughs.

"Forget you punk", she pointed at Voorheeze. Then she said, "you too Nita". Mama B was always calling people punks as she stuck her tongue out making a face. They all started laughing.

Clark had stopped at one of the local food shacks that everyone loved and picked up the food. "Lagina's" was one of those diners that still made that good down-home food. And they made that shit swell! Since everything on the menu was so good, Clark just ordered the entire breakfast menu and a couple of things from the lunch menu. He figured with his mom and siblings all eating, that shit would disappear quick.

Mama B had first dibbs on everything, it was only right considering she was Moms. Once she got what she wanted, her three cubs went to town. They had a ball and enjoyed each other's company. Only God knows when the last time was that she had all her kids at home at the same time. This was indeed a treat for her. Mama B didn't know what she did to deserve something so special, but she thanked God for it. They ended up spending the entire morning and part of the afternoon together.

A call from Tut had Clark leaving the apartment abruptly after a few hours.

**** **N. D.** ****

Clark sat in a parked car on Euclid watching the house three doors down from where Tut was parked. Tut had received a tip that one of the niggaz who shot at them the other day lived in the house. The niggaz name was Little Jeff. He was a young nigga who was beginning to make a name for himself with his pistol play. He was rumored to run with a clique of wild niggaz who were all about that pistol playing.

Clark had been sitting in the car almost an hour and was tired of waiting.

"Text them niggaz and let them know we going in." Clark finally spoke, neva taking his eyes off the house.

He wasn't with all this waiting shit. There hadn't been any activity at the house. He was ready to make it happen.

Tut received a text message immediately after sending the message.

"They ready, dad." He told Clark.

"Let's go." Clark exited his Charger and walked toward the house with his gun in hand. Tut walked a little off to his right with his banger out as well.

De'Kari

Three houses down in the opposite direction, Black Rob and Drew came walking up the street. Both were carrying assault rifles in their hands. Drew had an all-black AR-15 with an extended clip. Black Rob carried a Russian AK-47. No one spoke as they walked right up to the porch.

The next-door neighbor, an old, retired, bus driver was just coming out of his house. When he looked up and saw what was playing out, he turned around and went right back in the house, closing the door behind him. He'd gotten to the nice old age of sixty-eight by minding his own fucking business. He wasn't about to change up now.

Clark didn't hesitate, he kicked the front door in with one boot. Once he did, Black Rob was through the doorway so fast with the AK pointed and ready to go that you wouldn't believe he was 250lbs. Drew was right behind him with the AR. They each went in their own direction searching and securing the house. It didn't even take 40 seconds to secure the house and note that no one was there.

"What you wanna do Rogue?" Black Rob asked as he came out the back.

"Nigga we gone wait! Mothafucka gotta come home sooner or later." No sooner did the words leave out of Clark's mouth, Tut's phone started ringing.

"Nigga, dey got me pinned down Rogue! I aint gone make it Blood help me!" Mack Sauce yelled into the phone, his words fumbling over themselves, soon as Tut picked up.

"Nigga where you at?" Tut didn't waste anytime with bullshit. He could hear the gun shots in the background as Mack Sauce yelled in the phone.

Bocca! Bocca! Bocca!

Return fire echoed even louder in the phone. Mack Sauce was running out of time.

"Blood I'm right in front of Oakwood!" Tut was out of the house so fast there wasn't time for an explanation, he would explain on the way. All he yelled was "Get to Oakwood now!"

They made it to Oakwood Market in record time.

Scuurrr! Tires came to a screeching halt as everybody that had gathered around the scene being nosey scattered trynna get out the way. When the doors opened on both vehicles with niggaz jumping out with big shit in their hands, mothafuckas disappeared fast.

Drew was the first one to hop out when the cars came to a screeching halt. Everybody in the town knew who Drew was and what he was about. Nobody wanted any problems after seeing him bounce out holding that Choppa. Black Rob swung the AK toward the crowd, just praying he found somebody who remotely looked like they were wit that shit or was out of pocket.

"Damn! Blood"! Clark was the first one to spot Mack Sauce. He was on the other side of his throwback 5.0 Mustang stretched out.

"Damn dad"! Tut said as he came around the car and stood next to Clark, shaking his head.

Mack Sauce's body was laid all twisted the fuck up between his car and the fence. It looked like he was using his car as a shield the way it was shot up. His banger laid on the ground next to his body with the neck jacked back, a clear sign that he ran out of bullets. His body had at least sixty bullet holes in it. A few feet away was his cell phone.

There was no time to mope around or grieve. The police, no doubt, would be on their way. If they arrived any time soon, shit was going to be ugly. They needed to handle business and dip.

"Get the phone." Clark told Tut.

"I'm already on it, dad!" As soon as the police went thru that phone not only would they have all of their numbers in the phone, but the last person he called was Tut. The Pigs would be all over that and that would bring heat down all around them.

"Yo Clark!" Everyone turned around guns ready.

Clark tried to identify who it was. It was a woman's voice but that didn't make a difference, it could be a set up. He finally recognized her when she started jumping up and down and waving her arms.

"What's up Sonya?" He called over to her not wanting to deal with any bullshit.

"Yo Cuz! I seen everything! That shit was crazy!" She yelled back to him hella animated, swinging her arms and shit.

This got their attention, so he waved her over while walking in her direction. When she got within a couple of feet she told him.

"Cuz I swear to God that shit was crazy. I'm talking some right out the movie Wild, Wild West shit! For real!" Her animation was good for a movie but was too much for what was going on at the time. The little nigga was laying there dead as a doorknob.

Sonya was an O.G. smoker. She and Clark were like second or third cousins or some shit! She was cool peoples and though she was a smoker, he neva recalled her being on no fuck shit. So, they heard her out.

"So, the little cutie that's stretched out over there was coming out of the store wit a bag in one hand talking on his cell phone. Suddenly four cars came speeding up Bayshore!" She was making all types of hand gestures and shit. Drawing the crowd back as she acted out the antics of what happened.

"When he saw all the cars he dropped his shit and started to take off down Oakwood Street but as soon as he did that like four or five more cars came flying up Oakwood! Seeing that he didn't have no-where to go the little, fine mothafuckas pulled his cannon out and stood his ground. But Cuzzo I'm telling you something like fifteen to twenty lil niggaz jumped out of them cars. Lil cutie ran behind his car and did his thang! I'm telling you cousin, he popped like three or four of them too"! Sonya was all out of breath, swaying back and forth on her feet.

"Where they at?" Clark asked now looking around for some bodies.

"They picked all of them up and put them back in the cars." She told him with a look on her face like nigga is you serious, that's what anybody would've done. Then she looked like she was trynna recall something.

"Oh yeah! Cousin that aint the crazy part." She did a little shimmy with her feet and swept her arm out across her body like a magician.

"The craziest part of it all was they was Babies!"

"Huh? Fuck you mean Babies?" He asked her wondering if she had gone crazy.

"Ba-Bies! I mean little ass kids, couldn't have been no older than sixteen.

As soon as those words left her mouth, the sound of the sirens could be heard in the distance.

"Good looking out Sonya." He told her while handing her a knot of hundred-dollar bills.

"It's nothing cousin. I love you! Be safe. Tell you mama hi for me!" She was talking so fast he barely could make sense of what she was saying.

Clark wasn't listening to shit she was saying anyway, hearing the sirens meant it was time to go. They got the fuck outta dodge before them people showed up.

Back on O'Connor Street, Clark was trynna put shit together in his head. Shit was adding up. When mothafuckas tried to hit the spot over in Menlo he first thought it was somebody looking for a come up, nor-mal jack boi, street shit. But then them mothafuckas tried to take him and Tut out at Johnathan's and now this.

Clark didn't believe in coincidences. These weren't random acts that just happened to occur. Somebody had actually declared war on his team.

"Whatcha thinking dad?" Tut walked up with a whole XL pizza in his hands.

Clark looked at the pizza then said, 'I'm thinking somebody de-clared war on us and aint told us."

Gorillaz in the Bay 2

"I was just thinking the same shit!" Tut said with a mouth full of Pepperoni pizza.

"I want you to find out who the fuck it is. We need to handle this shit." Clark was thinking sooner than later.

"I'm on dat shit, dad! Whatcha think about Sonya saying it's a bunch of kids?" Tut took a couple bites off a new slice while he waits for an answer.

"I don't know Rogue, that shit crazy!" Clark couldn't quite wrap his head around that part.

"What I do know is we lost two niggaz. We gotta make some noise, the streets is watching."

"Speaking of which I'mma ride back through that nigga spot and see if I get lucky." Tut was ready to knock some shit down. "Damn right the streets are watching, niggaz gotta clap back". The only thing that he loved more than food and pussy, was knocking some shit down.

"Nigga you bout to eat that whole pizza?" Clark couldn't help it he had to ask, he was hungry as fuck!

"Nigga you aint getting none! So, I guess so. "Grabbing another slice out of the box. Tut was serious as fuck. He was knocking the whole thing down.

"I'm just saying nigga I can't get a slice?" Clark asked as his stomach growled.

Tut huffed and puffed hella dramatically. He stared at his box for a minute then smacked his lips like he was angry.

"Here greedy ass nigga." He pushed the box towards Clark, looking real pissed off about sharing his shit.

"Good looking out Rogue." Clark smirked as he grabs the box.

When he grabbed the box, he realizes why the fat mothafucka decided to pass it to him. He opened it to double check and Tut busted out laughing. All the pizza was gone. Clark was furious that he had been that gullible, but more so because he was hungry.

Tut damn nearly threw up all the pizza as he laughed so hard.

"Come on nigga let's hit the little taco shack on C Street, my treat." Tut could barely talk from laughing so hard.

"You mothafuck'n right it's yo treat after you pulled that fuck move." Clark told him as he walked toward the car.

"Yall niggaz won't something from Lil Mexico?" Tut called into the house at Drew and Black Rob. Once they both called out their orders, Clark and Tut headed off.

They walked inside of the taco joint and were glad that it wasn't crowded like it normally was. A minute or two later they placed their order. After they were done placing their orders Tut told Clark he was walking to C Liquors, which was two doors down from the taco shack, right next to Price Barber Shop.

Tut needed a beer and a pack of blunts. As he walked up C Street, he was thinking to himself how much he loved his block. He only wanted a couple of things from the store, but he ended up getting twenty-four dollars' worth of shit. Grabbing his bag, Tut headed to the door. As soon as he walked out the door and turned left, Lil Jeff was sitting right there in his car talking on his phone. Tut didn't hesitate, he reached into his waist band for the Desert Eagle.

Lil Jeff was the nigga whose house they had gone to on Euclid when Tut got the call about the stash house in Menlo.

BOOM! BOOM! BOOM!

The first shot went right through the windshield and into Jeff's chest.

Jeff fumbled trying to grab his banger that was sitting on his lap. In his fearful state of mind, he couldn't grab a hold of it. He looked down to get his bearings straight to grab the gun but by the time he looked up Tut was standing at the drivers' side door. Jeff shit his pants.

"What's up, Blood?" Tut taunted him. The fear that Tut saw in Jeff's eyes was priceless! These were the moments Tut lived for.

BOOM! BOOM! BOOM! BOOM! BOOM!

 Each bullet smacked into Jeff's body causing it to shake back and forth like it was doing the *"Thizz*: dance.

Even though the police were known for driving down C street, Tut strolled toward Clark with his banger in hand, without a care in the world. Clark was waiting in the car with the food in the back seat.

BOOM! BOOM! BOOM!

Tut neva saw the little nigga coming up behind him trying to knock his head off. The nigga was tying his shoe when Tut walked out the store and started busting, so he just stayed down until Tut walked away. Then he stood up and started creeping up on Tut.

Clark saw the nigga when he raised up. Knowing that the he had the advantage over Tut, Clark didn't waste time, he started yanking through the open driver's side window. Two of the slugs caught the little mothafucka in the stomach. He folded like a lawn chair. Tut spun around, then walked over to the little nigga and stood over him and aimed at his head.

"Nooo!" He yelled so loud it shocked Tut.

Clark flew out the car and over to where the boy lay squirming in agony. Clark knelt and picked the little nigga up with ease. The nigga was in too much pain to resist. Clark rushed him to the car and threw him in the back seat right on top of the food. Tut was already in the

Gorillaz in the Bay 2

passenger seat by the time Clark hopped inf. This was the opportunity that Clark had been waiting on. Now he would get some answers!

De'Kari

CHAPTER IX
(Parking lot of Mama B's)

Snniff!.... Snniff! He lifts his head back after snortin the two fat lines of cocaine, so he can get a good drain.

"Got Damn! Styles wasn't lying this that fire!". He says to himself as his entire face immediately goes numb.

When Clark left Mama B's house, Voorheeze took that as a cue to moving himself. Shit, he had things to do. He picked up his cell phone and punched in the number as he pulled out of the parking lot.

"Hello." The caller finally picked up after five rings.

"What's up lil cousin?"

"There you go wit that little cousin shit Rogue. I told you nigga I'm the big cousin." Steve tells him as he laughs into the phone.

"Whatever nigga. You help me bust this move and you'll be big cousin all day, today. Until then you just a little nigga." Voorheeze is always clowning around and fuck'n with Steve.

Growing up they were like brotha and over the years Steve was the one nigga who neva switched up on Voorheeze. Even through all the times Voorheeze was in and out juvenile, jails and prisons. So, in Voorheeze eyes Steve was his brother. Hell, he had always considered Steve more of a brother than Clark when they were growing up.

"For real though cousin, tell me something good." Voorheeze needed for Steve to come through for him.

"Oh nigga! You want me to tell you something good?" Steve antagonized him.

"Yeah nigga, tell me something good." Voorheeze repeats.

He knew knows his cousin is playing but the coke Voorheeze anxious. He was is concentrating on the conversation and on his rear-view mirror. An all-black Lincoln Navigator has been behind him since he got on the freeway, this was making him nervous.

"Nigga, I'm getting money and pussy! And you know that's good." Steve is having a good time fucking with his cousin only because he knows that he did come through for him.

"Naaw check it out I got something I know you gone like rogue."

"Now that's what I'm talking bout! What's good? What you wanna do?" "Where you at?" Voorheeze is amped.

"Nigga I'm wherever you tell me to be, whenever you say be there!" Finally, some good news for a nigga.

"Alright, I'mma text you an address. I'll be there in half an hour." Steve tells him.

"Alright, fa'sho that." Voorheeze noticed that as he changed lanes, so did the navigator.

"One." Steve calls into the phone as he picks up the book that he was reading to finish the chapter.

"One!" Voorheeze drops the phone.

The navigator is still behind him. Voorheeze is wondering if he is just being paranoid after all the coke. The Thornton exit is coming up. He switches lanes only to see the Navigator follows him.

"Man fuck this shit!" he says aloud. "We gone get this shit over with right now!" Voorheeze might not be the aggressive one, but he ain't neva been one to run from nuttin.

He reaches over and grabs the cannon from the passenger seat and places It on his lap. Things must be working in his favor because as they approach the intersection the light turns red. As he stops, he throws his whip in park. The Navigator angles to pull alongside of him. Voorheeze is already out with the Desert Eagle down by his side.

"Pitch black at night or broad daylight a mothafucka can get it!" He thinks to himself.

When the Navigator gets right next to him, the passenger window rolled down and his arm rose up with his big ass cannon.

"What's up nigga!" CJ yelled out the truck.

That was the only thing that stopped him from shoot'n. It took him a second to recognize who the nigga was. When he did he just shook his head.

"What! You gonna shoot, you gone shoot yo cousin in broad daylight?" CJ was laughing while he asked the question with his eyes beaming from the crystal meth.

"Nigga, you know you can't be playin games out here, rogue, it's ugly! Nigga I almost knocked you down." Voorheeze tucked the cannon and walked over to the other side of the Navigator so he could be on the driver's side.

"Nigga you always paranoid. Ain't nobody out to get you, besides you know I keep a big, ugly, bitch." If only CJ knew the shit that was brewing under the surface.

The signal light had turned green already, but the drivers just went around them honking their horns. Voorheeze climbed back in the whip and decided to talk to CJ through the window. After all, this was Fremont. Niggaz don't hop out whips and talk in the middle of the intersection like they do in the hood, not in Fremont. He called his number out to CJ then drove off. Voorheeze had to meet Steve, and nothing or nobody was gonna fuck that up.

Voorheeze double checked the address in his phone, the address matched up, but he see Steve's car, so he figured maybe he is early.

Gorillaz in the Bay 2

He posted up in the car and while waiting he took another 1-on-1 of the coke. Five minutes later a Tesla truck pulls up behind him. Without any thought or hesitation, he clutched the cannon resting on his lap.

Both Falcon doors lift and to his surprise, Steve steps out of the vehicle. Steve stands 6'4" and weighs 290 lbs. with high yellow skin and clean-cut waves. The real image of a pretty boy. Contrary to his size which is so intimidating he has the most sincere sincerest and inviting smile ever. Plenty of niggaz look at Steve and see the pretty boy square that he is. But don't get it fucked up! Steve might be a square, but he's still a beast. Test him and you will regret ever forcing the kids hand.

Steve's father was in the game real heavy back in the day. He also played in that corporate field. Seeing both worlds, Steve chose the smart route and it was paying off nicely for him. He was the hottest young real estate agent in the Bay Area, which is why they were there.

"Cousin, what's up, nigga?" Voorheeze asked as the two briefly embrace. "Rogue, I see you, I see you." "Yeah you know! That's just my new lil work thang right there. Ain't nuttin' major". Steve responds with cockiness and a big ass smile on his face.

"Oh okay, I see nigga. Yo new lil work thang, huh?" Voorheeze teased, making sure he put the emphasis on 'Lil' as he makes quotations with his fingers.

"Louie suit and shoes. Clear diamond bezel Rolex and the Tesla... but it's a lil sum'n sum'n." Voorheeze imitates Kat Williams as he is talking shit, his hands all waving while he bends down.

"You know how it is, you gotta dress to impress. Persuasion foe the occasion." Steve's doing his best Don Juan. They both break out laughing.

"Naw, for real though, you gone like this when you see it". Steve talks to him as he leads him up to the house.

The house is perfect. It is exactly what Voorheeze had in mind. It's a two-story Victorian with a wrap around the drive-way. Venetian shades the windowwindows for the heat. They're in the Hayward Hills right down the street from the college. Across the street from the house are four more houses which are on the inside of the mountain. This house sits on the outside of the mountain and it is the only house on that side of the street. It's a four bedroom, three and a half baths with a living room and a family room that has a seven-foot old brick fire place which gives the room a Gregorian feel. The kitchen is state of the art, and the backyard covers an acre and a half of the mountain. From the backyard, on a clear day you can see across the Bay.

Once they finished looking at the house, they stood in the family room discussing a few things.

De'Kari

"Yeah dis him right here." Voorheeze thinks about her as he stares over at the fireplace.

"You sure, cause we can look at a few more if you need to rogue?" Steve figured he would have to show him at least three or four different places before he made his mind up.

"Yeah cousin, I told you I didn't need nothing fancy, Rogue. It had to be something nice though. More importantly, it needed to be out the way." He got closer to Steve and lowered his voice when he spoke to him.

"The most important thing is that it's out the way, Rogue." He was telling Steve he didn't want anyone to know about the house.

"Nigga! I get it. This yo lil tuck spot. You ain't gotta worry about me telling nobody shit." Steve adjusted his tie and gave Voorheeze a serious playful look. "And you damn sho aint gotta worry about me popping up here…unless it's a problem with the money. Or it's poker night, Nigga." They both started cracking up.

"Nigga, the money always gone be straight. Speaking of poker, when is the next game?"

"Nigga on Friday like every week." Steve tells him in a high-pitched voice. He's surprised that Voorheeze would even ask him a dumb ass question like that.

"Whose house is it at this week?" Voorheeze had missed the last five or six games. In fact, he hasn't made it to a poker game since T'Ridas birthday.

"It may be at that nigga Anthony's house this week. Holla at Linell, he'll know."

"Aaight, now how you wanna handle dis money thang? You wanna take it now or you want to let Lily filter it?"

Steve thought about it for a minute, Lily was Voorheeze's accountant. She was damn good and trustworthy. Years of living with her older brother Juan, changed her life. She graduated from college and had a degree in accounting.

If Steve accepted the responsibility, then he would have a few hundred grand at his disposal to make some moves with. Steve was street-smart as well.

"Shit leave it wit me, I'll take care of it."

"Aight, come on, it's in the trunk." Reaching into his pocket for his keys, Voorheeze headed to the front door to leave.

Steve locked up the house, then made his way to Voorheeze. He grabbed a small duffle bag out of the trunk and is now standing by Steve's Tesla with one hand under his jacket. No doubt his hand is resting on the handle of his cannon. Although his head was facing Steve, his eyes were on constant swivel.

Gorillaz in the Bay 2

"Here you go, Rogue." He holds the bag out for Steve.

Steve looks at the bag. "How much is in there?" He might not be in the game, but he's been in the hood all his life. He knows that if that bag is full, it's too much in there.

"Nigga, it's a brick in that thang. I just picked it up and I ain't about to start counting stacks of dough out in this bitch." He lifts his arm signaling for Steve to take the bag.

"I know what the house cost nigga. Just take care of that and you can do what you do with the rest of it until I need it." They only wanted five hundred for the house, but Voorheeze knew that Steve would get this legal hustle on with the rest. That was better than it just sitting in one of the stash spots.

"Nigga stop thinking about it. Take the shit and throw it in yo trunk. I don't give a fuck where we at, a nigga ain't trynna stand in da street with over a half mill in his hand just waiting for someone to try and take it." Hearing this snapped Steve out of his momentary hesitation.

"Aight, just give me a heads up about that game." Considering he's the one with the heat, Voorheeze waits for Steve to toss the bag in and gets in himself.

"No doubt."

"Aaight! One." He calls out making his way back to his whip.

"One!" Steve yells out as he's pulling off.

**** N. D. ****
(Across the Bay)

Clark was sitting up with O.G. Peppi Hanks getting some game from him.

"I'm telling you young L.R. put you pride in your pocket. You dealing with some young stupid mothafuckas. You can't reason with stupidity young L.R. Naw Naw just hear me out now." Peppi doesn't let Clark who was about to say something speak.

"Listen, you'sa stand up little nigga but that's only because you cut from a different cloth than the rest of these mothafuckas. They aint got no rules dawg! No rules, no morals and no fucking sense. The only way to war with them is a full-on frontal attack. All Gas, No Brakes! Young L.R. you gotta go H.A.M."

Clark could see the Beast in Peppi start to rise and show its ugly head.

From time to time, Clark would bounce ideas off of the O.G.'s head. Peppi Hanks done seen and been through enough shit to make him timeless. He was a beast in the street, but he always had a solid head on his shoulders. So, Clark asked his opinion on carrying out the war.

"Plus, I'm telling you Dawg I did my research on them. Lil Pepp got at me and so did June Bug, they say it's enough of them mothafuckas to start two gangs! Nigga you can't beat that picking mothafuckas off two or three at a time." The O.G. finally paused to light a blunt.

"But Big Brah, how da fuck I'm gone look calling for help for a bunch of kids?" That's what'd been eating Clark.

Pep blew the smoke out and hit the blunt one more time. He looked at Clark as if he had a butt naked midget with two heads feeding him ice cream on his lap.

"A lot of good niggaz died behind not understanding a mothafucka or down playing a situation. Let me ask you something Dawg, how old were you when you jumped off the porch? Now what about when you first put in work?" He saw that he finally had his young homeboy thinking about shit. He went in for the kill. "Now truthfully, how old were you by the time you was a G to this shit?" Peppi nodded his head up an down and hit the blunt again.

Clark had neva looked at it that way. He and his cousins were doing shit by age nine. By age thirteen you couldn't tell him shit. He already had a couple of bodies under his belt. Hell, his second stint in Juvenile Detention stemmed from a robbery they'd knocked off. When S.W.A.T. kicked in the door they found four guns, money, brass knuckles and a bunch of stuff linking them to the robbery.

They were going to take Voorheeze in for the robbery because he was holding the shit until Clark stepped up and rode his beef. Hell, by fifteen he was a well-respected figure on the block. Niggaz respected his mind, but feared his G.

"Damn nigga you gone pass the Backwood?" He asked Peppi.

"I guess you starting to see clarity…" Peppi joked.

"All of a sudden you wanna hit the blunt. There's the tree you betta roll yo own. You know I aint passing it Dawg." They both started laughing as Clark reached for a Backwood.

**** **N. D.** ****
(East Palo Alto)

They pulled up to the abandoned house at the back of the G (the nickname for the Gardens also called G-Town). It wasn't a secret in the hood what this house was used for. On any given day, at all times of night, the neighbors could hear the cries and screams of torture that came from within.

Gorillaz in the Bay 2

Tut carried the nigga that Clark shot into the house and down to the basement. They had brought countless niggaz down to the confines of this basement.

"Lay the lil nigga on the table." Clark said as he dug inside an old moldy chest for a tool.

As Tut dropped the nigga down on the table with a loud thud, a cloud of dust rose up causing him to choke. He fanned his hand in front of his face attempting to clear the air. The smell of mildew that lingered in the basement was so strong it made their throats itch.

Clark walked over to the table with an old rusted carpenters screw driver in his hand. He looked down at the nigga who was holding his stomach as he was groaning from the pain of the two gunshots. He looked to be fourteen or fifteen.

"It's simple lil homie. Tell me what I want to know and save yourself a great deal of pain. Or you can act like you're hard and I betcha I make you religious." He was looking dead in the niggaz eyes.

"W-what you wanna know man? I need a hospital". He cried out, then groaned some more.

"I wanna know why you niggaz on me and who the fuck are you?" Clark asked thru gritted teeth.

"Okay we… we declared war on all of yall…" He had a coughing fit. "B-because…

Clark was leaning down close eager to hear the answer.

"… because yall some straight bitch ass niggaz!" He erupted in a violent fit of laughter.

He laughed so hard that he let out a big ass fart! He knew he was dead the moment they tossed him in the car.

"Aarrrgh! Aaarrrrgh! Shit!" He screamed out. The sound of his tune changed faster than a mothafucka the moment Clark shoved the screwdriver deep into the hole of one of the bullet wounds.

When the pain was unbearable. He inadvertently lifted off the table, Tut grabbed him and held him down.

"Okay lil tough ass nigga." He was wrenching and shaking the screwdriver while he talked. "I respect tough niggaz but you gone respect my gangsta!"

He moved so fast that Tut didn't even notice until the screwdriver was piercing a new hole inside of the boys' stomach.

The howl that escaped his mouth was cut off by one of Tut's massive paws as he covered the lil niggaz mouth.

"Whoaa! Whooa! Hold up nigga! Tough mothatfuckas don't scream like a lil bitch, nigga. You gone answer my questions, tough nigga?" Clark asked him.

He weakly nodded his head up and down, yes.

Clark was all smiles now. He looked at Tut and nodded telling him to move his hand.

"Why you niggaz doing this?" He knew the nigga would break.

"C-Cause yo mama was too much of a bitch to do it?" Tut's smile was bigger than the smile that was on Clark's face moments ago.

Clark looked at Tut, "what you think?" He gave the nigga credit, he had heart.

A devilish smile crossed Tut's face! Before Clark could say anything...

Whack! Whack! Whack! Whack! Whack! Whack!

Blood sprayed everywhere as Tut stabbed him repeatedly. The shocked look on Clark's face was priceless. It caused Tut to start laughing while he was stabbing the corpse. Clark was shocked because he neva seen Tut grab the knife he was using.

It's a good thing extra clothes were stored in the house for shit like this. They were covered in blood.

"We aint gone find out shit now." Clark said out loud.

"We wasn't gone find out shit anyway Dad." Tut responded.

Gorillaz in the Bay 2

Chapter X
(Union City, CA, a few months later)

Levell walked into the Texas Roadhouse Restaurant at Union Landing Square. He was super tired, hungry and he needed a drink. Levell was a good dude with good morals. Originally, he was from Mississippi, but he had moved out to California years ago. That street life, he'd ' been there and done that. His past resume would actually scare motha-fuckas. For many niggaz in the game, it's a good thing that he left the streets. He chose to walk away and turn his life around.

Now Levell was a hard-working construction worker. Every day he went to work he would bust his ass and break his back and at the end of the day, he would be okay with that because no matter what he was doing, he put his all into it, that was the type of man he was. Days like today, tested both his strength and resolve.

Dudes in construction had a habit of talking to people like shit be-cause they knew you couldn't touch them if you wanted to continue to work. Fighting would get you kicked out of the union. That was a rule Levell could neva get used to. Which is why he needed a drink. So, when his brother called saying he needed to holla at him, Levell didn't even think twice about it, he was there!

"Hello Sir, may I help you?" The hostess was fucking beautiful! She had a deep chocolate complexion with a hint of cinnamon and the juiciest set of lips a man could imagine. Her Rhianna cut just made her "come fuck me" eyes look even more sexy. Her 38 DD breast sat so perky on her frame that her poor little uniform looked like it was on its last stitch trynna hold them in. Her ass was so phat you could see it from the front. All of this was on a 5-foot, 6-inch, one hundred sixty-pound frame. She was used to receiving attention from everyone, both men and women drooled over her without shame.

Levell neva even noticed her. He walked right past her looking for Voorheeze. She was wondering why he wasn't ogling her like every-one else or even paying attention.

She made sure to stomp a little extra so her humungous ass really bounced up and down in them little ass spandex shorts she had on. She peeped over her shoulder just knowing that she was gonna catch him staring at all that ass she was shaking. To her surprise, he wasn't look-ing at her ass at all.

"Yeah, he gotta be gay, but the first nigga didn't seem like he was gay. Shit, he might be one of the D.L. ass niggaz. One of them gay thugs." She tells herself this because the scenario that she just created in her mind is far easier to believe than to believe that Levell just isn't interested in her.

She doesn't consider that there are other possibilities. Levell is happily married to the woman of his dreams, Rochelle. Levell doesn't just love her, he idolizes her and worships the ground she walks on.

"Batman! Voorheeze noticed them before they got to the table.

"What's up, Robin!" Levell shouts just as loud. Both showing a complete disregard for etiquette or consideration. Their response to each other is genuine, like two brothers who haven't seen each other in years.

They embraced using that one arm gangsta hug after slapping their hands together hard enough to make them sting.

"I see a nigga gotta send a distress call out in order fo yo wife to let cha out, huh? Voorheeze joked as they broke the embrace.

"Naaw you know after a nigga break his fucking back at work and putting up with all the bullshit. I just want to get home to my queen". His wife is the only thing that makes him feel sane at the end of the day.

The hostess is standing there with the dumbest look on her face after hearing that comment. She just knew they were gay.

"What's wrong with you lil thickems?" Voorheeze sees the dumb ass look on her face. He's wondering if they offended her somehow.

"Huh? Oh nothing, excuse me, I'm sorry. Here is your menu and your server will be with you shortly." She stumbles to get the words out. She was so embarrassed that she can't even look at them.

"What's your name lil thickems?" Voorheeze asked her.

"Excuse me?" She hadn't yet recovered from her embarrassment. The question throws her further off guard.

"Your real name? I like lil thickems, cause god damn, it fits! But we may be somewhere, and it may not be inappropriate to call you that." He licked his lips while looking her up and down the entire time.

She caught his little slick remark about sometimes they may be somewhere.

"Oh, so you just know that we will be seeing more of each other?" Although she's talking slick, she really is feeling everything about the big dark chocolate nigga in front of her. She does her best to hide her smile.

When Voorheeze first strolled into the building with his Cavalli jeans and Maui alligators on she was hooked. "Are you really that confident?"

"I'mma be honest with you sexy. This aint got nothing to do with confidence. I'm just sure about what's going on and what's gonna be going on." He picked up his drink and took a sip.

"And what's that?" She asked. Damn she just loved a man with confidence.

"When my brother and I are finished, and I leave this joint, you're leaving with me." There was no doubt in his words.

"Oh, I am, am I?" the dumbfounded look was back on her face.

"Yeah you're leaving with me."

"Just like that, huh? You not even gone ask me what time I get off or nothing?" The pretty hostess just wanted to see how far he was willing to take his shenanigans.

She was hoping that he was for real, because her mind was already made up. A sista needed a nigga like him. She could leave early if necessary and she could tell that he would be worth it.

"I don't ask questions that are irrelevant. When I leave lil thickems, we leave." He stated matter of factly.

"If your shift is over that's wonderful, you won't have anything to worry about. If it ain't then you'll quit, but you still won't have anything to worry about. Now let me talk with my brother and eat our meal. Just make sure you're ready in about an hour." His tone left no room for questions.

The only reason people couldn't tell she was blushing was because of her complexion.

God damn! She couldn't believe the audacity of that sexy, black, mothafucka! The puddles forming in her panties were a testament of how he turned her the fuck on. He had her so fucking horny, she didn't trust speaking.

"Okay." Was all she could manage to get out. She said it so low it was barely audible.

As she turned to leave Voorheeze called out, "say uh thickems…"

"Yes?" She turned around all smiles. Her pussy hoping, he would say 'come fuck me now!'

"What's your name, ma?" She had clearly forgotten all about that. That's how mind blown he had her. She blushed again and smiled before she said, "Danika."

"Danika, I'm Voorheeze, Ma." He had a puzzled look on his face, a thought came to mind, but he let it go.

Levell had been sitting back watching his bro at work the entire time. Admiring and respecting his get down. Voorheeze was a natural when it came to the ladies.

"Okay Voorheeze, I'll be ready." The look on her face when she said that reminded Levell of a child that just came home with straight A's on their report card and handed it to their parents.

Voorheeze watched that big ass booty as his mind was trynna reach back into his past.

De'Kari

"Okay mouthpiece! Big mothafuck'n Voorheeze, aka Casanova." It's a given that Levell gave Voorheeze his props. What else could he do, that bitch was bad!

"You know me big brah." He grabs his shot glass, Levell does the same thing.

"on the real though big bro, thank you for coming. I need you bro."

They both gave a salute and then downed their double shots of Patron Anejo. It's a tradition of theirs. Whenever they are out for drinks, they start with a double shot of Patron Anejo and a Tokyo Tea. These are Voorheeze's favorite drinks.

Their ritual started out one day when Levell was curious as to what the drinks tasted like since Voorheeze ordered them all the time. Levell ended up liking them and their ritual began that day.

"First tell me something, big brah, why did you look like that when she told you her name?" Levell wasn't a poker player but he was able read Voorheeze's face.

"Rogue, I went to elementary school with this chick named Danika. She was my (A-1), ace boon coon." Voorheeze thought about way back when and smiled at the memories. "She was a little Tom Boy, but secretly I used to have the biggest crush on her. She neva knew it though. Only person that knew was my nigga Dontae Johnson. I was wondering if it could be her."

"What makes you think that could be her, if you haven't seen her since elementary school? How do you know she stayed in the area? Levell asked, then took a sip of his Tokyo Tea.

"You know Clark stayed in the town 24/7. He used to run into her. He told me she asked about me a couple of times. But you know I been moving a thousand miles an hour." Voorheeze answered him, then reached for his drink.

"That'll be some real shit if that's her." Levell told him as he picked up his Tokyo Tea again.

(A Tokyo Tea is like a long island ice tea except you use 7-up instead of cola and you add melon liqueur).

Voorheeze was thinking the same thing, how could it be her. As far back as he could remember, Danika was a cutie pie, but she was a gangsta to the core, even for back then. She was a real tom boy. Hence, she was his Ace Boon Coon, aka, his A-1. Another thing was Danika just like Nolyn, was flat out skinny. But then again, he thought in elementary everybody was skinny. Well except for Salieh, but that's a whole notha story.

The waitress arrived and took their order and it's a good thing that she was butt ugly or Levell would have had to sit and wait while Voorheeze spit game at her too. Not that he minded one bit watching his nigga do his thang, but he really wanted to know what was up with the distress call.

Levell was strictly about business. Whatever the business was he gave it his full, undivided attention. It was funny because she was uglier than dog shit, but she was full of confidence. Levell damn near shitted on himself when he saw the way she kept licking her lips and eye fucking Voorheeze. The nerve of the little mud-duck. She did have some big firm tits, but they couldn't make up for her face. After she took their orders, she turned to leave and they both yelled out at the same time, "God Damn!" They couldn't help it.

Her ass was twice as big as the hostess. It was so big and round it looked fake. She looked over her shoulders and said, "I know, huh", with a smile on her hideous face and kept walking.

"Rogue, that ain't right." Voorheeze was slowly shaking his head while reaching for his drink.

"Shut-up! Nigga you'd still hit it." Levell teased.

"I know! Nigga dats why it ain't right!" They both erupted in loud cold, gut-wrenching laughter.

Life or Death, if you were friend or family he would give his all to protect you. If you crossed the line the reaper would appear. That's who Levell was.

"You know I'm with you." He told him. It was that simple.

"Vell, this ain't no hood shit, brah." Voorheeze tried to warn him. His conscience told him to keep it real.

"Nigga, what I just tell you!" Just that quick, Levell's temper reared its ugly head. "Nigga you my mothafuck'n brotha! I don't care if we go to war with the motherfucking president of the United States of America, nigga! If you need me, I'm there!" But Voorheeze already knew this. That's why he loved Levell so much.

They were just alike. Two rabid dogs who just wanted and needed to be loved. Loyal to a fault to the ones that loved them. Deadly to those that betrayed them or went against them.

Voorheeze looked around to make sure no-one was paying them any attention then he dug something out of his pocket, it was wrapped in a handkerchief. He slid it across the table. Levell was careful himself to survey the area with his eyes before barely lifting the handkerchief and looking. To his surprise, he was looking at a police badge. He looked up at Voorheeze confused.

"I got six more just like it." Voorheeze told him with no emotion. Before Levell could respond at all, the waitress arrived with their food and a refill for their drinks. She also had a big ass Kool-Aid smile on her face.

De'Kari

"I know you're feeling Danika and y'all bout to hook up and everything, but I know you got some good dick. I can tell just by looking at you. Yes, lord I can spot good dick a mile away. Here's my number. And yo ass better call me." She smacked herself firmly on her gigantic ass and said, "I know yo fine ass ain't scared of this big olé ass. Not with them big ass arms you got." The look she gave him was somewhere between "I'll fuck you until you have a heart attack" and "Nigga, if you play with me, I'll fuck you up."

After she left he filled Levell in on everything that was happening now, and everything that had transpired since T'Rida's funeral. Gunz had already gone to Philly and was doing his thang. A.J. had stepped up to the plate and so far, he was knocking shit out the park. With Big-Roc supporting him as his enforcer they were in the midst of a full scale all out overnight take over.

A.J. was seriously re-inventing Oakland. He'd even tried expanded out in Emeryville and had a small part of Berkeley on lock.

The little beef with Young Nigga Mafia was now a full-fledged war. They were taking losses every day. Bodies were turning up every day. And true to their title "Young Nigga Mafia" were nothing but little niggaz! Real live kids. But they took to this street shit like veterans of the game. Shit got so hectic that Clark had to bite his pride. At one of the War Room meetings he requested the help and support of the Wolf Pack.

No-one could figure out where these little motherfucka's came from, but it was hell of 'em. Even the Al-Qaeda niggaz were going crazy dealing with these little niggaz! Things had gotten so bad with shoot-outs and bodies stacking up, that the police stepped up patrols and formed a new special task force. Niggaz had to lay low for a while. "Little Bitty Bhag Dhag" looked like a ghost town.

He'd saved the best for last in honor of T'Rida's memory. Voorheeze personally took it upon himself to declare war with the Milpitas Police Department. His sister's words that night at Benihana's had played in his head the night he killed the first cop in Milpitas.

"I knew him well enough to know that he would be on you tough right now. For what you are doing to yourself, this ain't the answer baby, you gotta find another way." Those were the words that sent him on one.

Voorheeze had found another way! REVENGE was that way! He even had a couple cases of T-shirts and hoodies made with a picture of T'Rida on them and R.I.P. written above them. On the back the definition was spelled out 'Revenge Is Promised!' Each and every time he went to kill a police officer he would wear one of the black hoodies.

Gorillaz in the Bay 2

So far Voorheeze had killed seven cops. His plan was to take down the entire force. Or at least as many as it took to ease his pain.

He told Levell about the dope he'd started back snorting and all of the alcohol he was consuming. What he didn't tell him about was the dreams. The dreams were really the reason he called Levell. Sometimes he didn't know what reality was and what wasn't. Sometimes he would see shit that wasn't there. Silently Voorheeze believed he was losing his mind. He just wasn't gone tell anybody that shit.

"Look, let me go home and tighten up some shit with my wife and make sure the house is secure. Then it's whatever you need, big brah." The two of them have been over this for years. Levell is older than Voorheeze but he respects Voorheeze just as much as Voorheeze respects him, so they both refer to the other as Big Brah.

Voorheeze didn't want to bring Batman out of retirement, but he knew that in order for him to win the war that he'd started he would need the aide of the best. Batman was the best. The two of them had gotten so close and were so much alike that everyone began calling them Batman and Robin, the Dynamic Duo. But once Batman met Rochelle he quickly changed in the name of love. When everyone else felt some kind of way about the change, Voorheeze was the one to encourage it. They were truly brothers.

"Big Brah, I love you, blood! And I'm sorry I did this to you." Voorheeze knew what was coming.

"Nigga what good is family if they don't get you into some shit?" Levell joked as he always did.

With that they got up to leave. They neva even asked for the bill. Voorheeze just dropped $200 on the table and that was that. They approached the front and Danika was there, ready to go.

The two exited the doors of Texas Road House together. Levell didn't know exactly what to expect when he first got the call from Voorheeze telling him that it was "Safety and Security" and he needed him. As he walked through the doors, he knew this he walked into the restaurant as Levell, but it was Batman who was walking out.

De'Kari

CHAPTER XI

"Ooh boy, you better stop playing! You know this ain't yo car!" Danika told him as Voorheeze approached the Lambo.

"It ain't? Whose is it then?" He smirked as he dug into his pocket to pull out the key fob. "I don't know, but you better get away from it. Out here trynna get me shot by fronting like this yo car!" She was looking around the parking lot dead serious, all nervous and shit. Making sure nobody was watching them.

Danika had met her share of broke ass niggaz who fronted like they were ballin. She didn't think he was one of them at first, but now she was starting to get mad that she took off early. She's happy that she wasn't dumb enough to take him serious enough to quit. Fuck this she thought to herself, getting ready to walk away.

"Trust me lil mama you ain't neva in danger when you're around me." He pushed a button on the fob and the alarm disengaged, the doors lifted, and the engine purred to life all at the same time. Danika's jaw dropped in utter amazement. She turned to look at him. When she started to say something, he shook his head no and moved to help her get into the car. Then he walked around to his side and climbed in.

Danika couldn't believe it! She was actually riding in a Lamborghini. She could feel the power under her ass. The car drove so smooth it felt like she was floating instead of driving. She didn't know if it was new or not, but it had that new car smell. The pure power that rumbled throughout reminded her that this was a powerful race car. The seats where so soft against her body, it felt like she was sitting on a pillow of feathers. The allure of it all was mind-blowing. She didn't have anything to say now.

"You're sure hella quiet over there, lil mama, you alright?" He kept that smirk on his face.

"Don't tell me you've neva seen a nigga steal a car with the key."

"Boy shut up. You know I'm over here feeling all embarrassed and shit." She told him as she crossed her arms over her chest and pouted like a little kid.

"It's all good, beautiful. But you're too old to be judgmental and making assumptions. You should've learned that a long time ago". Seeing that she was still acting uptight, he wasn't trying to fuck the night off, he decided to smooth it out.

"But don't feel bad, beautiful, assuming is a common occurrence. Especially when it comes to a young black man. Now some assumptions are actually accurate. But some aren't. That's why it's best not to make 'em."

De'Kari

Look at this nigga, he just thinks he so smooth she thinks to herself.

"You're sure putting it on thick with the compliments. So now I'm beautiful. What else you got? You must really be trynna get you a piece." She laughed as she told him this.

"First of all, I can't compliment truth. Secondly, I already told you at the restaurant that you're mine. So, I don't need a piece, I got the whole thing." He took his eye off the road for a second and looked at her.

"Is that right?" She was playing stand off-ish but everything about his confidence and swag had her pussy screaming 'nigga fuck me now!'

"Life is too short and far too hectic to bullshit and beat around the bush, I will always give it to you straight." Experience taught him best.

"Since you don't beat around the bush you won't mind me asking you what do you do for a living that allows you to afford this car? Or is it a rental? And how do you know I'mma let you claim me?" She's feeling herself now that he's relaxed her.

"Naw I don't mind as long as you can accept the answers." His response sort of seemed like he's playing games but the tone in which he spoke said he was dead serious.

"I can accept anything I ask for." She was just as serious.

"Okay. I'm in da game, heavy, but let's just say I manage people." He didn't have time to sugar-coat shit.

"Manage people? Oh, so you a pimp?" She cut him off with a look of disgust on her face.

"There you go again with that assuming. I can't stand pimps so no I ain't one. I've been a hustla all my life, one way or another. Now I've moved up to management. That should answer your question on that. I don't rent shit. This is all me! I didn't buy this, it was given to me as a gift from my brother before he was killed.

"As far as letting me claim you, you already did that the moment you came with me, you and I both know it. So, we can stop playing that game. The only question is do you have it in you to be wifey? Or are you gone show me something to ruin it?" Voorheeze reached inside of the compartment and grabbed a blunt.

Danika noticed the gun, but didn't say anything, his comment had her at a loss for words.

"I know good when I see it, I know bad when I see it, but more importantly I know special when I meet it and you're special; Period, point blank! On top of that, you're beautiful and thick, just the way I like it! Why would I pass that up? Anything that you're lacking I can teach you, because intelligence is learned. So, unless you're scandalous or trifling, you gone be my wife!" Nothing else needed to be said.

Gorillaz in the Bay 2

This nigga is just too much. He's fine as hell, got money and got way too much confidence. It's only been two hours and already he was laying the law down. And hold up, did he propose to me? Before she could say anything to him, his phone rang.

"Yeah what's good?" He listens for a second before stating, "Hold up brah, I don't even know you my nigga. Put blood on the phone."

Some nigga named Johnny was on the phone claiming that he knew Fernando and that Fernando told him to call. When Fernando finally got on the phone, Voorheeze began speaking.

"What's up lil homie, long time no hear! But brah, you know not to let somebody I don't know call my phone."

Fernando is saying something on the line as Voorheeze is exiting off 880 onto Tennyson. It's good blood only cause it's you, don't trip. But what do I owe the pleasure of this call?"

"Oh yeah, say no more on the phone, what time?"

"Aaight, where at?"

"Tell yo peeps I'll be there." Voorheeze hung up the phone and dialed a number.

"Hello?"

"It's the What Dat Do King. What it do?"

"What's up brother?"

"I need you and Chiba to dress the kids for church and be ready for choir practice." He tells French Tip as his mind is racing.

"Alright, when we going?" Was all she asked.

"In da morning. Meet at the W. R. by 9:00am."

"Alright brother, I'll see you in the morning."

"Aaight, one." After he hung up the phone, he made a U-turn and jumped right back on the 880 heading south. Since he had to meet French Tip at the War Room he figured he might as well stay at his place tonight.

Fernando was a Norteno that he knew from prison. Blood was a solid little nigga with heart. Fernando would have been a good candidate to set up shop in Redwood City. But them niggaz were too busy gang banging to make some money.

"So, you really do manage people, huh? Her question brought him out of his thoughts.

"One thing I'll neva do, Thickems, is lie to you. No matter the consequences I'll always keep it real with you. And I'll only ask that you do the same. No matter what I'll neva judge you unless you lie to me. So, you'll neva have a reason to lie to me." She could understand and respect that.

The two-story house they pulled up to wasn't anything spectacular. It wasn't even something to write home about. Danika was expecting something way more extravagant considering the car. But she wasn't the type to be attracted to a nigga because of money, anyway.

It was a good thing she didn't say anything either. The inside of the house took her breath away. Everything was brand new and state of the art, from the furniture to the appliances. The floor plans were identical to the War Room as far as the first floor.

The second floor consisted of three bedrooms and a third living room. There was marble floor and mink carpet throughout the house. Danika neva even knew a person could have a mink carpet.

There were six bedrooms, four and a half bathrooms and three living rooms. Every single room had eighty-five-inch flat screens. The master bedroom had a smart T.V. in it. The T.V.'s in the living room were 3D. These were T.V.'s that weren't scheduled to come out for another couple of years. The kitchen counters and the center island were made of marble. Butter soft leather sofas were throughout the house.

The best room was the back den. It had three televisions that sat on three different walls. The fourth wall which was the wall facing outside was made of very thick glass. There was a heated swimming pool directly in the middle of the room that led under the house out into the back yard. The east corner of the pool had a waterfall. When he hit a button on the big ass remote in his hand the waterfall split to reveal a fully stocked mini bar. A fully stocked refrigerator and a cooler full of beers sat on the side of the bar. There was a pool table on one side of the swimming pool and poker table on the other, inside the den.

"Since you couldn't make your mind up on what you wanted to do, I figured I'd show you your new house and then we could get acquainted. Gone and make yourself comfortable while I throw on something to relax." He showed her how to use the remote and was gone.

She did exactly what he said and got comfortable. Now with her jacket off, (her shoes were already taken off at the door), a wine cooler in her hand that she got out of the refrigerator. Danika was sitting on the couch relaxing and listening to the O'Jays on the iPod she'd found that belonged to Voorheeze. She connected it to the music system that was set up. The system was so expensive and so clear, it felt like Eddie Levert was in the room singing to her.

Her eyes roamed around the room. She glanced at the swords hanging on the one wall briefly. Then became interested in the adjacent wall which was covered with photos.

Giving in to curiosity, Danika got up and walked to that wall. She noticed that Voorheeze was in almost every photo. Most of them were different events. As she paid closer attention to the photos, she noticed the other people in the photos.

A couple of photos in particular caught her attention. The first was of him and the now infamous T'Rida. Everybody knew who T'Rida was. The shit with him was hood legend. Not only was he one of the richest niggaz in the Bay; but that nigga went out like a true Gangsta! Everyone in the hood respected that shit. If he knew T'Rida then he must be somebody reputable.

The second photo was of her homeboy from the hood, Clarence, although everybody calls him Clark. Clark was in his normal dress of Red Monkey jeans and a white-T and Voorheeze was wearing some beige expensive suit with $300 custom made Bostonians. They were polar opposites, Voorheeze was much bigger than Clark, yet it's clear Clark is older. Clark was hood and Voorheeze was gangsta. Voorheeze is mugging the camera whereas Clark is smiling. Two men standing together yet in totally different worlds.

He came into the room wearing Sean John black silk pajama pants and a white, wife beater covered with a black silk robe. Danika had to take her eyes off him before her lust got the best of her!

"Way back when I was younger. I went to school with a girl named Danika. I used to have a crush on her. She neva knew though." She looked again at the picture of Clark and wondered if it was possible.

"And what school was this?" She asked feeling nervous.

"It ain't around here sexy, so it doesn't even matter. Plus, that was a lifetime ago." He made his way over to the bar and made himself a drink.

She figured if he wanted her to know he would've told her considering how much he's shared with her already. So, she didn't push the issue. Instead she asked him...

"So, you knew T'Rida, huh?"

His mood got solemn as he sat down on the couch. She saw the change on his face and came and sat down next to him. She placed her fingers under his chin and lifted his head up. She could see the severe pain in his eyes.

"You guys were that close, huh?" The tenderness in her voice tugged at his heart.

"He was my brotha."

There really was something special about her, he could feel it. With all her beauty, you could tell she was ghetto underneath all the polish. Her face said fashion model, but her eyes screamed Ride or Die Bitch!

De'Kari

Before he knew it, he told her all about T'Rida and himself, from childhood up. He just left out Neva Die and all they do. He got up to fix him another drink and instead went inside the cooler behind the bar and pulled out a gold bottle. He popped the cork and poured two glasses and carried them back to the sofa along with the bottle.

"The day of his birthday bash, brah bought me the Lambo and the chain I had on earlier. The chain signifies something, I'll tell you more about that maybe another time." He handed her the glass of champagne and sat back down.

"He wasn't my blood brother, but sometimes blood ain't thicker than water". Truer words aint neva been spoken.

"What about that picture of you and Clark? It seems like you know him well too?" She just had to know. She was dying to know, yet she didn't want to know.

"I should know him well, that's my big brother." He stated matter of factly. She couldn't believe her ears. They must be playing games with her. Did he just say that was his brother?

"LaMont? Menlo Park Belle, Haven, Letroy and Dante, big head skinny LaMont! Boy you mean to tell me that you're LaMont Simpson?" There was no polish in that. All ghetto.

"Damn lil skinny ass Tom Boy, Danika! Looks like you grew outta that Tom Boy shit." He said indicating her body.

"I can still fight though. Boy, I outta beat you up. Talking all this 'I'm Jason Voorheeze crap, when you're little o'le LaMont." She poked her large chest out and made a deep voice when she mimicked his name before she punched him in his chest.

"Be careful before you hurt you hand." He teased her.

"Oh yeah?" She threw another punch at his chest and to her surprise he tapped her fist down and wrapped his arms around her in a playful squeeze. It happened so fast she dropped the Champagne flute with the Cristal in it.

"I can still get the best of you though." He told her as he looked into her eyes. They were begging him to kiss her and he was about to, but reluctantly he let her go. He didn't want to rush things.

They sat and talked for hours. They told each other their life story, and all they endured over the years. He was so open and honest about everything that she felt compelled to be as open and honest with him about everything. Their laughs came close to tears and then they laughed some more. It was wonderful.

Danika had been waiting for a man like this all her life. Someone that could make her laugh and could listen to her all without judging her. His comments about certain things in life shows her that he didn't see mistakes and poor decision making he saw choices and lessons learned.

After all these years who would have ever known LaMont Simpson would grow to be her ideal man.

"So, let's get back to when you said you were crushing on me..." She said with a seductive look on her face.

Voorheeze wanted to fuck the shit out of her, but he knew if he did later she would feel some kind of way about getting down on the first day. Especially after their long conversation. He wanted her to be a keeper. He didn't need anything fucking that up.

"What's there to talk about? I wanted you back then and I want you now. Back then you were my road dawg, I didn't know how to play it but now I do."

"And how is that?" Sexuality dripped off her.

"It ain't gone be the way you think." He stood up and walked over to the bar.

The sun had come up hours ago, so he knew it was time for him to take care of business. He grabbed a box and then escorted her to the master bedroom. As he began taking his clothes off, he talked to her.

"Okay, look! No one has ever been here, Period! Bringing you here shows you that I mean what I say. There's something special about you." He walked in the closet and when he came out he had a knot of Franklins in his hand. "Do you have a license?"

She was so caught up in the moment that she forgot all about her car. "Shit, I left my car at work."

"Don't worry about it, here!" He reached in the night stand and pulled out a set of Mercedes keys. Then he gave her the knot of money, which was ten thousand. He was doing so much she didn't have time to think.

"I gotta take care of some shit. I'll be back later. Get you some sleep. When you wake up, if you gotta take care of something, that should be enough. If you need more, open that box right there." He pointed at the box that he had brought from the bar.

"If you gotta go somewhere the Benz is in the garage. But I'm beggin, please under no circumstance do you bring anybody here or tell anybody about this house. My mama doesn't know where I live." He walked towards her and took her in his arms. He kissed her so deeply and so passionately that he literally took her breath away.

"D, if I was playing games I would've fucked you hours ago, I want a wife, not some ass. If you're here when I get back, then you're with it. If not, the money is yours and I'll pick the Benz up from your job. If you are with it, last night was your last night working there."

De'Kari

He left her speechless as he walked to the shower in nothing but boxer briefs.

To say he was big would be an understatement. He was 285 lbs. of chocolate muscle. Not that steroid supplement muscle, but that break a sweat and get it in the gym muscle. He didn't have wash board abs, but that was okay with her. The print in them boxer briefs told her not to give a fuck about a six pack. The way he just put it down, made her thank God he ain't gave her none of that pole. She would be hooked fa'sho then. Every time she saw Clark and asked him about his brother, Clark would always say, "Brah hella business I'm telling you, he on some other shit." Now she knew what he meant.

She wasn't going to be rude and climb into his bed without taking a shower, so she got undressed and headed to the bathroom to climb into the shower. They were grown, they could take a shower together without doing anything she figured. When she opened the shower door he turned to face her. She couldn't help herself she had to look. When she did, "Oh Shit No." She exclaimed and closed the door.

That big mothafucka terrified her, yet at the same time enticed her. He climbed out the shower and wrapped a towel around himself. "It's all yours thickems."

"Don't be laughing at me, you could've told a bitch you had a garden hose attached to you, I knew it was a catch to all this shit. Boy move!" She blurted out as she brushed past him. He grabbed her as she was passing and gave her another one of his heart stopping kisses.

"I'mma be gone by the time you get out the shower. The alarm code, my cell number and remote for video surveillance monitors are on the night stand." He paused for a minute while hugging her tight.

"I really hope you're here when I get back." Danika's legs barely carried her to the shower, and he didn't even fuck her.

**** **N. D.** ****
(East Palo Alto)

Now the average mothafucka would avoid enemy territory whenever he was at war. Needless to say Tut Tut wasn't the average nigga. He didn't give a fuck about a war and he didn't give a fuck about them little niggaz.

His moms lived on Illinois and he drove over to his mom's house in his car, fuck a rental! He needed some of that good down-home cooking that only moms could whip up. He crossed the front yard on his way out, scanning the street as he did looking for anything out of pocket. But he knew them little mothafuckas wasn't that stupid. There was nothing suspicious on the block.

Gorillaz in the Bay 2

He didn't know it but this mom lived right next door to their headquarters. He also didn't know that he was being watched at that very moment. It was so dark outside, he wouldn't have seen the two niggaz in the Jeep Liberty anyways.

Five minutes after leaving his moms house he was pulling into Sho'Man's Market for some Backwoods. Being full wasn't the same without some Grapes to smoke after the meal.

He parked and hopped out the car thinking about getting a bottle too while he was there. He said what's up to the two dope fiends that were standing out front. That saved his life! When he saw the look on their faces he didn't think twice...

BOCCA! BOCCA! BOCCA! BOCCA!

That thang came off his hip like he was a Gunsmith in the old Western days. Tut's instincts had become so honed in over the years that he sensed exactly where the danger was coming from before he even turned around.

Even the two dope fiends were speechless because the little mothafucka had jumped out the Jeep with a Mac 11 in his hand ready to rock. He neva got the chance to squeeze the trigger.

BOCCA! BOCCA!

Tut didn't pay no attention to the nigga on the ground. He was chasing after the driver who'd sped off.

This wasn't their first rodeo, instead of running for cover the dope fiends were betting on whether he would get the driver or not.

BOCCA! BOCCA! BOCCA! BOCCA!

When the driver sped off Tut started shooting through the back window. Glass rained down like water and one of the bullets made it. He saw the driver snap forward like he was at a Bust Rhymes concert.

Tut ran to the driver's side and hit him twice more in the head. He then raced to the body on the ground and fed him two more to the head.

"O.G.! Dis yall Day. Good looking." He told the two dope fiends when he made it back to his whip. He tossed them a phat ass rubber band loaf. They saved his mothafucking life and because of that, the $5,000 he tossed them gone keep them high all week!

Tut got the fuck on!

De'Kari

Chapter XII – Pack Pride
(Later that morning)

"Hello?" Clark put his fork down and answered his phone.

Ordinarily, Tieka would have a fit that he would answer the phone while they were eating dinner, but she knew the amount of stress he was under, so she didn't say anything.

"What's up dad?" Tut asked through the phone.

"Make it happen," was all Clark said.

"No doubt", just that quick the call was ended.

Y.N.M. was becoming a huge pain in the ass.

At first Clark figured his team could handle it, but he didn't realize there were so many of the little mothafuckas. Hell, even still he didn't know how many of them mothafuckas there were. It seemed as if every time they killed one, four more would pop up. What Clark did know was he had taken some major losses both financially and on the killing field.

He realized that he was hesitant to send the pack in even though he had been given the green light. Pride still wanted him to be able to take care of the problem without help. Common sense said get help. What Clark hadn't taken into consideration is the fact that he and his team played by rules. Rules of the game. These young mothafuckas were everywhere. They didn't care about police or consequences.

That phone call put an end to the debate. Clark just told Tut to let Johnny Spitz know to send in the wolves.

After the phone call, Clark picked up his fork, but he knew his appetite was ruined. He needed the wolves, but in his mind, it would make him look weak to the family because he had to call for help. Little did he know everybody was going to need help with Young Nigga Mafia.

"Baby don't worry about it. You made the right call." Tieka got up from her plate and walked over to him. She knew everything that was going on. Clark was a cocky nigga, which made him careless at times, so he didn't care about discussing business in front of her. She stood behind him and massaged his shoulders. He was so tense his muscles felt like concrete rocks. Tieka knew what needed to be done. She bent down and kissed his forehead then his lips while her hand slid down to his lap.

He was already hard with anticipation. She grabbed his python and squeezed it through the basketball shorts he had on.

"Let me take care of you, Baby." She grabbed his fat dick out of the shorts and got on her knees. Tieka just loved how big his dick was.

It drove her crazy. She licked her lips, ready to savor his taste. She teased him at first letting her tongue circle around the base of his head. Then she licked the pole from the bottom to the top before taking him fully in her mouth.

Her mouth was so hot and wet, Clark had to lean his head back and close his eyes. Her head game was off the hook. First, she pulled back slowly, then swallowed him again. She kept the slow pace up only for a few minutes before she started really going to work.

"God Damn! Do yo thang!" He was biting down on his teeth, that shit was so good. Tieka was bobbing her head up and down as fast as she could as the spit ran out of her mouth and down his shaft. She used her hand and jacked his dick while she sucked it. As she went up and down on him she would twist her head. At the same time her hand would slide up and down his shaft slowly jacking him off.

Slurp, slurp, slurp.

Is all that could be heard in the house. She had so much spit on his dick her hand glided up and down with ease. He couldn't take it anymore. Clark pushed her head away and picked her up off the ground as he stood up. Without saying a word, he ripped her blouse and bra off of her and hungrily sucked on her titties.

Tieka loved that rough shit and he loved giving it to her. While he sucked on her titties, he reached down and brought his hand up under her dress. She wasn't wearing any panties which set him off; the touch of her bald wet pussy really drove him crazy. As he slid two fingers into her hot, waiting pussy Clark bit down on her nipple.

"Ooh, fuck! Baby." Tieka moaned out as the pleasure sent waves through her body. She could feel her skin turning hot. While his two fingers fucked her pussy, he rubbed her clitoris with his thumb.

"Ooh please! Clarence, please fuck me." Her pussy was on fire. She didn't want his fingers, she needed his dick.

She was getting light-headed. Any minute now Tieka was going to cum. As he released her nipple to move to the other one, her nipple stood at attention. He reached down with his free hand and lifted her dress in the back and smacked her hella hard on her phat, yellow ass! She shook her ass in response. Right at that moment, he squeezed down on her clit.

"Oh, Fuck! God Damn I'm cummin, Daddy!" As she screamed she held his head tight against her tit. All kinds of electricity ripped through Tieka's body. Her body shook so violently her free tit was slapping him in the face. So, he bit down a little harder on her nipple. Once the orgasmic wave passed and she stopped convulsing, he spun her around and bent her over the table. He didn't give a fuck that she landed on his food.

Gorillaz in the Bay 2

He lifted her dress and stared lustfully at her phat yellow ass. There was a red palm print from where he'd spanked her. He rubbed it for a second, then smacked her again. Tieka squealed. Clark didn't waste time sliding in slow. He rammed his entire dick into her hard and fast in one mighty thrust.

She loved it! His size and girth filled her completely up, testing her limits. Clark grabbed both ass cheeks and begin grudge fucking her. Tieka thought she was in paradise, she loved every moment of it.

"Ooh, Yes! Ooh fuck this pussy! Fuck me!" She threw her ass back on his dick just as fast and as hard as he was thrusting into her. Whenever he gave her the dick, she knew to hold on. He was pounding away so hard and her pussy was so wet, it sounded like someone was plunging the kitchen sink. Her pussy was spitting juices at him. The table was shaking so hard that stuff was falling off and crashing on the floor.

Clark didn't know how but her pussy got even wetter at that moment. He removed both hands off her ass and then smacked both ass cheeks at the same time while he shoved his dick all the way in her.

"Fuuuuuck!" He roared like a lion.

That did it! Her walls clamped down on him so hard as she erupted that he bust off too.

Tieka had some bomb pussy. He's was so glad she'd come back into his life.

****. N. D. ****
(Later that night in East Palo Alto)

As he drives the van down the pitch-black street, the look in his eyes tells what time it is. He doesn't know what these niggaz were thinking when they did whatever they did to have Clark summon him.

He really doesn't give a fuck either!

His number was called, so now it's time for him to do what he do. His team is well known all throughout the Bay Area (natives call it the Yay Area). Hustla's throughout the Yay tell stories of the hardest niggaz bitching up after meeting them. Hands mothafuck'n down! The name of each member of the team puts fear in the hearts of niggaz. But his name, his name puts fear in the hearts of goons and killaz! Straight up he is raw and uncut! His name will tell a mothafucka what he's about.

Tonight, niggaz will be reminded of what that is!

Murda!

De'Kari

He stopped at the corner of Clark St. and Bay Road. From here he can see the group of niggaz out on Illinois hustling. He counts at least eight or nine bodies. Bodies because in his mind they are already dead.

He drives across Bay Road entering Illinois Street. To his left the wooden plaque reads *Welcome to Nairobi Village*. As he reads the sign, Murda thinks to himself, "It takes a Village to raise a child, but a child can destroy a Village"! He smirked at the irony. As Murda approaches he has caught the attention of the group out on the block. His count was close, but he was off by five. There are thirteen bodies on the block. The average mothafucka would rethink what he is about to do, considering how much they out number him. But Murda ain't the average nigga, something these niggaz will soon find out.

Knowing they outnumber him thirteen to one makes him excited, if that is possible. Some of the niggaz mean mug him like they're just the hardest mothafuckas to walk the globe. Murda slows down until the black electrical van is in the middle of the group. Immediately hands go to their waists in preparation for whatever. After all this is E.P.A.

"Brah I got eight!" Murda calls out through the open window as he bobs his head up and down smacking his lips as he awaits a response.

"Nigga park that shit and get out! Nigga dis "Illa", we aint serving no cars! Some big black nigga yells out.

Murda throws the van in park and begins to open the door.

"Not in the middle of the street you stupid mothafucka! The same nigga shouts out. Murda thinks he sounds like a lil bitch with his tough guy act.

"My bad young blood." Murda calls out as he fakes like he's about to get back in the van. Instead his right arm comes up.

Toot! Toot! Toot! Toot! Toot!

The tech nine starts spitting. The sound suppressor not only blocks sound, but it stops the flames from coming out the barrel. The first nigga to catch some heat is the loud mouth mothafucka. Then Murda just sweeps the crowd. The moment he started firing he began walking towards the niggaz he was shooting.

A couple of the niggaz were truly gangstas, they didn't try to run like the rest of the bitch ass niggaz. They held their ground and tried to whip out their shit. These weren't Village niggaz, or G-Town niggaz, or Midtown niggaz.

These were P.A. niggaz, and P.A. niggaz didn't do no running. Straight up!

Unfortunately for them, they were dealing with a murderous nigga. So, they died too. A couple of bullets flew past his head yet

Gorillaz in the Bay 2

Murda neva flinched. Ten seconds later there were thirteen bodies scattered across the pavement laid out in different positions.

Murda climbed back into his van, he placed a new clip in the tech nine then put the van in drive and continued down the street.

Boca! Boca! Boca!

Murda swerved a little as a reflex, then threw the van in park. He snatched the Tech off the seat and looked for whoever the fuck just sent lead his way. It didn't take but a second for his well-seasoned eyes to pick the mothafucka out of the night.

Toot! Toot! Toot! Toot! Toot! Toot!

He let the Tech spit.

He shot through the passenger window as he as climbing out the driver's side door!

Boca! Boca! Boca! Tink! Tink! Two of the shots just missed Murda head and went through the windshield.

Toot! Toot! Toot!

He sent another burst at the nigga. To his surprise the nigga wasn't crouching down like a bitch. He was standing on the side walk firing away. Police sirens could be heard but neither of the two shooters gave a fuck!

Ced was getting tired of going shot for shot with a big ass van separating him and whoever the bitch ass nigga was.

Ced was just parking his Mustang and getting ready to hit the block when he heard the shots. As he walked down the street he could see the black van in the middle of Illa (nickname for Illinois Street) where the shots were coming from. When they stopped, and the van started down the street he figured fuck it! He'd neva seen the van before so he wasn't worried about one of his niggaz being the driver. So, he figured the van must be shooting at his niggaz, with that thought in mind he lit that mothafucka up. The police sirens got closer!

Taat! Taat! Taat! Taat! Still Murda was letting the Tech sing!

"Fuck!" He yelled as he realized he was going to have to let the nigga breathe. He sprayed another burst then jumped in his van and made that first left on Michigan Avenue. He drove down until he hit Baylor Street and turned right. Fuck the speed bumps. He sped all the way down the street. At the corner he busted a left and headed towards the Dumbarton Bridge.

When Clark reached out he didn't give any specifications. He just gave him a location and told Murda to make a statement. Thirteen killed at once. Statement made.

The Wolf Pack is hunting!

(Earlier that day)

De'Kari

The sound of his cell phone woke Clark up out of a good ass sleep. After their hard sex session somehow, he and Tieka managed to make it to the bedroom and fuck again before passing out.

"Hello," the sound of his voice is covered in sleep.

"Nigga it's two o'clock in the afternoon whatcha doing sleep, dad?" Tut's high pitched voice came through the phone like electricity.

Clark got out the bed so that Tuts loud ass voice didn't wake up Tieka.

"Nigga I'm up now what's up wit it." Clark sounded like an old cigar smoker.

"Brah, I just got that intel back on dem two thangs we were looking for on dat Menlo thang."

"Oh yeah?" A couple months ago somebody killed the two niggaz who had gotten away from the failed robbery of the stash house on Sevier. Nobody knew who killed them and Clark wanted to know so he had his niggaz put their ears to the streets.

"I'm telling you Dad, yo aint about to believe this one." Clark could hear in Tuts voice that he was holding on to something heavy.

"Speak nigga, dis ain't no fucking game show! You trynna build suspense and shit."

"Aaight aaight nigga damn," Tut choked on the weed smoke because of the laughter.

"Dad it was some Mex from outta town."

"Fuck outta here! Ain't no Mex gone slide thru Menlo and knock some shit down." That shit was unbelievable to anybody.

"I'm telling you, Dad, some lil Norte nigga named Beast. They say the little nigga out there in Redwood going ham, Dad. Say he the nigga dat got lil Mexico on fire." Tut let the blunt hang off his lips and put his hand on his 40 as he watched a strange car roll thru the area.

"You said Beast?" Clark was making sure he heard him correctly.

"Yeah Beast, dad." The car was turning back around so Tut came up off the hip.

"My brother on his way to meet up with a nigga named Beast today. Let me hit that nigga and let him know what's good."

"Off top, dad. It looks like I'm finna get off into some shit anyway." Tut said placing his finger on the trigger.

"You need me?"

"Naaw, I'm straight, dad." Clark could hear in Tut's voice that he was focused.

CHAPTER XIII
(Over on C Street)

The car was a four-door silver Volvo. Tut didn't know who was in it and he really didn't give a fuck. At the first sign of some outta pocket shit he was squeezing. He had an extended thirty, hanging off his forty, and he was going to let all thirty fly.

The Volvo was a couple of houses down and steadily coming. The forty was already cocked all he had to do was squeeze, but something wasn't right. He only saw one person in the Volvo. If this was a move there should at least be two people in the car. As it neared him, the Volvo slowed down, and the driver's side window rolled down.

"Fuck it!" He said to himself as he raised his hand ready to pop off.

"Nigga if you was gone bust you should've been squeezed nigga!" JuJu's head came sticking out of the window smiling.

Tut lightweight was pissed off at JuJu for playing so he figured he would teach him a lesson. "See that's what I'm saying about you Menlo niggaz Dad. Keep coming 'round here thinking shit sweet until a nigga accidentally light that ass up!" he said raising his banger.

Right then three more bodies popped up in the car. The entire Volvo was full.

"Na ain't bout to be no lighting dis mothafucka up!" Mall calls out from the back seat. "Fuck around and have dat ass doing da Harlem shake out in dis bitch."

"Aaight Dad! I see you niggaz in a real good mood. What's up?" Tut lowers his shit.

"Brah we got da deep on one of dem niggaz so we ridin" JuJu lifts the Mac-11 off his lap for emphasis.

"Say no more Dad! I'm ridin!" Tut ran and jumped in his bucket, an all-Black 2000 Toyota Eclipse Super Charger.

Their target lived in the new apartments off University Ave. and Sac St. Considering the tension between Sac St. and Menlo, JuJu was certain this shit could get ugly. He picks up the phone and calls his childhood homeboy.

"What's up playa." Micky answers on the first ring seeing JuJu's number.

Mickey is a MMN (Menlo Park, Midtown Norteno) nigga but at the end of the day JuJu knows it's all Norte.

"What's up Rogue, my niggaz just got word that y'all got a snake sliding on the under in them apartments on the corner of Sac St."

De'Kari

"That ain't possible rogue. We keep our grass cut short." Mickey knows it's a scrap that's been creepin through over there.

Him and his niggaz was getting ready to move on him tonight. He couldn't expose game to JuJu. They were niggaz and all, but he wasn't bout to discuss a body with nobody.

"Call your peeps, Rogue, and let 'em know we comin thru. We sliding down Runnymede Street right now Rogue back to back"! JuJu hung up the phone before Micky could respond.

He knew the lil nigga would want to politic about it, but now wasn't the time.

When they reached University, they made a right. The plan was to flip a U-turn at the corner of Bay Road and come back up University and park on the corner of Sac Street. But shit don't always go as planned; especially in "Lil Bitty Bhag Dhag!"

Out of nowhere JuJu just pulled over to the right.

"Rogue, dats da car right there!" He yelled out pointing to a four-door blue scrapper on deuces across the street at Pal-Market store.

Mall, Stone and D-Roc didn't hesitate to hop out the whip with big shit in their hands. They started across the street. JuJu was mad that he had to be the driver on this one. He loved knock'n shit down.

Tut didn't know what the fuck was going on but his forty sat nicely on his lap ready with his head on swivel.

They had just reached the island in the middle of the street. Cars did any and everything they could do to get out of the way of the three masked gun men in the middle of the street with machine guns.

Shit this was E.P.A. and mothafuckas already knew what time it was!

Three Mexican dudes came out of Pal-Market lost in their own world. They were oblivious to the death that stared right into their eyes. Spooky's instincts told him to look up. He had been talking to his girl about what he was going to do with her when they got back to the spot.

He had his left arm draped around her shoulders. When he saw the three niggaz in the middle of the street he froze, and time stood still for a second. Then all hell broke loose!

Faaat! *Faaat! Faaat! Faaat!*
Tat! Tat! Tat! Tat! Tat! Tat! Tat! Tat!
Braaaaat! Braaaaat! Braaaaat! Braaaaat!

All three shooters opened fire at once! The big Mexican didn't know what was happening. One minute he was drinking a Jarrito, the next thing he knew the bottle exploded and a sharp pain tore thru his throat as a bullet from the Mac-11 ripped a chunk of his throat off.

Gorillaz in the Bay 2

Something smacked into his chest then his shoulder, his arm and his stomach! He was getting hit all over! Even when a missile from D-Roc's AK-47 flew thru his face and exploded out the back of his head, he didn't know what hit him. His body tumbled to the concrete; dead before it fell.

Spooky finally broke free from his momentary paralysis and grabbed his banger off his waist. But he was too late. The force of all the AK bullets Stone sent his way knocked him off his feet and through the big plate glass window in front of the store. Cars were going in all directions trying to get away, some crashing in to each other.

Like horses being freed from the starting blocks the last dude and the chick took off with no hesitation. The chick ran up the sidewalk toward Sac Street while dude ran in the street.

Bullets were flying everywhere.

JuJu and Tut broke into action. They both hit the gas and cut the wheel to the left. The cars jumped the small island.

Tut jumped out the car and let the forty talk.

BOCA! BOCA! BOCA! BOCA! BOCA!

He cut the last dude down and jumped back in the Eclipse. Mall, Stone and D-Roc jumped back into the Volvo and JuJu sped down the sidewalk! He would be damned if he was gonna miss this opportunity.

The little chick was running and screaming. Yelling shit in Spanish and English. Fear gripped her heart and had her running extra fast.

"Help! Help! Please somebody help me!" She neva saw the car as it barreled down on her.

Pop! Pop! Pop! Pop! Pop! Pop!

JuJu let the Mac-11 go. As the bullets riddled her body she dropped only to be run over by the speeding Volvo.

Just like that, both cars raced down University and hopped on the freeway. JuJu and them headed one way going toward San Jose while Tut was headed for the San Mateo Bridge.

"Hello?" The voice answered the line.

"Aye Rogue, I'm on my way to Oakland I'mma stop off and get me a nice hot cup of coffee." Tut said into the phone. Just that fast he was exiting 101 onto 92 East getting ready to cross the San Mateo Bridge. He needed a new paint job fast!

"Aight I'll let them know." Voorheeze said before hanging up the phone. Then he called the Koffee Shop to let them know that Tut needed his shit painted.

**** N. D. ****
(Later that night in the Gardens)

De'Kari

An all-black Dodge Caravan drove down East Bayshore. It crossed the intersection at Pulgas Avenue. There weren't any vehicles behind the Caravan making it much easier to pull over and turn into the Light Tree Apartment complex.

The driver pulled into the first parking spot. No one said a word. Everyone knew the plan. When they were ready, the first guy opened the door and three stepped out.

They looked like identical triplets of death as they made their way to the back of the complex. All three wore all black all the way down to their combat boots. Long jet-black dreadlocks flowed down their backs. The only difference between the three was there was two males and one female.

The female carried a Galil, which is the smallest assault rifle in the world. It's low recoil and lightweight makes it perfect for a woman. The two niggaz on the other hand, both carried AK-74's. One with a 300-round drum, the other a 180-round clip.

As the three crept into the small alley that lead to the back driveway, laughter and shit could be heard. Since the female was in command of the hit, she was leading the way. She stopped abruptly, lifting a closed fist in the air, signaling for them to stop. She braved a look around the building and was so giddy she almost couldn't contain herself. There were thirty or so people all out in the back of the complex, grooving and doing their thang.

She turned to her team and gave them another signal. In unison they stepped from around the building.

Taat! Taat! Taat! Taat! Taat! Taat! Taat! Taat! Taat!

The three assault rifles letting off at the same time was a sound like no other.

Complete pandemonium broke out as everyone tried their best to get out the way.

Blockka! Blockka! Blockka!

Above the saw-like roar, the sound of a hand Cannon could barely be heard as someone tried to display their gangsta. Sadly, that was the dumbest shit they could do. All three shooters directed their sights in that direction. In three seconds, forty plus rounds hit his ass! That didn't scare everybody off.

Bocca! Bocca! Pop! Boom! BOOM! BOOM! BOOM! Bocca! Bocca!

A few Niggaz were returning fire showing no fear, but most were trying to get the fuck out of there.

Hearing the horn sound, the three of them back-peddled while shooting. One by one they jumped into the Caravan. Just before she jumped in, Terry screamed out "Mafia Bitch!" Then she let out another burst of bullets as the driver hit the gas and did it moving.

**** N. D. ****
(The next day)

"I want yall to feel good about what you've done so far, but I don't want you getting so caught up with yourselves that you forget that this is only the beginning!" Sutton surveyed his team as he spoke.

There were over seventy young Wolves gathered in the backyard on Illinois Street.

"One thing about them and their wanna-be Mafia shit, is they adhere to and abide by those wanna-be Mafia rules."

His hazel eyes glistened with fire burning in them! "Niggaz wit us, Anybody can get it! And we aint listening to shit!"

The backyard erupted with shouts and cheers at his words.

He waited for the noise to die down before he spoke again.

"Now that shit dat sis and her team did…" He was careful not to use any names.

"Dats dat shit I'm talking about! But we will celebrate when it's over. Right now, it's war! Yall said that you wanted the City…. Then go take this fuckin City!"

**** N. D. ****

"*If this broad don't hurry up she gone fuck around and get left*" he thinks to himself as he checks his watch for the umpteenth time. Clark had been waiting on Tieka for almost forty-five minutes. They'd only been back together for a short period of time, so he wasn't trynna fuck things up by spazzing out, but she needed to hurry the fuck up.

Clark's temper could get the best of him sometimes and with the way things were going with them little niggaz he was already on edge and teetering over it.

"Tiek! Come on!" He called out to the back room.

He had to bust a couple of moves before they handled their business.

"You ain't gotta be all yelling my name like you done lost your mind or something." She told him in a tone that was seductive and sassy.

"God damn!" He was speechless when he saw her.

She had her hair pinned up in a French twist wit a Chinese ribbon twisting down the front. Her purple top with the hot pink Baby Phat kitten on it, looked like it took a miracle to fit her breast in it. But the white seven jeans that she had on were so tight, spray paint would not have fit her curves any better. Her purple and pink Chanel shoes and matching bag only set her outfit off right.

She was bad as fuck and she knew it; tonight though, everybody would know it.

"Coming down the hall looking like that! Fuck the concert, let's get back in bed." He told her as he grabbed his dick.

"Boy quit playing," she burst out laughing.

He wasn't playing but fuck it, they'd already made plans. Clark tucked his Desert Eagle in his waist band and they headed out the door.

Outside Stunna and Keak sat in a Black and Red Lincoln Navigator with tinted windows. The smell of platinum cookies the smoke from the blunts they were smoking was very loud. So loud you could smell it outside on the sidewalk.

Neither one of the killaz wanted to be here on a baby-sitting job. They were Wolf Pack and the pack was hunting. Especially Lil Keak. He was only sixteen but hands down, no questions asked he was by far the deadliest of the pack. Sutton wasn't as deadly as Keak, but he was just as cold.

They were bout that action, not sitting and waiting around. But, war had been declared and they both knew that in war you protected the heads.

Who better for the job? The best or in this case the worst. Tonight, they basically were body guards in the shadows. Their job was to trail and protect.

The first stop they made was over to one of Clark's money spots on Camellia Way. He pulled up to the house, hopped out and ran in. A couple minutes later he was walking out with a small leather carrying case. He jumped back in the truck and pulled off.

He really didn't want to leave his niggaz in the midst of an all-out war, but Fantasia was in town having a concert at the Oakland Coliseum and Fantasia was Tieka's favorite artist. One night while he was rollin off a couple of e-pills and a molly she had asked him to take her.

He said yeah just to shut her up, so she didn't fuck off his high. Wasn't no way he could back out. He tried time and time again, but she wasn't having it. But he'd just popped two Molly's in the house when he grabbed the money, so he wasn't tripping.

In fact, he wasn't tripping off nothing. Maybe if he was sober he would realize the dumb ass moves he was making like going to the spot with her in the car.

But the E and molly had his mind on a different level; he wasn't on his security. If Clark had been, he would have neva let Tieka see his stash house; no matter how good the pussy felt or how long he harbored deep feelings for her. He hadn't seen her in over ten years. Technically he didn't know shit about her. But, his mind was cloudy, and he wasn't thinking straight. He glanced over at Tieka, damn she was beautiful!

He was in a brand-new Mercedes G-wagon. He had the prettiest female for miles in the passenger seat. His trap duffle had fifty bands in it. Plus, he had two killaz riding behind him......Naw you couldn't tell him shit!

**** N. D. ****
(Union City)

"Look! My lil man hit me last night. He a Northerner out of Red-wood City. All he told me was he heard that I had a little problem in the town and that we shared the same problem." French Tip was loading bullets into the extra clips she brought for the two Glock 40s she had, while Anne was sharpening one of her kitana's. But they both were paying close attention as Voorheeze let them know what's up. Anne was taking this assassin shit to another level with all her knives and shit like she was Lara Croft in the Tomb Rader movie.

"He set up a meet with his big Homie, some nigga named Beast. Now this my lil Homie and he solid but y'all know me; strapped and ready for whatever." Strapped and ready was the only way to be.

"You ain't got no idea what he talking about?" French Tip asked him as she finished loading a full clip into her banger and grabbing another.

"I think it's that situation with brah. But I ain't gone make no assumptions. We gone head over there and see what's what."

Anne spoke up for the first time, "Alright let's roll!"

(An hour Later)

The average fool would see French Tip and Anne by his side and wonder why Voorheeze would bring two women to a Mobb meeting. A fool indeed. These were dangerous women. French Tip is one half of the leadership of the deadliest female assassin squad in the country.

Anne went from being their rising star to full fledged star. Hell, Anne was not referred to as "Chiba" which means "female or lady wolf" because she was the face of the She-Wolves. She was as vicious as a real She-Wolf.

They rode in French Tip's pink challenger. Voorheeze didn't think pulling up to a mob meeting in a Lambo was a good look, so, he too was in a dodge challenger. His however was triple black. Black paint, black rims and black interior. Not to mention he rode behind deep, dark tints.

They pulled up to the park and could see a small group of Mexicans assembled by a picnic table waiting. Before getting out Voorheeze pulled his zip-lock bag of powder out of the glove box and took two huge snorts.

By now Anne and French Tip had made it to the door and was posted up on security waiting for him. Voorheeze lit a cigarette and got out the car. As he climbed out the car he received a text from Clark.

The two women were two steps behind him, one on each side as they approached the group. French Tip's eyes took in everything. Anne's hand was in her Berkin bag that hung on her shoulder wrapped around the barrel of her 9MM which had an extended clip on it that held fifty rounds.

"What's up Voorheeze?" Fernando stepped out of the group to greet Voorheeze with a one arm gangsta hug.

"What's up lil homie? Your phone call sounded pretty interesting." While the two embraced, Voorheeze quickly sized up the rest.

"That's right Homie let me introduce you to my Big Homie." The dude that Voorheeze had already pegged as a threat if there was a problem, stepped up.

Voorheeze didn't give a fuck about the Mexicans number. Being out numbered didn't bother him. What did bother him was meeting in the middle of a park in broad daylight. This was some new shit. The cocaine making him alert to the point of paranoia wasn't helping.

"Yeah homie so that's what I mean about yo problem." The nigga Fernando called his Big Homie once he filled him in on shit.

Voorheeze only caught bits and pieces of what he said.

"Yeah Fernando informed you right, the little mothafuckas I'm dealing with is beginning to become a problem. But in actuality, my brother is dealing with them Y.N.M. niggaz."

"Who the fuck is Y.N.M." Some older chick with fire in her eyes asked.

"Well from what my peoples figured out it's a gang of young mothafuckas from P.A. and Oakland but it's a possibility that their bigger then we think."

Voorheeze didn't know who the small chick was but there was something about the fire in her eyes. It was like he could strangely feel some type of kinship with her.

"Well what I'm just trynna figure out is what's the connection between them and Coast Side." Antoni stated stepping back in the conversation.

Voorheeze had a puzzled look on his face.

Gorillaz in the Bay 2

"Coast Side? You mean Coast Side Locos? Ain't that them Surenos from Half Moon Bay?"

The South Siders had been making some noise lately. Voorheeze remembered them kicking some shit off at a Hoodstarz show a little while back over in South City.

"Yeah it's this mothafucka named Danny but he goes by Spooky. He been giving my homies some problems. He's CSL."

Voorheeze knew the name and hearing what dude just said, connected the dots for him.

"Brah Spooky wasn't just CSL. Spooky was Y.N.M. this I know for a fact. But I'll tell you this he won't be giving yo homies no more problems." He took a moment to let that sink in and then added, "But all this shit is starting to look like Y.N.M. and CSL are rock'n together.

"Look Homie, I don't mean no disrespect to you or your organization but if we join our resources it would make it that much easier to deal with these Putos. They've already formed an alliance why don't we?"

There it was. Antonio got to the point of the meeting. He couldn't see himself beating around the bush.

Voorheeze weighed the pros and the cons with working with the gang bangers in his head. On one hand it opened a new liability because most gang bangers were hot headed and always had a point to prove. On the other hand, more bodies meant more muscle. Plus, maybe now he would be able to talk these dudes into hustling. At the very least attacking CSL while his brother hit Y.N.M. would take some of the pressure off Clark.

"Check it out brah, I'm all about the bullshit for real for real. But brah-brah, I don't take orders, I give them, and I been doing this for a minute cause I know what I'm doing." The little chick caught his attention again as he spoke. There was something about her. Danger radiated off her body.

"So, if you and yours trynna rock wit me then rock wit me. But brah we move as a family. One cohesive movement. Any moves and decisions you and I will come to an understanding and make together."

Voorheeze could tell Antonio commanded respect and was used to calling shots. But what the lil gangsta didn't know was Neva Die was Black Mafia! Organized, Unified and Extremely Deadly!

"Homie, I respect how that sound. I'm wit that. So how you think we should handle this?" Beast wondered.

"That's easy homie. We make a statement. And we make that bitch right now!" He grabbed his Newport's out his pocket and put one in his mouth looking back at his little sister as he did so. Like always French's face didn't betray any signs of what she was thinking.

De'Kari

"Now see homie, I like that attitude. I'mma need about an hour to get all my homies ready. Where you wanna meet?"

"Shit right here is fine with me. All I gotta do is make a call and give my squad a time and a location and they'll be there. Just make sure to let yo peoples know when they see a fleet of black and red or black and pink vehicles slide thru, that's my team."

"Sounds good fam, by the way they call me Beast. With all the shit going on I forgot to introduce myself."

Voorheeze thought of the text message he just received from Clarkola, "Beast? I've heard of you brah. You that same Beast that did the damn thang over in da Lo, not too long-ago wit dem 'stick up kids?"

"Yeah that's me!" Antonio told him while they locked eyes. At the same time letting his hand fall to the butt of his Glock 40.

French Tip wasn't with the bullshit nor the talking. She figured that mothafuckas yapping, instead of letting the bullets fly, was a quick way to get killed. The moment she saw that look in Antonio's eyes, a twin 9MM appeared from nowhere in her hands.

Voorheeze wasn't her Boss, he was her big brother. The one who used to come up to the school house and deal with the bullies. The one who held her as she cried when her dad used to beat on their moms. She was damned if she let something happen to him. She was ready to pop off!

The moment Anne saw French Tip move she quickly went into action. She pulled her nine from her bag so fast no one saw the movement. But they saw the long ass fifty dick hanging off that thang.

"If yo hand move anotha inch, I promise you I'm knocking yo head off!" The only reason he got a warning was because French Tip knew he was just trying to be cautious.

Everybody got tense.

"Naw Brah it ain't even on that page. Everybody fall back." The comment was meant for the Wolves. "Let's just say you beat my mans to the punch. Dem lil niggaz hit one of my brother's traps. So, believe me, we were on dem niggaz."

"Alright then." Antonio said dropping his hand down to his side. He showed no fear.

"So, we'll link up in about an hour or so." He didn't get the name Beast by succumbing to fear. Having the weapons pulled didn't raise his heart rate at all. But he respected the ladies speed and efficiency.

Esmeralda put away her 38 that no one saw materialize in her hand. She stepped closer to get a better look at Voorheeze.

"This is my Mom. She's the brains of my hood." Antonio introduced.

"Please to meet you Ma'am." Voorheeze extended his hand.

Gorillaz in the Bay 2

"You look real familiar. You and her. "She pointed at French Tip. "I've seen a picture of you, long ago. You wouldn't happen to be related to Cantelope by any chance would you."

"How do you know Cantelope?" He was curious now.

"Let's just say I took a liking to her when she was younger. My name is Esmeralda, but they call me Black Widow."

"You're playing right?" He asked. Seeing that she was dead serious he told her "My cousin used to always speak highly of you. I know exactly who you are. Say Beast, normally when I deal with someone it's done with a certain level of caution. That's just how I rock. But if the Black Widow is your moms, Rogue, I extend both arms to you off the bat based on her resume. Brah I'mma fuck wit you real tough."

"Thank you for the show of respect." Esmeralda told him. Respect was real important to her.

"Now that we're all on the same page let's take care of this business." Antonio was ready to get it poppin.

Voorheeze hit Clark, and Johnny Spitz up and told them to meet him at the War Room. He had already told French Tip to buzz Cantelope in on what was what. He would let them link up and take care of this shit. Right now, he was feeling the powder. The coke had him in the building, definitely feeling himself. He had some cops to kill.

De'Kari

Chapter XIV
And So, It Begins
(Back in Union City)

She was the definition of perfection to many men. The type of woman every man dreamed of, squares, playas, gangstas, dope fiends, d-Boyz, hell it didn't matter she was what they all wanted. What they all fanaticized about while fucking their old ladies. This chick was what the convicts envisioned while beating their dicks in their cells at night.

She was 6'0" and 220lbs of pure, dark, chocolate thickness. Her hair was all natural, thick, healthy and down past her shoulders. Her juicy 38DD breast sat up just right. Not too perky, not too much sag. Her ass was just as big as Tieka's if not bigger. It sat perfectly at the top of her long, firm thick legs. The type of legs a nigga would want wrapped around his head.

She was outright breath taking. She had the most beautiful smile he had ever seen! But her two best qualities above all was her intellect and her huge heart! Her heart was bigger than mother Teresa's. Yet there was no room for him in that heart.

Sniff! Sniff! Voorheeze' face was so numb he could no longer tell if he was getting a drain or not from the coke. Thoughts of her constantly haunted his mind. He'd stopped at the AM/PM on Alvarado Niles to get some gas and something to drink.

He figured he would play with his nose before he pulled off. He didn't know why she'd popped in his head at the moment. Lisa was neva far from his thoughts. Hell, he was in love with her and she didn't know it.

But why would he think about her now? Guilt, that was why. Even though they weren't together, and she was married to some nigga who didn't deserve her, in his mind she belonged to him and he belonged to her. So, whenever he slept with another woman Voorheeze would feel guilty like he was cheating on Lisa. He was heading home to beat the brakes off Danika's pussy and his conscious was fucking with him. Lisa was on his mind and in his heart.

Voorheeze was able to pull up the camera monitors inside the house on his phone, so he knew Danika's answer about staying or not. He'd called her as he was getting off the freeway to let her know he would be there soon. When he called the house phone she didn't pick up until she heard his voice come over the intercom.

"This nigga is on some next level high tech shit" she thought as he told her he was on his way. It was a little after 12:30pm so she was laid in the huge California King bed waiting on him.

De'Kari

All day she had been driving herself crazy trying to figure out what she should do. Last night was some real fairy tale shit. All the shit La-Mont was doing was foreign to her. She was a hood chick, she wasn't used to all of that.

Voorheeze turned onto Santa Elena Way and drove to the end of the street. He pressed the garage door opener as he approached the house and then pulled into the garage of the War Room.

"Beep! Beep! System disarmed!" The automated voice called out.

Danika looked over at the monitors on the wall but didn't see any movement. She knew damn well she heard the security system say, "System Disarmed."

She was laying butt naked in bed as a surprise for Voorheeze. Since she was all alone in a strange house Danika had grabbed a big ass knife from the kitchen and placed it on the nightstand. After hearing the security system, she grabbed the knife and went to investigate. She walked all through the house and didn't see anyone.

Shit, she was ready to give it to a mothafucka if she had to. She figured something must be wrong with the alarm system since she didn't see shit. She would just have to tell Voorheeze about it when he got in, she thought to herself.

Danika made it back to the bedroom still naked and her heart damn near jumped out of her chest.

"Hey you." Voorheeze was standing in the middle of the bathroom getting undressed.

"Hey you my ass! Boy you scared the living shit out of me. Now you're intriguing and alluring, I'll give you that. But this Houdini shit, you better get to explaining that before we have a problem!"

"A problem? I'm trynna figure out how you gone threaten a nigga with a knife while you're butt ass naked with a body like that and think a nigga bout to take you serious." He couldn't help but laugh.

By now Voorheeze was fully undressed and the way his pole was standing at attention saluting her took Danika's mind off what she was saying. She couldn't believe what she was seeing. Her knees damn near buckled at the sight.

"Just let me wash up real quick and I promise I'mma lace you up on everything." He didn't wait for a response, instead he just turned on the shower and hopped in.

Ten minutes later he walked into the room with a towel wrapped around his waist and baby oil covering his body smelling like Chrome cologne. He laid across the bed on his stomach facing her with a smile on his face.

"So, since you're here, I guess it's safe to say you're feeling what I was saying last night about us?"

Gorillaz in the Bay 2

"Honestly LaMont, it is a bit much. I mean I haven't seen you in twenty years and if you take Belle Haven out of the picture then hell I just met you last night. And you talking about 'Wifey' come on now how am I supposed to take that serious?" Danika really needed to see where his head was.

"Look it's like this, first off I don't play games and ain't got time for them. I say what I mean, and I mean what I say. My granny raised me that way. Life ain't promised to nobody. Everything we do each day is a risk. So, I don't waste the time. I don't have time to be pussy footing around, when I want something I go for it. The moment I walked thru them doors of the restaurant I knew I wanted you. I just had to tend to my business first." The way he licked his lips when he said that sent a trimmer through Danika's body.

"As for just meeting you, yeah I was low key crushing on you back in the day. But even if we had just met it would not have mattered. See when you first meet somebody your spirit tells you right away if that person is good or not. Your soul speaks to you, most people have just stopped listening to their spirit or their conscience whichever you prefer to call it. But they listen to what they've been told and taught over the years about what a person should or shouldn't be. What a person is or ain't supposed to look like and most importantly what we are supposed to want and not supposed to want." He reached out and took her hand in his.

"Thickems listen, I don't need nobody showing me, trynna teach me or tell me what I want. I know what I want! And you're laying right here." He pulled her close to him. The part of the blanket that was covering her body fell away. She was exposed and breathless, yet she didn't feel vulnerable. If anything, for the first time Danika felt safe and secure. Hell, she felt like she finally arrived somewhere. But she didn't know why she felt that way.

Before an answer could come to her, Voorheeze's lips were covering her hers. His mouth stealing her breath away.

The kiss was deep, sensual, tender yet full of passion. His tongue invaded her mouth in search for hers. Finally, their tongues intertwined in a game of tag that sent jolts of electricity from Danika's tongue down to her clitoris each time their tongues met. He pulled back from her finally breaking the kiss.

Her body screamed, *"Give me more! Yes, let me feel that again."*

"Thickems I don't do anything normal I'm as unorthodox as a person can get. But if you rock with me, you'll learn to trust me, and believe me I won't lead you astray." His words dripped with sincerity.

De'Kari

"I'm here so that means I'm at least willing to see how far it can go. Only you can make it not work. Only you can push me away." She tells him in the softest voice.

As a response Voorheeze pulled her completely on top of him. The weight of her body laying on his was perfect. Her soft skin had the slightest hint of cocoa butter on it. They kissed like long lost lovers reunited, it was that powerful.

Danika could feel the print of his rock-hard dick pressing firmly against her as she lay on top of him.

Just as he had assumed, her ample ass cheeks were firm yet soft to the touch. His hands caressed her ass as they kissed.

"Mmmm…" as his hands squeezed her ass she couldn't help the moan that escaped her lips.

Her pussy was so wet by this time that her juices flowed down her thighs and puddled on him. Her heart was racing as her body temperature rose.

The cocaine in his system told Voorheeze to *'beat that pussy up and give her that dope dick!'* But he knew he had to finesse the pussy and that's exactly what he planned to do! He laid claim to the pussy.

Danika's entire body tingled from his caresses; she was on fire. Reluctantly she broke their kiss and slowly began to make her way down his body kissing and licking a trail as she went.

Voorheeze was excited and nervous at the same time; like he was losing his virginity all over again. When she got to his stomach her tongue circled his navel.

Just when she started to go lower he stopped her. In one swift motion he picked her and flipped her on to her back. The ease in which he was able to pick her up with one arm attested to his strength and this sent another thrill down to her pussy.

He stared at Danika's body for a moment licking his lips, the suspense building. Then he kissed and licked her from head to toe. Voorheeze made his way back up her legs very slow. Once he reached her inner thighs he gently bit down on each thigh.

"Ssss!" She was going crazy. Her pussy was tingling like fuck. Danika's breathing had got deep and heavy. She opened her legs wider, encouraging and yearning for him to go further. When his mouth touched her, she shot through the roof. She jumped at his initial contact. His tongue trailed up and down her outer lip, one and then the other; his tongue was hot and moist. The moment his mouth encircled her stiffened rose bud, a climatic explosion shot through her body.

"Oh! Shit! Oooh!" The shock of reaching a climax so quickly caused Danika to scream out louder than she intended.

126

Gorillaz in the Bay 2

He sucked on her clit as the waves of pleasure shot thru her body. Once she finally stopped shaking he dipped his tongue into the pool of cum that was flowing out of her and then continued fucking her with his tongue while lapping up the juices.

"Oooh shit! Mmm mmm!" She moaned over and over while grabbing onto his bald head.

Once he'd successfully licked all of Danika's juices up, Voorheeze licked her clit again and then gently bit down on it. She was starting to cumm again! She held his head in place with both her hands, she bucked and fucked his face until the orgasm passed. By the time he rose up finally getting ready to penetrate her, Danika had already lost control of her senses.

He positioned himself above her, his face covered in her pussy juices and slid inside her. Her walls felt like warm satin.

"Mmm." Danika bit down on her lip and moaned as he entered further and further into her. Just when she thought he was all the way in, more and more of him invaded her walls. Danika felt a spark exactly where he touched and probed. It felt like she was going to lose her mind. At that point he plundered her mouth with a kiss, knew that he was stretching her, so he waited until her walls adjusted around him. He slowly began gyrating his hips in small circles. The friction it was causing on her clit was building another climax. Voorheeze slowly pulled out of her until his head almost fell out, then he paused.

It was all about mind control and he knew he could hold out longer then she could. She tried thrusting her hips up, but he didn't budge. His size and girth felt so good when he was in her, Danika needed it again. She grabbed his ass with both hands and tried to force him into her. Finally, one word escaped her lips.

"Please." It was barely audible.

Just a little louder than a whisper but he heard it.

That was the confirmation that he needed. She'd surrendered to him. He slammed the full length of himself into her repeatedly.

"Yes!" she screamed out "god dammit! Fuck me!" Fuck her he did.

He went to town on that pussy. His balls slapped against the base of her ass cheeks. He pulled her leg over his shoulder to get deeper penetration. She couldn't decide if she wanted to scream, bite her lip, or call God's name. What she did do was surrender to the will of the dick. Every time Voorheez's big dick went in her, lights flashed in her mind. Danika matched him stroke for stroke. After a while he flipped her over on her knees and fucked her doggystyle.

That was his mistake! Danika was throwing it back at him just as hard as he was pumping, and she rotated that ass while she was doing it. Sweat fell from his face onto her back like rain.

The sight of her big phat round ass smashing into his pelvis as his dick disappeared into that pussy was too much for him to handle. Voorheeze could feel his balls swell and his stomach tighten up. He bust a nut so powerful into Danika that when it shot into her it immediately made her cum again.

After they caught their breath and recuperated, they talked for a little bit. Voorheeze told Danika about the War Room and its purpose.

After T'Rida's death they needed a new location for their meetings; it was a wrap for the Milpitas house.

Always putting safety and security first, Voorheeze bought the house on Santa Elena Way as well as the house directly behind it. He had a tunnel dug underneath them to connect the two houses with no one knowing about it. Once the tunnel was complete the workers were killed so no one knew the tunnel existed. Not even the members of Neva Die who met at the War Room knew about the tunnels. And no one at all knew about the house, at least that's what he thought. Danika was the first person he'd told.

If things ever got hot for the squad and they needed to get out of the War Room they were good. They talked and fucked and talked and fucked. By the time they were finally done fucking, her pussy was sore; it was a good pain.

**** N. D. ****
(The next day)

"You mean to tell me that my officers are coming up missing, Lord forbid they may have been murdered and you sorry sons of bitches ain't got no fucking answers for me!" Captain Sweeney was furious. You could see the veins in his red neck bulging and pulsing underneath his reddish skin.

"Sir...I...we...I'm mean..." Lt. Boots began but the words wouldn't come out.

"Sir my mothafuck'n ass! I don't want no god damn excuses Boots! If you gone open your mouth it better be because you got some god damn answers for me!" Captain Sweeney didn't give a fuck that he'd disrespected Boots. He needed his men to get off their asses.

The entire Homicide Division was present and accounted for except for Russo whose been missing for almost three months now. He was the first one to go missing, and since then a string of cops had disappeared. Not just cops, but good cops. Cops that Sweeney knew personally. Though he couldn't prove it, Captain Sweeney suspected foul play.

"Captain w-we understand you want answers. We want answers too, these are our brothers were talking about. But we can't create evidence that ain't there." Detective Peters spoke up.

"Don't give me that shit. Peters, you and Urena didn't seem to have a problem creating evidence with that Rogers case." He made sure to look at Lt. Urena as well. "Don't think I've forgotten about that little stunt either. You two are still on my shit list so you better come up with some answers. This god damn department keeps receiving all these awards for outstanding police work. Well god dammit, let me see some outstanding fucking police work! Find my goddamn officers!"

Sweeney stepped from behind the podium and started heading out of the room. Silently everybody was glad to see him go. For a little guy, Captain Sweeney could be over bearing.

Overall, he was a good guy. On any given Sunday you could see him being caring and understanding. Maybe feeding the homeless or helping at risk youth. But when he was riled up he was a real pain in the ass!

"Costa! My office now!" He yelled out to the Sergeant as he reached the door.

Sergeant Costa was a good cop. He came from a family with a long line of good cops in their family. Hardworking and proud people!

Costa did his job, was hard dedicated and straight forward. Yet he had compassion too. As he stepped into the Captains office, he walked up to the desk prepared to take a seat.

"Don't sit down this won't take long!" Sweeney barked out. He pulled his handkerchief from out his pocket and wiped his forehead.

"I want you to take that kid Hedgecock with you. He seems like a good kid. Good instincts and maybe some potential. I don't want him getting caught up with them riff raffs if I can help it.

"Whole departments going to shit, but I'm trying to save what I can. Sergeant you're a good man and a fine officer, so I know the kid will be in good hands. Now get out of my office and earn your paycheck!" Sweeney neva looked up. Not once.

"Yes, sir." Like the good cop that he was, Sergeant Costa gave the only response he knew.

Back in the locker room he caught up with Hedgecock.

"Hey Rookie."

Hedgecock looked up from polishing his boots "talking to me?"

"Yeah you. Cap says you're riding with me. Meet me downstairs in five minutes. Polish your damn shoes at home!"

De'Kari

"Yes sir, Serg." Hedgecock felt embarrassed by the way Sergeant talked to him.

Costa walked to the back of the locker room where his locker was located. Strapping on his bullet proof vest he put his shirt back on and grabbed his bags. Before he closed his locker, he looked at the picture of his wife as he always did, said a quick prayer, grabbed his amino acid shake and closed his locker.

This was his daily routine. Hit the gym every morning before work and pray before he went out into the field he did them religiously.

Once he and the rookie got in the car and was on their way, Costa figured a little light conversation just see where the kid's head was would be better than trying to lecture him off the bat.

Most Sergeants were down right ass holes. They used their rank to bully the officers around with intimidation, but not Costa. He had good people skills. After all he was considered the "Go to Guy."

He had transferred over from the San Mateo County Sheriff's Department to the Milpitas Police Department as a special favor for Sheriff Laiens who is a longtime friend of the family.

When Chief Vieira reached out to Sheriff Laiens for advice and assistance not only did he give some wonderful advice, but he also recommended lending the Chief a few of his up and coming stars and a couple kick ass veterans. Those Veterans were Sergeant Costa and a couple, Lieutenants Boots and Urena.

After an hour of riding around showing Hedgecock a thing or two while feeling the rookie out, Costa figured it was time to do some police work.

He had placed a call earlier to Brenda Russo and asked her if it would be okay to meet with her. He wanted to get a feel for young officer Russo and who better to paint a picture then his wife.

Costa turned his unmarked Marquise and headed towards her house.

**** N. D. ****
(Somewhere in East Oakland)

Nina was furious!

The night after Wendell 's death it seemed that the little mothafucka who he was meeting just vanished. Her and her sister searched high and low for months. They combed through the streets of East Palo Alto with no success.

Then yesterday she had been craving some soul food, so she drove over to Soul's Restaurant in East Oakland. As she was ordering her food she heard someone call out.

Gorillaz in the Bay 2

"God Damn!"

Knowing it was some disrespectful ass nigga checking out her ass, she spun around furious, ready to put the mothafucka in his place.

Nina couldn't believe her luck! She turned around and was staring the little nigga that they had been looking for straight in the face.

Instantly she changed her mood and demeanor and played the role. Nina let him spit his little weak ass game and even allowed him to pay for her and her sisters food while taking his number. She knew Trina wasn't going to believe this, hell she didn't believe it.

She excused herself and went to the bathroom to call her sister and tell her about it. Needless to say, Trina neva did get her Soul's that day.

Now sitting low with her sister ducked off in a black impala with tinted windows, Nina she watched the house down the street. She couldn't believe what she was seeing. There were twenty or thirty little mothafuckas all hanging out in the house, the yard, and in front of the house.

It looked like a normal hangout for kids, like a clubhouse. They had been sitting there long enough to see that it was a dope spot as well. Dope fiends would be served near the corner while other niggaz who looked like D. Boyz would pull up and go into the house, only to come out a few minutes later carrying a small bag. Nina knew they were copping some work. It looked like they didn't give a damn about the police, they did everything in the open like it was legal.

Earlier today they both witnessed why. A cop cruiser was about a block away when a loud whistle sounded out. No doubt warning them that the police was coming. They expected to see the group disperse.

Instead they witnessed the craziest shit that they had ever seen. All thirty of them reached somewhere or another, some inside their pants, others in bushes, some behind cars. But they all stood tall holding guns, machine guns, and assault rifles in their hands in a challenging way, daring the police to stop.

The police car sped out of there like they were in high pursuit. If Nina wouldn't have seen it, she wouldn't have believed it.

Like the good girl that she was, Trina was taking notes, so she could give Voorheeze and Cantelope a full report. Nina loved her sister to death, but she couldn't believe that she was actually sitting there taking notes with a pen and a pad like she was back in school. Nina smiled and shook her head at her sister. Trina was crazy! She was always "Miss Goody Goody!" but she was deadlier then a baby rattle snake when crossed.

Tonight, was a very insightful night for the twins, but just when they thought it couldn't get more insightful their minds were blown.

De'Kari

"Trina. Girrrl you better look at this." Trina knew whenever Nina was on to something juicy, she could hear it in her voice.

Trina stopped writing and looked up. She was just as surprised as her sister to see a Black and Pink Camaro pull up to the house. Everybody in the Yay Area knew exactly who drove them black and pink Camaros with matching rims.

Trina felt betrayed! Nina wanted to jump out and set it off! Whoever had just pulled up to that house was unmistakably a She-Wolf.

They waited eagerly to see which one of their sistah's was betraying them all. The driver's door opened, and she stepped out

"That low life cunt! Stank ass hoe!" Nina couldn't believe who it was. Not her, it couldn't' be.

Trina picked up her cell phone and looked for a name in her contacts. All hell was about to break loose!

Anne was tired, hungry and cranky. All she wanted was a hot bath, some food and as much sleep as a girl could get. She hated long drives and lately that was all she had been doing. She'd moved out of her parents' house with her little brother nearly eight months ago. He was beginning to be a handful and she was spending more and more time over in the Peninsula. So, she had gotten her a little apartment in Fremont, the half way point between Oakland and East Palo Alto. The apartment wasn't much but it was her own and it was clean. She was too tired to drive all the way home. Anne knew that she couldn't make it, so she decided she would stop off at her parents' house in Oakland and stay the night. After all she hadn't seen her little brother in almost a year.

It was the She-Wolves that had assisted Beast with that problem in Half Moon Bay with CSL. After the incident there was a little back lash, so, Anne and a couple of the others had to lay low for a while. Anne went to Stockton.

She quickly grew tired of that Valley life and decided she would take her chances back at home. Stockton was cool, but nothing was like the Yay Area. Not to mention that valley weather was just way too hot for her.

As she got closer to the house, Anne almost lost her mind. She wondered if maybe she was looking at the wrong house. Was it possible she had driven down the wrong street? The big rod-iron fence, the old faded yellow paint and the front awning told her it wasn't the wrong house. Anne didn't speak to anyone as she confidently marched up to the front door. Most of them were smart enough to avert their eyes, yet some had the nerve to stare her down. They were all kids. She didn't understand it.

"What's up big sis?" Just as she was climbing the porch, Sutton stepped out of the house.

"You tell me." Anne responded as she continued to walk directly into the house, "Boy we need to talk."

There was no way she was going to have this discussion in front of his little friends, she wanted privacy.

Needless to say, the conversation led to a debate, which led to an all-out heated argument. Anne couldn't believe Sutton would disrespect their parents' house the way he was doing. She tried to reason with him, but he was just as hard headed as their father. He even had the nerve to tell her that she had abandoned him for Neva Die.

As her instincts screamed out to her, she couldn't shake the feeling that she was being watched. Maybe if she wasn't so pissed off she would've been more in tuned with herself. Maybe then she would've looked to her left as she passed the impala and saw the two silhouettes that stared at her as she passed.

**** N. D. ****
(Milpitas, California)

Lt. Boots was still pissed off due to the way the Captain spoke to him earlier today in the A.M. briefing room. Boots was a damn good Lieutenant and a hellavah officer. He was transferred over to this department to help aid in the restructuring of the Homicide Division and help he has. In the short time since he had been here he'd already solved four homicides that were giving the other detectives problems.

Boots was in his mid-thirties tall, lean, relatively handsome, despite the fact that he was bald. A factor he considered a reason for his bad luck with woman. Neva in a million years would he realize that his anal-retentive attitude is what runs the women away. That and the fact that he lived for the job.

To Lieutenant Boots it was all about fighting crime and making the world a better place. He didn't see any other way. This is what drove him day in and day out. He was the type to work 12-hour days at the office and still take his work home with him. A damn good cop but a poor candidate for man of the year.

He just happened to be in the area when the call went out about an alarm at Milpitas High School. On a normal day he would neva take a call like this, but the cops who patrolled this area were both busy with disputes at the moment.

There had been a rash of break-ins lately. Meth heads stealing anything they think could get them a few dollars for their next fix. The school superintendent was worried about the new state of the art computer lab that cost a few hundred grand. Because his family had political ties, the Superintendent had been able to stir up some ruckus. As was his nature, Lt. Boots decided to help out.

When he pulled up to the high school everything looked in order. decided to take a look around. Not only would it satisfy his curiosity, but he knew it would shut the Superintendent up. He took a look around the entire campus once. Nothing caught his attention. Satisfied that the school was okay and that everything was in order, he radioed it in "3641 Dispatch."

"Go for dispatch."

"Ah yeah I'm over at the high school. I've had a thorough look around and don't see anything. Everything looks to be in order, cancel; the call." Boots spoke into his chest radio as he made his way back to his car.

"3641 you say cancel the call. Is that correct?"

"10-4 dispatch."

"10-4 the call is ..."

LT. Boots opened the door to his car and paused for a second. Something was wrong. His instincts spoke to him. He glanced around but didn't see anything. When he sat inside of the car, he wiped his fingers on his pants legs. As he did so, the hairs on the back of his next stood up.

Why was there liquid on his fingers? It wasn't raining, and it's been a while since he had gotten the car washed. Something was wrong!

At the moment, he smelled the gasoline for the first time! Suddenly all the doors to the car locked themselves. Boots reached over for the door handle and yanked on it. Nothing happened! He yanked harder and harder still nothing happened. He reached over to the passenger side door and attempted to open that door. It didn't budge. Worry and panic tried to sneak in, but he wouldn't allow it to!

Focusing so much on getting out of the car he didn't see the 5'10", middle aged black man glaring at him through the windshield. He seemed to appear out of nowhere. Boots felt like he was being watched and finally looked up. When he saw the man standing in front of his car staring through the windshield with a sinister smile on his face, he lost the battle with both fear and panic.

The look in the strange man's eyes paralyzed Lt. Boots. He had neva seen a more hateful set of eyes. Now with fear sending adrenaline throughout his body, the stench of the gasoline was getting unbearable! By now the liquid had time to soak through the bottom of his pants.

Gorillaz in the Bay 2

Boots looked around and realized the entire car was soaked. Gasoline was all over the place. Gasoline was poured all over the inside and outside of the car; that's what the liquid was on his fingers when he got in the car. Then Boots remembered the man that was outside the car.

When he looked up he noticed two things. One there was a second larger bald man standing next to the first guy with a gun in his hand. Boots didn't move. They already had the drop on him. The new guy was smoking a cigarette and laughing. Then he tossed the cigarette at the windshield. The car erupted in flames.

"3641 Dispatch!" He panicked while yelling into his radio, "1216 officer in need of assistance. I repeat 1216 officer in need of assistance at my last location! Need immediate backup!" by now he was practically yelling into the radio.

"Copy that 3641! Assistance is on the way."

"Every available unit we have a 1216 officer who is in need of assistance, all cars in the vicinity of Milpitas High School."

Lt. Boots could hear dispatch radioing help, but he wasn't paying attention to it. He was desperately trying to get out of the car.

He knew the odds were against him, but he had to do something. Even if the fire didn't get into the car, by the time back up arrived the smoke and fumes would kill him. He had to act! He reached for his service weapon and felt a hot white piercing pain shoot through his arm. Then another in his shoulders! He couldn't move his arm. He looked down at his arm and saw blood, he was shot!

Voorheeze lifted the Desert Eagle and sent two more missiles into the cop's other arm. This way he couldn't shoot his way out of the car. He would indeed burn to death. Batman had rigged the car's locks with his knowledge as an electrical engineer.

They both knew the amount of time the cop was locked in the car with the windows closed would cause the fumes to build up. Even though they wanted to see the rest, they knew they had to leave. There was no need to watch, they already knew what would happen next.

The pain from the gun shots were excruciating. He had neva been shot before. Boots was praying that his colleagues would get there in time. His heart raced as heard the sirens, he knew they were getting closer. Then it happened!

The built-up fumes inside the car seeped thru the bullet holes and ignited! The car was an instant furnace! The entire inside of the car was engulfed in flames. The intense heat and burning was too much to bear!

Lt. Boots made his final fatal mistake! He screamed! The moment he opened his mouth, he felt the most agonizing pain he had ever felt

De'Kari

in his life. The heat from the flames seared his mouth, esophagus and lungs instantly. His death was quick, but those seconds leading up to his death were the worst of his life!

The squad cars raced down the street with sirens flashing and blaring. It sounded like an alien war cry! Car after car zoomed by! There were so many cars, it looked as if they were responding to a bank heist with hostages. None of the speeding cars paid any attention to the construction truck as they flew past.

Batman smiled as Voorheeze pulled out a Newport 100, lit it and rolled down the window. "It's gonna be a hot summer!" he said to no-one in particular

Chapter XV
(Voorheeze tuck spot in Hayward Hills)

Voorheeze sat back down on the couch. He picked the keyboard remote back up and turned the volume down on the tv. Turning his head from side to side, he tried to see if he could hear anything. This is the seventh time he's done this in the past hour.

Not only that but he has double-checked the alarm system making sure the alarm was on four times. He'd checked his desert eagle each time. His phone had been ringing but he wasn't going to answer. He was convinced that his phone may be tapped.

SNIFF! He picks up the bottle of Remy and takes a gulp just as the doorbell rings. After checking the monitors, he buzzes his guest in.

"Damn! Niggaz ain't locking doors around this mothafucka or something!" His tone full of irritation at his brother's lack of security. The coke got him on full beast mode.

"Nigga as paranoid as you are, I'm surprised you ain't got shit rigged to a five second delay before this whole bitch lockdown."

Clark jokes as he walks into the room with an athletic sized Nike gym bag.

"Well I don't nigga so next time lock the fucking door!"

"Whatever nigga save that tough shit for them." Clark wasn't trynna hear that shit today.

Voorheeze picked up the keyboard. He hit a couple of keys and the front doors locked. Next the alarm activated. He replaced the keyboard in his hand with a plate of coke on it, the size of a mountain. He made two huge lines out of the coke, each line about a gram. *SNIFF! SNIFF!*

"God damn Nigga!

"What?" Voorheeze looked up confused. He wiped his face put the plate down and reached for the bag. He unzipped the bag, looked at the contents and nodded his head in satisfaction. He reached into the bag and removed two stacks.

"Here!" He tossed them to his brother

"What's this for?" Clark was dumb founded

"Nigga you looked out, now I'm looking out." Voorheeze told him as he stood up with his head tilted to catch the drain.

"Rogue I don't need yo money."

"I don't either." Voorheeze said. Dead seriously. "Now give me fifteen minutes and I'll be ready."

"What if I wanna go outside? Nigga am I a hostage in dis bitch? God damn!" Clark joked with him.

De'Kari

"Folsom on lockdown!" Voorheeze called over his shoulder dead serious.

A little while later they were pulling up to Jing Jing's in San Jose off First Street. On the ride over Clark gave Voorheeze an update on what was going on as far as A.J. and his team. The duffle bag was from A.J.. The shipment arrived like clockwork with no problems. However, somehow the last pick up of money had been overlooked by Voorheeze. Voorheeze had asked Clark to pick it up for him as a favor, because he could have sworn he saw a burgundy Jeep Cherokee following him. The first of the two bags were safely tucked away before Clark had brought the second to Voorheeze.

Upon entering Jing Jing's, they were led inside to a Hibachi style grill, where their little sister was already waiting. She rose and greeted them both.

"Hey brothers!" She hugged Clark first, and then Voorheeze. Clark mumbled something then sat down.

"What's up beautiful" Voorheeze said, returning her hug.

All the women that were close to him, he always greeted the same. It was either "beautiful or gorgeous", except for her. *He could neva greet her that way. How would she respond? She didn't even know that he felt about her the way he did. She wouldn't dare look at him that way. Whenever he greeted her, it was always cordial and respectful, but neva intimate or personal.*

After placing their order and having a pint of hot Saki brought over in a little kettle made of bone china, they conversed low and briefly before the chef took his place behind the grill to work his magic. It was truly an amazing sight. The grill itself was approximately four and a half feet in length and two feet wide. A table was formed around the front and sides in the Japanese tradition. There were eight other people seated around the grill.

"Have you decided what exactly we're going to do about our little situation?" French Tip asked Voorheeze.

The restaurant was loud and lively enough for them to hold a conversation in discretion.

"What little situation?" Clark was just putting his rice cup down from taking a shot of the hot Saki.

"Naw, I got some things in mind, but I wanted to get you guys insight on 'em. Voorheeze ignored Clark.

"Rogue, what are you talking about? Clark didn't like being out of the loop.

French Tip filled him in on the phone call she had gotten from Trina about Anne showing up at the house where the Young Nigga Mafia cats were. Considering the damage that they had caused to him

138

and his team over the past few months, Clark was ready to get into that ass. Normally, the level headed and thinking one, Voorheeze was already finding her guilty as well as ready to pass judgement. French Tip was the voice of reason. She brought up a few valid points. Like Anne's body count for Mobb alone spoke of her loyalty. Add the fact that she knew where multiple cash spots and stash spots were, and neva once was there a problem or a dollar taken.

"I'm just saying, Chiba wouldn't pull nothing shady like that. She's not built like that" French was expressing her trust and love by calling Anne by her handle.

"Man fuck that shit! She's an Oakland hoe, and all them Oakland mothafuckas are shiesty." Clark wasn't giving Anne the benefit of the doubt.

Too much blood had been spilled already. He had lost too many people. One, was too many to him, and he was well past that number.

"Check it out! We ain't going to bite each other's heads off behind this shit. Clark, I feel your pain rogue, and about betrayal; you know I feel just as adamant about it as you do. But, sis got a point. As much work as Anne has put in for dis damn family, we at least owe it to her to explain this shit." He reached for his Saki, and downed it, all the while looking at his baby sister. "But make no mistake about it, this is Neva Die over everything. If she's guilty; She-Wolf or not, I'mma knock the bitch's dick in the dirt."

The last thing Voorheeze wanted to do was wrongly convict one of his own. T'Rida had brought Anne into the into the Family, so, if the wrong decision was made, he would feel like he was crossing his brother in the grave.

But he wasn't gonna to let a Judas escape freely either. He decided it would be put on the table at the next War Room.

**** **N. D.** ****

French Tip had his mind going a hundred miles an hour, and she didn't know it. Immediately following their dinner, he was on his shit. He placed a call to his little cousin. Steve couldn't believe what he was hearing! First, he thought Voorheeze was playing some type of practical joke on him. After reassuring Steve that he was dead serious, Steve instantly went into gear. His commission off this move, would net him over a million dollars.

Next, Voorheeze put in a call to Sam and J Styles; his two Lieutenant's, and let them know, he needed to see them. The phone calls didn't stop though. He called Cantelope next. He thought about calling French Tip, then thought twice about it. To him, she was just a little too adamant in Anne's defense. Until he saw where her head was at, he would have to keep his sister at a distance. At least that was what the cocaine was telling him.

SNIFF! SNIFF!

He tilted his head back after snorting two lines to catch a drain and not let in run back out of his nose. As he drove, he thought over all his decisions, analyzing them and making sure that he made the best possible moves.

(East Oakland)

Sutton sat in the house playing Madden in the front room with Young Sav, Stacks, and Pistol. They were his most trusted. Only one was missing; Roscoe. Chanelle and Monique were off in the dining area, playing spades. Normally, Sutton would dominate any of them when it came to Madden. Tonight however, Young Sav was getting into that ass. Sutton was a die hard 49'ers fan, so naturally, he was the 49'er; while Sav, born and raised in Oakland, was an Oakland Raider.

He was up by two touchdowns, but there was more than enough time for Sutton to stage a comeback. He hiked the ball; play action pass. Young Sav's defense, bit on the play action. Sutton got Brandon Lloyd open for the deep ball. He let it soar through the air for a guaranteed touchdown. Out of the middle of nowhere, the cornerback leaps and intercepts the ball!

"Fuck!" Sutton yells in frustration. "What the fuck was that?"

"That's that Town Bizzness niggaz." Sav laughed and taunted as he is still working the controller trying to make it a pick six.

Sutton is desperate not to let him score. He knows that if Sav scored the game would virtually be over. He has enough time on the clock to make a stop and still come back. But if Sav scored right now the game will be over.

Sutton's phone rings.

"Naa nigga don't pick that shit up! Let it ring! I don't want no excuse when I pull off this V.I "Sav yells out.

Sutton grabs the phone while still trying to bring him down.

"Nigga you aint gone get no victory you bout to lose this shit, watch!"

"Hello?" He answers the phone.

"Hey sexy, what you doing?" It was the little chick he met the other day. He could tell by her sexy voice.

"Shit, I'm just chilling wit my peeps for the moment."

"Don't lie nigga, you gettin yo ass whopped right now!" Sav yells out in the background as he completes another first down.

"Who is that?"

"Don't mind him. That's just the neighborhood retard. We normally let him over at night to eat dinner. Everybody started cracking up. Sutton isn't laughing though when Sav scores another touchdown making the score 35 to 17.

Sutton stands up and drops a 20-dollar bill on Sav's lap. Fuck that game! He knew he was gonna lose. His mind nor his heart was into it. He was still replaying the argument that he had with his sister and below the surface he was seething. Sutton wasn't like Anne. She was loving and caring but under the surface dangerous and deadly. Sutton on the other hand just didn't give a fuck. If Anne didn't know her place he would surely put her in it and if she didn't stay in it then he wouldn't hesitate to send her to their parents.

He resumed his conversation and made his way to the back room for some privacy. Maybe lil mama could take his mind off things.

"Sorry about that, I had to get up and get some privacy." He told her as he finally made it to the back room.

"So, what, you just sit around the house all day playing video games."

"Naa. Today just happened to be a relaxed night for us." She fires back

"Who's us? Don't tell me that you got a woman." Nina put a little attitude with it trying to play the role.

"Naa baby, us is my peeps." He tells her quickly. "One day if shit goes good you'll meet them."

"Oh, so it's like that, huh?"

"Don't take it personal, baby! You don't take every nigga you meet home to yo parents, do you?"

"Hell no!"

"Okay then it's the same thing."

They talked for another 20 minutes or so. It really was good therapy for him. Lil mama was a little feisty. He found that cute. The two of them made plans to hook up the next day and he couldn't wait. But for now, he had a schedule to keep.

****** N. D. ******
(The following night at the War room)

"Tonight's meeting aint going to be our normal updates and assessments!" Voorheeze paused and looked around the room. "Tonight, I could really give a fuck about money and territory." He paused again. This time he stopped pacing around the room.

De'Kari

His look was totally off. Instead of his normal sharp dressed self, Voorheeze was thugged out. His Mauri Alligators were replaced with black Timberland boots. His silk threads were gone. Replaced by black jeans and a black G-unit tank- top and on the top of that was a bullet-proof vest. The most alarming addition was the big ass Desert Eagle that he was gripping.

Johnny Spits and Stone just sat there unphased. French Tip and Cantelope knew what was going on. Still, French Tip was nervous. She didn't like seeing her brother like this. Dee Dee and DJ were looking at A.J., trying to get a read on what he wanted them to do. They were thinking since they were the only ones from Oakland, this shit was about them. C- Murder was idly playing with his Bowie knife looking like he didn't have a care in the world.

"As yall know now we've been at war for quite some time in East Palo Alto with some little mothafuckas. For months we didn't even know who we were fighting. Finally, the homework paid off, at the same time the streets started talking. When I was first told that we were locked in a full fledge war with kids I couldn't believe it. I figured somebody made a mistake somewhere until more intel poured in. "He reached for a stack of manila envelopes and started passing them out while he spoke.

"The group calls themselves Young Nigga Mafia."

He kept talking but Anne wasn't listening. The last thing that she heard was Young Nigga Mafia. She had been hearing her brother and a few of his buddies say that name. She was praying this was a coincidence. Her little brother couldn't be running around with niggaz this dangerous.

"I want yall to open the manila envelopes. Look at what and who we've been dealing with. Then I want you to tell me what I'm supposed to do?"

Everyone was paying full attention to their envelopes, no one saw the twins walk in followed by Stunna and Keak. Stunna took up position by the sliding door, the twins directly behind Anne while Keak blocked off any path towards the front of the house.

Voorheeze continued "I've had someone following the nigga we found out was the leader, but the little mothafucka managed to slip 'em . Thanks to the twins we found him again."

For the first time everybody noticed their presence. They also noticed how they were positioned behind Anne. She couldn't see them, but she could tell how everyone was looking in her direction that they were there. The fear she just had, she knew was indeed true.

"Imagine their surprise when they follow him back to their headquarters only to see one of our own there."

Gorillaz in the Bay 2

Anne looked up from the stack of papers and photos she was looking at. She dropped everything that was in her hands.

Voorheeze was holding up an enlarged picture of her parents' house. Last night with all those little fuck-ups surrounding the house and her car. She reached for the photo not believing her eyes. She started to stand but was held down by the twins.

She looked from one shoulder to the other at the two hands holding her in place. "Voorheeze what the fuck is this?" And why do you have a picture of my car?"

"This was taken last night"

"I know when the fuck it was taken, I was there." Everyone knew that Anne didn't curse. She was starting to lose her cool.

"Chiba the question is why in the fuck was you there?" Voorheeze didn't like the way she spoke to him. She-Wolf or not he'd fill her ass with hot shit.

"That's my daddy's house!" Anne spit out furiously. No one was expecting to hear that, "Up until right before that shit in Half Moon Bay, it was my house. I got tired of driving back home every night, so I got an apartment in Fremont. I left the house to my little brother and his friends." Reality was now starting to sink in; her little brother was a part of this Y.N.M. thing.

"Your little brother huh?" Voorheeze walked back over to where he got the stack of folders from. He picked up a picture and turned around.

"Why?" A long single tear escaped her eye and burned as it rolled down her face. "Voorheeze... I suggest you have a damn good reason why you are standing there holding a picture of my little brother in your fucking hand." The tear already fell but no more would follow. They would be replaced by indescribable anger and rage.

"This is your little brother?" He was just as shocked as everyone in the room.

"She aint know cuz. A blind nigga can see she aint fakin." It was Cantelope who spoke up. She knew when a broad was fakin or not.

"I didn't know what?" Anne spit out on the verge of some Tasmanian Devil shit.

"Anne your little brother is the leader." There was no sense in building up to it, so Voorheeze told her flat out.

Anne remained quiet for a long time. Everyone watched her. Some feeling pity for her, some trying to understand, everybody waiting to see what she would do.

"And you thought I was in on it? Thought I would betray the family?" She shook her shoulders free of their grasp. "Get yo mothafuck'n hands off me!" Anne slowly stood up. "I'm dedicated and motivated

De'Kari

but most importantly I'm loyal! I would have neva accused any of yall of shit let alone treason. But I'll tell you what. Do what you want to his team. I'll take care of my brother. If anyone of you touches my brother, I'll kill everybody in this goddamn room." As she made her way out of the room Keak stood in her way with his Dessert Eagle pointed at her head "Bitch I don't care who you are. Take another step, I'll put a hole in yo shit!"

"Let her go!" Voorheeze called out. Then making eye contact with Keak he gestured for him to follow her.

After Anne left the rest of Neva Die continued to have their meeting. They discussed the new information regarding Anne and Y.N.M. Clark and Johnny Spitz where to design a strategic plan to finally deal with Y.N.M. A.J. strongly offered their assistance in dealing with Oakland members which the family accepted. Once that was figured out they conducted their normal meeting.

Sales were down across the board. It would seem that fiends were switching from crack to Crystal Meth. At first Meth users were the young white crowd as well as bikers. Now, it seemed the tweekers (coke smokers) were now riding the crystal bubble instead of the crack pipe, A decision was made for further research to be done on this.

After the meeting everyone left except French Tip. She was concerned for her brother. She knew his pride would neva allow him to admit when he was weak or bothered. Still she was concerned.

"Are you okay Brother?" she asked with the sweetest voice a human could possibly have.

"I'm good, Booger. Just a lil tired that's all." Booger is a nickname he started calling her in 2002.

"Maybe you should take a break from shit for a bit and relax a little. You know we can handle these little niggaz." She could see how much strain he was under and it was killing her.

"What kind of leader would I be if I just kicked back right now in the middle of a war and possibly treason?" He got up to make himself a drink, "You want one?"

"Naa, I'm good. So, when am I going to meet this new love interest of yours? You've been hiding her for months now." She figured she would change the subject. The last thing that she wanted to do was stress him out even further.

"I don't know sis. Soon I guess. I aint been hiding her especially from you. I've just been real busy. I tell you what. Why don't we all go out to eat next week or something? You, Ray, Danika and I."

Playing 'Meet the Browns' was the furthest thing on his mind right now, but he would neva deny his little sister. They made it a date. She

144

Gorillaz in the Bay 2

gave her brother a kiss and a hug and then left. Voorheeze locked up the house before heading to the tunnel.

The moment he stepped through the hidden door and into his master bedroom, Danika was all over him. She damn near knocked him down when she jumped into his arms raining kisses all over his face.

"Hey baby! I was hoping you would come home early tonight." She exclaimed when she jumped in his arms.

"Hey Thickems!" one arm went around her waist while his other hand cupped her gigantic ass cheek.

"I missed you, Daddy!" She tells him

before her mouth attacks his in a lust-filled kiss

Finally allowing him some oxygen she asked, "Are you hungry, Daddy?"

"Starving."

"Okay! While you jump in the shower I'll go warm your plate up" She gave him one more kiss then unwrapped her legs from around his waist and walked out of the room. He watched her as she switched away. The thong she was wearing getting swallowed up greedily by her ass cheeks.

While in the shower, the hot water cascaded across his back, relieving some of the stress and tension in his body. As Voorheeze relaxed he couldn't help but to think about her again. Her flawless skin, her breath-taking body. Danika calls out from the room bringing him back from his fantasizing.

"Hey, my lil sister is dying to meet you" He calls out in response as he steps out of the shower.

"Do you think she's going to like me?" The nervousness evident in her voice.

"Of course, she gone like you. Babe your perfect. How can anyone not like you?" He gives her a kiss on the lips as he lays across the bed next to her.

After saying his prayers and giving thanks for his food he picks up his fork and digs in.

"Ooh Shit!" He calls out after his first mouthful, "We just can't let her taste your cooking. Once she finds out that you can cook better than her, she gone hate yo ass!" Voorheeze jokes.

"Boy quit playing!" That comment made her feel good.

After he finished his dinner she opened her legs and gave him his dessert, which he greedily accepted. After making love they fell asleep.

(Somewhere in the Yay Area)

De'Kari

The tears cascaded down her cheeks. Anne made one hundred attempts to wipe them away or stop them from falling but she couldn't remember the last time she cried or the last time she felt a pain so severe. She didn't even cry when her parents were killed. The day was so vivid in her mind. It was like it happened yesterday. When she heard the news about the car crash she was devastated and felt a sense of dread, but she didn't feel any sorrow. Anne couldn't grieve. She didn't have time to. She had to focus on her little brother. Sutton needed her.

She did any and everything she had to do to ensure that her baby brother would be okay. From messing with busters who had a little money, to doing small hustles on her own. Whatever she had to do. Anne made sure that the bills were paid, and there was food in the house. That's how she ended up being with Melvin. He was a buster and a chump, but he would break her off.

Melvin was how she'd come to meet T'Rida. Melvin and his stupid ass cousins made the mistake of robbing one of T'Rida's spots. That first day they kicked her doors in, Anne knew right away that there was something special about T'Rida. It was him that attracted her. Him that turned her on and flamed her dedication. Her loyalty was pledged to T'Rida.

Back when she saved his life in that shoot out on Beech Court. She'd acted on impulse because she was drawn to him. She pledged her life to this organization because it was his! Anne had hoped for a love affair with him, but it wasn't planned. Their affair was so powerful and electric. It was short lived, but it was theirs.

And now as she sped thru the rain-soaked streets thinking about her little brother. Anne couldn't help but to miss T'Rida. She needed him. There was so much she wanted to tell him. So much he didn't know. Time and time again she wanted to break down and confide in him, but she could neva find the time. Now, there is no time.

Her ringing cell phone interrupted her thoughts. She reached over and answered without looking at the screen

"Hello?"

"Look big sis. I'm sorry. I didn't mean to get at you like that earlier." The sound of Sutton's voice made the tears flow faster.

"How could you lil Demetris?" She banged the steering wheel so hard with her hand. "How could you betray me like this?"

Sutton was very confused "Sis I said I was sorry! A nigga was outta pocket, but I would neva betray you."

"Demetris, how could you and your nothing ass friends steal from and attack my people?" She wanted him to say it wasn't true. She needed him to tell her there was some kind of mistake. She wasn't prepared for what came out of his mouth.

"All is fair in War."

"What the fuck that supposed to mean?" Anne is sure she didn't hear him right.

"See sis, if you were playing on the right team, then you would know what that means." Sutton let out a sadistic laugh

"Look lil boy this is not no fuckin game…"

"No, you look Bitch!" He interrupted her. It's a game alright and when it's done Neva Die will be the loser. It's Young Nigga Mafia time bitch! And none of them crocodile tears you crying gone save you if you on the other side! Now since you're my sister, I'll give you a chance to save yourself. You got two days to make your mind up before I make it up for you!" He hung up the phone without allowing her to utter a word.

Anne couldn't believe her ears. She was blown away. This little mothafucka had the nerve to call her a bitch! Not once but twice! Here she was crying over the predicament, when all along he knew what he was doing. They could've killed her tonight or any other night. This mothafucka thinks it's a game.

"Mothafucka I changed yo shitty ass diapers and you got the motherfucking nerve to call me a bitch!" By now she was yelling at the top of her lungs, "I got yo bitch mothafucka!"

De'Kari

CHAPTER XVI
(Back of the Gardens)

It was a little after four in the morning. The club had been jumping like fuck. After the club, mothafuckas went to get some food and then it was off to Pussyville. The normal "Hood Shit". Clark took the little broad Vanessa to the Homestead Suites in Sunnyvale and wore her little-ass out. The way she had that little-pussy popping on him, he wasn't ready to call it quits just yet.

He had something else in store for her, but first he had to swing by his spot, on Camellia to pick up something. He ran in and took care of his business and then ran out carrying two black duffle bags. When he jumped back in the Scooby-Doo van, Vanessa instantly put her head in his lap. The windows were tinted so he figured fuck it and leaned his seat all the way back.

She was sucking his dick so good the nigga was holding his breathe. Vanessa was bobbing her head up and down on it while and turning and twisting her head. The result was a like a cyclone on his dick.

Just when he palmed the back of her head ready to really feed her his dick, his senses started going off like crazy, he felt like a thousand eyes were on him, like he was being surrounded. When Clark opened his eyes he literally almost shitted on himself. He was so scared that he farted in Vanessa's face. She gagged, lifted all the way up and opened her mouth like she was getting good and ready to curse him out. Clark immediately covered her mouth with one hand and wrapped his arm around her head.

"Sshhh!" He told her while looking around like a run-away slave. "Don't say shit V." He took his hand down from around her face.

"What the fuck is going on?" she whispered. Vanessa had neva seen so many police in her life.

"I don't know". Clark shook his head thinking about the two duffel bags he'd just thrown in the van.

Four kilos of coke and fifty thousand in cash was enough to get a life sentence and that's what was in the two bags.

"But we aint moving so be perfectly still."

Outside of his window it looked like a fuckin law enforcement convention. East Palo Alto P.D., Santa Clara Sheriff's Department, F.B.I. and the D.E.A. were all storming his uncles house. There had to be at least fifty fuckin 50 cops. Clark didn't want to move and risk someone seeing the movement behind the glass, but fuck it, he couldn't be a bitch. He had to let his folks know what was going on.

First, he hit his big cousin's cell phone, all he got was the voicemail. Next, he hit another cousin's phone only to hear his voicemail. "Fuck!" He yelled in his head. He didn't know what else to do. What could he do? They were already bringing somebody out in handcuffs. A little later came the "God Father", his uncle in cuffs. Clark could clearly tell he had been sleeping.

All types of thoughts ran through Clark's head, "were they really trying to hit his spot and ran in the wrong house by mistake? Was he next"?

Subconsciously he reached for his 40 and thought to himself he'd rock dis bitch like Red Rock Café before he went down, fuck that! There was nothing he could do but wait as they brought out bag after bag of shit. Faggott ass cops were like that. They just took shit for no reason. Shit that aint pertaining to shit. They took it just to fuck with you. And made it seem like you guilty of something.

He knew they would be stuck in that van all day, but it was better than the alternative. He looked over at Vanessa and whispered some encouragement.

"Shit bear with me until this pass through. Don't say shit and I swear to God I'mma take care of you!"

Her response fucked him up. She just licked her lips, dropped her head and went right back to sucking his dick. *Getting a nut couldn't hurt, fuck it!*

Clark didn't' know it at the time but he was actually witnessing one of the biggest raids in California's history by either local law enforcement or federal agents. The raids were choreographed actually by E.P.A. P.D., Santa Clara and San Mateo County Sheriff, F.B.I., D.E.A. and A.T.F. Simultaneously they hit over 21 Northern California Cities in an attempt to dismantle what they called the most sophisticated and organized group, the Al-Qaeda Gang.

A gang who in the words of the F.B.I. was one of the deadliest gangs to ever come out of California. When it was all said and done, one hundred and eleven people would get locked up in the sweep. All behind one informant ...... Ali Wali.

As he was getting ready to tilt his head back and enjoy the superb head he was getting, Clark thought he saw a familiar face. He strained to see but she was far away and there was just too much traffic going back and forth.

Her back was to him but from what he could see, the height was the same and so was the shape., hair and side profile. *But naw it can't be* he thought, *I am starting to act just like that nigga Voorheeze*, hell naw that aint her, he thought! Vanessa had her tongue circling around his head now driving him crazy. He closed his eyes, palmed her head and helped her go to work.

(Meanwhile in back of the Vill)

Most niggaz complained about their jobs, because either they didn't like what they did or they figured they didn't get paid enough for their services, but Murda wasn't one of those niggaz. He got paid ten thousand every week whether he worked or not. And usually he got hit with a little extra when he did work. But honestly Murda didn't give a fuck about the money, he loved his job. He was a little nigga and always had been. So, he'd been fighting all his life just to get a fair hand.

Finally, he just said fuck it! Since he wasn't going to get a fair hand, he'd make his own hand. He's been putting in work ever since. He walked out the back of the dykes and made a right on Illinois. On foot he followed Illinois Street all the way around to Tulane Avenue, looking for a victim.

This morning he noticed there was a lot of police traffic; marked cars and unmarked cars. But Murda didn't care, they had their business to tend to and he had his. They were fine to do whatever they pleased as long as they didn't get in his way.

A couple of houses up ahead he saw a few youngstas in the front yard. No doubt they were slanging (hustling). Murda got into character rubbing his nose, scratching his arm and looking down at the ground instead of directly in their faces. there were only two of them.

"Brah Brah, yall got some hard?" He asked, playing the role of a smoker looking for some crack.

"Damn O.G. what happened to yo clothes rogue?" The oldest of the two joked, they both started laughing.

Murda scanned the street discreetly with his eyes, watching for traffic.

"Naa what's up O.G., I'm just fuck'n with you, what you need Brah?" Again, it's the eldest who spoke. He appeared to be West Indian or something.

"Young' un I need dat Young Nigga Mafia hard. I heard yall got that Butta." Murda hungrily licked his lips.

"You know nigga! Da Mafia got dis bitch on lock!" This time it was the younger one who spoke up trynna be tough. Clearly, he was a poodle.

De'Kari

What's the old cliché Murda thought, *Young and Dumb*, don't know when to shut the fuck up. That's okay though, he just gave Murda the confirmation that he needed.

"How much you got O.G.?" The older boy called out.

"I got a big face", Murda replies. "100 reasons you no longer breathing."

BOC! BOC!

He hit the lil dumb ass one first. He couldn't have been no older than fourteen. The older one stared at his little brother, eyes wide open in disbelief as the entire right side of his little brother's head is blown off. He turned his head back around to face the old dope fiend.

BOC!

His mind neva had time to register the muzzle flash before his shit got knocked smooth the fuck off.

BOC!

The first slug ripped half of his face off. Surprisingly he was still alive. The second slug however knocked the back of his head off and cut out all lights.

Murda picked up the sack of rocks and walked back the way he came. Walking as if nothing happened. He made it all the way back around to Illinois and almost to the Dykes thinking about how the nigga was still alive with half of his shit knocked the fuck off, when he heard, "Hey you! Freeze!"

Of course, he played it off and kept walking and started singing like he was crazy.

"I said freeze mother fucker!" Fuck his command!

Murda was paying attention to the sound of his feet, he could hear the pig getting closer. Murda kept walking. He pulled the crack pipe out of his pocket and started packing the stem, then he turned around so the cop could see him take a full pull. Just as he thought this made the cop lower his guard.

"God damn junkies", he shook his head in disgust as he holstered his gun.

"Tis a fine, fine day sir, would you like a hit?" Murda stretched his arm holding the burnt pipe towards the cop.

"No, I don't wa...", he neva got a chance to finish the statement before Murda opened fire. *BOC! BOC! BOC! BOC!*

The cop fell on the pavement. Murda walked up and stood over him.

BOC! BOC! BOC! BOC!

Murda hated cops! He turned around and walked nonchalantly back to the Dykes where he disappeared.

The Pack was hunting......

Gorillaz in the Bay 2

(Union City)

Voorheeze was sitting in the living room with two AK-47's on the floor in front of him, two FN Herstals with extended clips by his side and an AR-15 in his lap. His eyes were glued to the news. The only time his eyes left the screen was to check the surveillance monitors or to pick up the plate of coke he was snorting.

Danika was laid at the other end of the couch staring at him like he had lost his natural mind. He hasn't said one word to her since his sister called 45 minutes ago. When she called, he turned on the tv in the room. A few minutes later he dropped the phone and kept watching the news segment. When it went off he bounced and grabbed the small arsenal and turned the tv on in the living room.

Voorheeze's phone kept ringing nonstop, he finally broke it. He refused to talk anymore. Now he just sat there snorting powder, watching tv and the monitors, and fuckin with his guns.

The news was saying in one of the largest busts in California history only the so-called suspected leader was still at large, but everyone else was apprehended. They had photos of the so-called leader, blasted on every channel. Voorheeze's heart went out to him because he was a good nigga and he didn't deserve to go down like this all behind some bitch nigga who couldn't hold his own. The fucked-up part about it was he wasn't even a member of the Al-Qaeda, so how in the fuck was he the leader.

"Babe you wanna talk about it?" Danika was trying to get him to focus on something other than the news and the dope.

"What's there to talk about? That's my family right there. My niggaz getting gaffled up and I can't do shit about it." He responded in a raised tone, but it wasn't aimed at her.

He just hated that he couldn't help. The game lost some real solid people today!

"I know Daddy. But why you got all these guns out? That happened hours ago?"

He looked at her like she had gone bonkers for real.

"Of course, it was hours ago. What the fuck dat mean?"

"LaMont I know you don't think yo peoples gone snitch on you." This time she had a "nigga please" attitude in her voice. Danika was from East Palo Alto and she knew Al-Qaeda niggaz were solid.

"What? Fuck no! My people aint about to go out backwards." He turned the volume down on the tv. "Look they say they got one hundred and eleven people. To my knowledge it aint even one hundred and eleven niggaz in the Al-Qaeda."

De'Kari

"That means they done snatched up a bunch of nobody ass niggaz in the process. *Sort of like casting a large net. You only want certain fish but you gonna end up catching a bunch of others as well."* He paused to let that soak in.

"The other mothafuckas are the ones I'm worried about. There is only one organization that they can tell on that's bigger than the Al-Qaeda. You wanna guess what organization that is?" He knew that she realized it now, he could see reality sinking in from the look on her face.

"Neva Die", she mumbled under her breath.

"Let me see your phone". He needed to check on his lil sis.

He dialed a number and waited for someone to pick up, but it rang until the voicemail came on. After getting voicemail for the second time he sent a text message.

Cantelope it's Voorheeze, hit me back ASAP on this number right here.

When she called him back a few minutes later, he could tell she had been crying.

"What's up cousin?" He spoke gently.

"Hey LaMont". He could tell she didn't want to talk by the sound of her voice.

"Cuz, we just gotta get to the bottom of this and find out what happened. I promise you if it's any fuck shit we gone handle it." Voorheeze meant everything he said. Cantelope was like a sister to him. Her pain was his pain.

"Alright Imma call you if I find anything out cousin." With that, Cantelope was off the phone. She didn't wait for his response, she was in too much pain.

The conversation with Cantelope brought him out of his trance. He looked over at Danika and could see worry on her face because of his behavior. So, he decided to open up fully to her. Over the months he had shared some things with her and she'd seen enough to know the get down. She just didn't know the magnitude of the get down. After their conversation she would know everything. Well at least everything that Voorheeze knew. At that time, he wasn't aware that the entire organization was brought down at the hands of one snitch.

"You know what?" Let's go have some fun?" Voorheeze jumped up. There's no sense letting the day go on being all fucked up because of something he couldn't control.

"What you got in mind Daddy?" Danika was just happy that he was out of the funk he'd been in.

"Shit let's go do some fun shit." He told her as he smacked her on her ass as they walked down the hall towards the bedroom.

Gorillaz in the Bay 2

When Danika first got dressed she came walking out she was in some little sexy get up. Voorheeze told her to throw some sweats and tennis shoes on, reminding her they were going to have fun not win a fashion contest. She changed her clothes and put on something comfortable, but it wasn't sweats. She put on some tights.

They jumped on the freeway and it seemed like only minutes later they were exiting at the Great Mall Parkway. A moment later, they arrived at the Great Mall. Voorheeze could tell by the look on her face that Danika thought they were going shopping. But that wasn't happening, he was thinking with a smile on his face.

They found parking towards the back of the parking lot since everything else was full and made their way to Dave & Buster's. She had a big smile on her face once she realized where they were going. Inside was jam-packed with a mix crowd. Some young, some middle-age and some old. They made their way to a booth in the back by the arcades. They both ordered a drink and finger food, then took off towards the games. They were having a ball playing games and being silly.

Three and a half hours flew by without them realizing it, they were having so much fun. Voorheeze only dipped off in the bathroom twice to get high so he wasn't too gone. The atmosphere was live. They nearly played every single game in there.

Voorheeze was playing Street Fighter doing his thang while Danika stood there watching and some nigga walked up to the game without even saying excuse me and tried to Deebo his way past Danika.

"Hold up bitch ass nigga! You don't see my woman standing there?" Voorheeze let the controls go and was instantly turned up. He stepped right in the niggaz face, fist balled, ready to rock. He turned from happy-go-lucky to a monster that quick. It was frightening.

The nigga that he was talking to was bigger than Voorheeze by at least 60 pounds. A big, defensive end looking nigga. First, he looked at Voorheeze like he was crazy until he saw the look in Voorheeze's eyes.

"What you talking bout homie?" The big nigga asked.

"Fuck you mean what I'm talking bout? Nigga my Queen right there and you bumped into her like a hoe on the strip." Voorheeze was so close in dude's face, he was literally spitting in the niggaz face.

A small crowd had formed.

"Bitch ass nigga! Apologize to my woman!" Voorheeze was ready, Fight or Fire it didn't matter to him. The stench of fear from the nigga was strong.

"I... I.. I'm sorry." The nigga stumbled as he looked around confused. He didn't know what Voorheeze was talking about, he apologized to wrong person.

"Not her! Nigga that's my woman!" Voorheeze told him as he pointed at Danika.

"I.. I.. I'm sorry Miss." The big ass nigga hunkering down and saying he was sorry was like that big olé nigga in the Green Mile saying, "Isa sorry Boss."

Voorheeze turned back to his game as if nothing ever happened. He placed his money card in the game and began playing. Just that quick he had forgotten about the issue. For the rest of the time they laughed, played and teased each other for the entire three and a half hours. Back in the booth they caught their breath and chatted about the night. Danika was teasing him about his anger and told him how sexy she found it that he would defend her honor without question.

Voorheeze senses was telling him that he was being watched. Without being obvious he scanned the area with his eyes. First, he didn't see anything. Then he found it. A white boy who had police written all over him, was over at the bar staring them. Voorheeze played it off, focusing on Danika, but on the low he was keeping the cop in his sights. In his mind he was wondering; Is it feds? How many of them are here?

After finishing their drink, they got up to leave. Just as he expected, the cop got up and followed them. He whispered into Danika's ear while handing her the keys to the Lambo, instructing her to go get the car. There was a large group by the doors allowing him a chance to make his move.

When the cop made it thru the crowd, he was standing outside looking around wondering where the man he was following went. He wouldn't have lost sight if it wasn't for the fucking crowd, he thought to himself.

"You know me or something man?" Voorheeze slipped thru the crowd outside by the patio section and was now standing directly behind the cop. One hand on his shoulder and the other pressing his cell phone into his lower back, faking like it was a gun.

"Hey! Hey! Let's just take it easy." The nervousness evident in his voice and how red his skin turned were clear indications that Voorheeze had the officer shook "Aint shit to take easy. Why da fuck you following me?" He spewed in his ear.

"Hey man I'm MPD."

"Rogue, I don't give a fuck if you Barack Obama! Fuck you following me for white boy?" This time he jammed the phone in harder as he spoke.

"Say man, you looked familiar... you looked like a possible suspect I.. I.. I was just trynna get a better look." He damn near pissed his pants.

Gorillaz in the Bay 2

Right then Voorheeze's cell phone began ringing.

"Wait a minute", the cop said struggling to turn around.

Voorheeze let him go and began smiling.

"Stop following people cop. The Streets aint safe." He told the cop while laughing.

Officer Hedgecock was red with embarrassment. He looked around and saw that everybody had been watching. "I could lock you up for assault", he shouted trying to save face.

"Yeah but you'll look like a fucking fool", Voorheeze called over his shoulder.

As he was making his way to the car, Danika walked up to him and began walking in stride with him.

"I thought I told you to get in the car?"

"You did. I wish I would be tucked away safe somewhere and my Daddy might need me." She stated flatly while pulling her hand out of the Berkin bag holding a .38 snub nose. She showed him that if he was rock'n, they were rock'n. They climbed into the Lambo and headed home. It had been one hell of a day!

Hedgecock was scared shitless. He'd heard all the stories about good cops who were killed off duty, he didn't want to be one of them. He just wanted to be a good cop. His fear was quickly replaced with anger and rage when the realization hit that the black mothafucka wasn't even armed. He felt so much like a jackass. Like the dweeb they used to call him back in school.

Hedgecock stared stupidly at everyone that was looking at him snickering and laughing. Some even pointed at him. He wished he could pull out his service weapon and shoot all of them in the face. He knew they'd stop laughing then! Instead he made his way back inside where he nourished another Samuel Adams. Hedgecock was trying hard to remember where he had seen the man's face before. Racking his brain over and over wasn't going to give him the answers he needed, so he finished up his drink and left. It was time for good old-fashioned police work.

Back at the station, Hedgecock was busy on the computer. He was running the license plate of the Lamborghini the black motherfucker was driving NVD276. Thinking, only one kind of nigger could afford a Lamborghini. The car had "nigger drug dealer" written all over it. Hell, he'd have to be a fucking rap star just to afford the car!

The name of the registered owner came back under a Thomas Smith. He knew the name but couldn't figure from where. A quick google search gave him the answer he was looking for. "Hot Damn it! I knew I was on to something." He said to himself.

De'Kari

"Oh yeah, what you got there? Sergeant Costa came walking into the room.

Hedgecock quickly shut the screen off and nervously looked up at the sergeant. "Uh…nothing. You know…uh….just checking some things out."

"Don't let me find out you're in here watching porn when you got the real deal at home." Seeing that he wasn't going to get any info, Costa left out headed for the gym. He'd just finished running six miles, now it was time to hit iron.

The moment Costa was out of the room, Hedgecock turned the monitor back on. Thomas Smith, whoever the motherfucker was, he was somehow related to one of the most hated niggers in California history. Although, it was neva proven it had been suspected that Smith was deep off into some heavy shit; drug sales, weapons, organized crime, etc. There were no open cases regarding him since he was dead, but that didn't' mean there was nothing there. The Captain said fuck the rumors and ghost chasing and ordered everyone get back to working on active cases they had.

Hedgecock believed that there was something to be found, now he was sure. He also knew that he couldn't go to the captain with what he had because he didn't have shit! He thought about bringing the sergeant in on his suspicion, but Costa was too much of an honor boy. He would tell him that the Captain said drop it and they were supposed to follow direct orders.

He decided to do some digging on his own.

**** N. D. ****
(Jack London Square, the following night)

"See lil mama, I told you, you were gonna have a good time tonight. And you were acting like you didn't ever wanna fuck with a nigga." Sutton was feeling himself as he walked hand in hand with Nina, his swag showed it.

"Lil Mama? Sweetheart, you're barely old enough to know me, let alone to be trying to finesse me by calling me lil mama." Nina had to admit the lil youngsta was fly, but she was only here tonight because of work, that's it and that's all!

Tonight, she would be doing everybody a favor. She was going to kill the little bastard and be done with this shit.

"A nigga might be young, but my dreams are grown! And so are my pockets. You looking at the next King of the Yay Area and I'm kinda thinking that you just might have what it takes to be my Queen."

Gorillaz in the Bay 2

He smoothly shot at her. Sutton knew his swag was through the roof, so he was talking big shit.

Nina let her neck roll and lips smack before telling him "Oh you must really be feeling yourself, huh? I just might have what it takes." She mocked his words.

He was baiting the trap for her. Waiting for her to bite.

"Well, I see we just gone have to show your lil ass something."

Bingo! Hook, line and sinker! He had a Kool-Aide smile.

"If you think you got something you can show me, then I'm game." He slyly slid that in there. "Oh, believe me Honey, I got something to show you alright." His little sexy ass thought this shit was a game, but Nina was going to show him just what the fuck she had in store for him.

They finally made it back to his car. The young gangsta grabbed Nina around the waist and stood face to face with her looking into her eyes. His plan was to kiss her a little bit and start the foreplay, but as he looked into her eyes something bothered him, throwing his game off.

It was there for only a split second then it was gone, but Sutton saw it! His instincts were too sharp! Instead of kissing her he grabbed her chin gently between his thumb and forefinger. Sutton stared into her eyes to see if he could catch a glimpse of it again, he couldn't. Instead of kissing her, he opened the door and held it open until she got in. He walked to the driver's side wondering what it was he saw. The glimpse was too brief. It was right there but he couldn't get it. He made sure to file it away in his mental and come back to it.

Soon as he sat in the driver's seat, his cell phone rang. He really didn't want to talk to his sister and that was who was calling. Reluctantly, he answered. "Hello?"

"Look we need to talk." Was all she said to him.

"I'm busy right now. I'mma have to hit you later."

She knew her little brother and his, 'I'm busy' right now and quite frankly Anne wasn't in the mood for none of that shit.

"Demitris, you can get some pussy later. Drop the little hussie off so we can talk. I'll be at moms and pop's house waiting for you." She didn't even wait for any acknowledgement whatsoever, Anne disconnected the line. He loved her gangsta, but he was going to have to teach her a thang or two about respect.

Needless to say, Nina wasn't happy about their night being ruined. When he told her something important came up with his big sister, Nina figured it was a sign. After he dropped her off at her car she planned to double back to his house and do what she does best. If Anne got in her way, then she would get it too.

Anne was beyond livid. She was a walking volcano of rage, but you couldn't tell by looking at her. On the outside she appeared as cool and calm as a frozen lake. She knew her brother would come. He might be feeling himself, but she knew that he still respected her authority. He would take his sweet time to defy her and she was alright with that, but she knew he was coming.

Anne had already made her mind up that she would in fact kill him tonight.

The only thing that was tugging at her heart was the fact that he would neva get the chance to meet his nephew. No one knew about her son except her cousin Jen, who was caring for him. When Anne had gotten pregnant things were real crazy and everything was happening so fast. She didn't' know that she was pregnant until she was already five months. By the end of her term she was barely showing. A baggie T-shirt and everything was concealed.

Once she had the baby she knew the life that she was living wasn't conducive to being a parent, so she called her big cousin and asked her would she care of the baby. Jen agreed in a heartbeat.

The last few months Anne was in the Valley living with Jen. These were the best days of her life being with her baby boy, a heavenly gift.

Anne wanted to share her joy with her brother, if no one else. But her first mindset was right, no one needed to know and that included her brother.

She wiped herself clean, flushed the toilet and washed her hands. She looked around for some air freshener but couldn't find any. When she walked out the bathroom and headed back to the front she was surprised to find Sutton sitting at the dining room table.

"I hope you sprayed up in there. Come up in my house uninvited taking a shit and stinking up the place." His voice was so snide and arrogant.

"Excuse you little nigga! I don't stink up nothing. And I might have moved out but this is still my Daddy's house!" Her tongue was as sharp as her tone.

"Look I'm not about to argue with you. Dad is gone so I'm the man of the house period! Therefore, this is my motherfucking house!" Sutton slammed his fist down on the fragile table for effect.

He spoke with an authority that Anne hadn't seen or heard from him before. It still didn't change shit.

Momentarily her eyes darted to her gun that she had left on the table. It was a quick dart. She didn't think he saw it, but he did.

Gorillaz in the Bay 2

"Tell me something little brother. Why did you betray me?" The sincerity in Anne's voice was not forced it was pure and genuine, she truly was hurt. "Everything I've ever done was to provide for you and make sure you were straight. Why would you go against the grain like this?" A lone tear slid down her face.

"That's the problem right mothafuck'n there! Let me tell you something. I don't explain myself to no mothafuck'n bitch!"

"Nigga what the fuck did you just call me?" Her hand moved so fast he didn't see her move. But Sutton could see that big ass barrel staring him in the face. He slowly stood out of his chair.

"What? I'm supposed tuck my tail because you holding that cannon? Bitch you got me fucked up!" If looks could kill he'd have already murdered her.

Viciously! Anne gripped the butt of the gun tighter while her finger gently caressed the trigger.

"Demitris..."

"Fuck you, Bitch!" He didn't let her get out another word.

Fuck it! Anne wasn't about the talking. She'd tried to reason with him, but her patience was gone.

Click! Click! Click!

The firing pin clicked on empty. She just tried to blow his fucking head off, but the gun was empty. What the fuck happened she thought. Anne had no way of knowing that Sutton took all the bullets out of her shit while she was in the bathroom. He smiled at her while he pulled his Glock out of his waist band. He didn't even hesitate.

BOC!

One shot to the head, it was over.

BOOM, BOOM, BOOM! Three rapid shots lifted Sutton clean off his feet, sending his body flying over the dining chair.

Sutton and Anne were so focused on each other, they didn't hear Keak open the front door and creep into the house. He had still been tailing Anne since the meeting at the War Room the other night.

Babysitting and watching mothafuckas wasn't his thing, but lately that seemed like all he was doing. This is one time he was glad that he was patient though. With Sutton out of the way it would be an all-out clean-up of the rest of his crew. It was time to bang out!

BOOM! BOOM! BOOM! BOOM!

He stood over Sutton's body and put four more slugs into his chest. Afterwards, he turned to Anne, but there was nothing he could do for her.

He walked towards the door just as Nina was opening it.

De'Kari

"Two points Wolf-Pack, zero She-Wolves," he told her as he walked out the house. She turned around after seeing the two bodies and followed. There wasn't anything to talk about.

**** N. D. ****
The next day

Voorheeze had a little time on his hands so he figured he would cook Danika one of his infamous meals. He wasn't just super turned up, in "street mode' all the time. He was a gentleman when he needed to be. Thinking about doing something good for his babe is how he found himself at the Whole Foods store in Redwood City on El Camino Real. He only ate the best and Whole Foods had the best and freshest food. Considering it was a nice day out, he expected more people to be in the store, but it was relatively empty.

Voorheeze made his rounds grabbing a few things. He turned on the aisle with the vitamins and saw a phat juicy ass bent all the way over looking at something on the bottom shelf. It had to be the size of a young Rhino. She had on tight fitting Capri pants, a casual blouse with heels on. He couldn't see her face though. He was so busy staring at her ass he didn't notice until she stood up that it was a white girl. An O.G. white chick at that. She noticed he was staring unabashedly at her ass.

"Sweet heart if you stare any harder, I'm afraid your eyes are going to get glued onto it." She smiled as she was talking. "Shiiiit, I'm hoping that more than just my eyes can get stuck on it." He was afraid that she would be one of them ugly thick broads, that was until she turned around, she was fine as a mothafucka.

"Do you make it a habit of molesting women with your eyes in the grocery store young man?" Her tone was serious, but there was an underlining hint of flirtation in her voice.

"Shit, I don't make it a habit of running into women with such a mouthwatering body attached to such a beautiful face." He looked her up and down licking his lips as he told her this. She walked up to him full of confidence.

She stood inches away from him when she asked, "What are you prepared to do about it?"

Drop that shit in your hands right here and let's go." Voorheeze had already dropped his stuff. He wasn't with the games at all. Voorheeze had neva in his life fucked with a white chick. Today he was going to cross that line.

She walked a little ahead of him as they walked out of the store. The more her ass swayed in front of him, the harder his dick got. With each step she took it moved and bounced like a giant ball of silk. Voorheeze walked her to her car then pointed to his Lambo and had her follow him. They arrived at the Ritz-Carlton in Half Moon Bay in no time. Voorheeze walked in the lobby to get the room. He must have had it written all over his face because when the guy behind the desk handed him his key card, he said "Sir, I hope you enjoy yourself." It wasn't so much what he said, it was how he said it. Like there was an inside joke that only they knew about. Voorheeze didn't think too hard on it, he just winked at the dude and kept it pushing.

Since he had neva been with a snow bunny before, Voorheeze figured he would take his time with her, give her that long, slow, deep stroke. He thought about this as they took the elevator to their room. He realized he didn't even know her name, but he wasn't going to fuck the mood up by asking. If she'd wanted him to know her name, she would've given it to him. The air inside the elevator was thick with lust. Finally, they reached their floor. This time Voorheeze walked in front of her, so he wouldn't be distracted by all that ass.

Sure, he had his thoughts and his plans of taking things slow, but the lady had plans of her own. The moment he opened the door she attacked him. Hungrily, Lustfully, she pushed him so hard up against the door, it slammed shut. She kissed him so hard and full of desire, then started biting on his lips that when she finally broke away from him, his lips were sore.

Meanwhile, Voorheeze's hands were having a field day roaming over her voluptuous body. A soft moan escaped her lips when he finally freed her ample breast from the restraints of her bra. He greedily covered them with his mouth. He sucked and slurped like he was trying to swallow them.

She reached up and grabbed his head pulling it backwards exposing his neck. She bit down on and suckled his neck sending electric jolts thru him. His dick was so hard it felt like he was about to burst through the zipper. She felt his bulge and knew he needed to be freed, so she reached down to undo his zipper.

His hand unbuttoned and unzipped her pants and found its way inside her panties. One hand was having fun gripping and squeezing her big ass, while the other delicately stroked and rubbed her hot and moist pussy. His thumb encircling the nub of her clit, while two fingers worked their way in and out of her.

"Mmmm... I want this dick", she whispered.

She finally got his dick freed from his pants. She glanced down to get a look at it and couldn't believe the size of it. This chick had neva seen a dick that big, she was going to enjoy this! Her tongue invaded

De'Kari

Voorheeze's mouth with hungry kisses while she continued to pull on his dick. They kissed hard, passionately. As Voorheeze stroked her pussy, his snow bunny shamelessly rubbed her pussy against his hand like a cat in heat. . Her pussy juices were dripping all over his hand. Faster, he rubbed her hardened pearl while she tugged on his pole.

He smacked her ass and pulled her even closer and at that moment, she bit down hard on his lip as her first orgasm invaded her body.

When the waves of pleasure subsided, she fell to her knees and took him into her mouth. She was spitting on his dick and stroking it. She was so excited that the saliva was running down her chin onto her breast as she gobbled his dick.

Voorheeze grabbed the top of her head and helped her swallow his shit. He couldn't remember the last time he'd received some head this good, but he wasn't trying to bust off in her mouth. He needed to feel that pussy! Needed to damage those forbidden walls and see what that pussy do.

He lifted her off her knees and led her over to the couch. He stripped completely out of his clothes and eagerly awaited while she did the same. She was a valley of snow-covered hills and curves. She had a mound of soft blond pubic hair covering her pink pussy that was calling out to him. He couldn't help it, he got down on his knees and made his way to her pussy.

She held her breath with anticipation. She had been dreaming of a big black hunk having his way with her for years, but she was always too shy to act on it. She didn't' know what came over her today. Maybe it was the stress that she'd been under or the neglect she was receiving at home.

"Oh my God, Yes!" She let out a loud moan as his thick tongue made its way into her hot pussy. Her sweet nectar bathed his tongue. He guided her to place her right leg on the couch, slightly bent, while he feasted on her. Nobody had ever given her oral sex this mind-blowing before.

"ooo… oh… OH OHH ooH OHHH YEAH! She started rotating her hips harder as she grabbed each of her breasts and alternated sucking from one nipple to the other. As she sucked her nipples her eyes were glued on him.

"Sssssss…yeah….ooooh….ooooh!" She could feel her orgasm building, she was ready to explode. Instantly she broke out in a sweat! She finally grabbed his head with both of her hands as she literally fucked his face.

"Oh Gawwwwwd! Ooooh! Yes!" Rivers of cum shot out of her pussy and covered his face and neck.

Gorillaz in the Bay 2

Voorheeze gripped both ass cheeks and continued sucking on her clit. When she stopped shaking, he licked her dry. He stood back up and sat on the couch. After putting on a magnum condom, Voorheeze guided her onto his lap and watched as her juicy pussy lips swallow every last inch of him. Once she had him completely inside of her, she looked at him with a devilish smirk on her face.

"Are you ready, handsome? Can you handle this big phat ass?" She asked as she looked in his eyes. The moment he opened his mouth to answer her, she shoved one of her sensitive nipples in his mouth. She began bucking and bouncing on his dick like she was a rodeo cow-girl on top of a wild bronco. The tittie he had in his mouth kept falling out while the other massive tit slapped him repeatedly across his face.

Voorheeze respected how she was taking the dick. He smacked her on her huge ass and grabbed it.

"Ride this mothafuck'n dick! Come on, take this dick! Show a nigga what you got!" He told her as he pulled her hair with one hand and grabbed her ass with the other.

She was racing to the finish line, but he wasn't done. He lifted her off him and bent her over the couch. That big round ass spread out twice as big. His dick jumped with anticipation as he guided his hard shaft to her opening. Voorheeze slid balls deep inside of her. He grabbed her hips and grinded in circular motions. She responded by rotating her ass in the opposite direction. Her poor little pussy just continued to cream, raining juices down her thighs. Once he started power driving his dick into her it was over. He slammed hard, fast and deep. She screamed and he was worried that something was wrong, but when she started moaning, he continued to long-pole her. The sight of his dick being swallowed by her swollen pussy lips drove him crazy. That big ass bouncing back against his thrust was the icing on the cake. Every time she threw it back, he spanked her which drove her crazy. The sensation was so intense, he exploded. He thought for sure he had busted the condom.

She had another jaw dropping orgasm, which caused her to scream out louder than before. After which, she collapsed on the couch and he dropped down next to her. They both lay there gasping for air with smiles on their faces.

"Well handsome, that was truly incredible." She told him once she finally caught her breath.

"Shit tell me about it. I didn't think you could move that thang like that." He responded to her while rubbing on her phat ass.

"I won't ever bite off more than I can chew." She told him.

De'Kari

"So handsome, what can I call the man who can fuck as good as you just fucked me?"

"You can call me Jason, ma. Jason Voorheeze." He told her as his dick began coming back to life.

"I like Jason, but Voorheeze is an interesting name." She told him as she grabbed his semi erect penis and slowly started stroking it again.

"And what's your name? With all this ass you got." He asked her as he positioned himself behind her. His dick was rock hard again.

"Beth.....awwwww...yes.....Bethanie Vieira." She told him just as he slid back into her hot wet pussy.

They fucked four more times before exchanging numbers and leaving the hotel. Both wondering why they waited so long to sample a taste of the other race.

Bethanie Vieira was walking stiff; her pussy was so sore and swollen. But she had a huge smile on her face. The vision of him eating and fucking her, she was definitely going to call him again. She could tell he was from the streets, so she would have to be careful considering her job. But she would most definitely be getting some more of that good dick.

The sky was nice and dark by the time she pulled out of the parking lot headed home.

Gorillaz in the Bay 2

CHAPTER XVII
Club Carsjanae's

The scene was crazy! The atmosphere was electric as always and everyone was feeling the vibe. Clark was in VIP with some of his team popping bottles and peeping out which chick they were going to take home or to a room. Clark decided to wait and let the crowd sort itself out instead of searching for a female.

Cream always raises to the top. Just like the best doesn't have to be looked for, it will always be seen. So instead of chasing tail, he sat back with a glass of Crystal and was feeling the beat. Rick Ross was pushing thru the speakers loud and niggaz was feeling that Miami shit. But when that old school Luniz "I GOT FIVE ON IT" came on, niggaz lost their minds!

"/Playa give me some brew an I might just chill / but I'm the type that like to light another joint like Cypress Hill / I spin Luniz, Spit lugees when I puff on it / I got two bucks on it but it aint enough on it /"

When the verse started every nigga in the club rapped right along with the song. Niggaz that were smoking were waiving blunts in the air in time with the beat.

The DJ followed that up wit the "Hyphy Remix", mothafucka's were loving it. It was no wonder Carsjanae's was the hottest club in Northern California. It was evident! The best crowd, hottest DJ's and VIP lounges were just the beginning.

"Are you not the talkative type or do you just have no one to talk to?" The voice was silk as he heard the words.

When he looked up, he could not believe what was before his eyes.

"Which answer would get you to sit down and find out?" He hoped his reply was sharp enough to leave an impression.

She stood just above 5"5" with honey-gold skin and a body unlike he had ever seen. C-cup breast, itty bitty waist with an ass that had to be at least 45 inches. Her long, silky hair looked wet as it cascaded all the way down to that ass. Surprisingly, her best feature was a face that only belonged in Heaven.

"Oh, I was going to do that already. No matter what the answer was." True to her word she swung that big ass wagon past his face as she sat on the sofa right next to him.

He caught a whiff of her perfume which smelled like cotton candy as she passed in front of him.

"Tell me something, is your name as perfect as everything else about you?" His question was as sincere as his desire for her.

"I'm sorry I think I'm going to disappoint you there."

"I highly doubt that."

"My name is Spiritual."

He looked at her like she was crazy. "Okay Ma, what is it? Something like Shaquita or Jacquanetta?"

"Honestly, my name is Spiritual." She laughed at his silliness.

For a moment he was at a loss for words.

"So, in other words you are indeed Heaven sent. I mean if I called you beautiful, I would be disrespecting you. Your body was sculptured flawlessly and now your name is Devine." Clark's nose was wide open.

"Wow! Now that is an impressive compliment", she replied. The red from her blushing giving her face a sunset glow.

"Would you care for a drink?" He gestured for the Crystal.

"Yes, thank you." She told him as she watched him pour a glass and hand it to her.

"So, tell me for real, what's up? How is it that you're this perfect and still single?" Clark wasn't trynna fuck off his chances, but he wasn't gonna sit and beat around the bush either.

"Well, for starters I neva said that I was single, and no one is perfect honey not even I." She took a drink of the Crystal after that.

They talked the remainder of the night. Oblivious to any and everyone but each other. Every now and then Clark would break the intimate connection they were sharing to refill their glasses. She truly was perfect to him.

He seemed like he really wanted to know so she told him her story.

She was originally from North Carolina, working as a marketing executive in a small firm. She ended up in California after being scouted by a large firm. She was in a marriage that was helplessly all but over. She and her husband had not been intimate for a couple of years and neva had any children.

Proof that nothing could stay perfect, midway thru the night, there was some commotion going on. Clark paid it no mind until Tut yelled out that it was Linell. Clark excused himself after asking Spiritual not to leave. He and the rest of his crew rushed outside to the back of the club where the altercation was taking place. Anybody that didn't move out of the way got mowed down. When they finally reached the front of the crowd, Linell was beating the dog-shit out of some Incredible Hulk looking mothafucka. It was literally some embarrassing shit, the way Linell was dog-walking the nigga.

The bouncers were holding everybody back, making sure nobody was trying to come to the nigga's rescue. All around the crowd was going bananas cause of the ass-whooping they were seeing. The nigga that was getting whooped stood 6"2" and weighed 290 lbs. solid muscle. He looked like that nigga The Rock back when he was still wrestling. To Clark, he looked like he should be up in somebody's octagon trying to get a UFC belt or something.

If you didn't know Linell, you might underestimate him because of his size and easy-going personality. If anyone in that crowd had underestimated him, they had a change of mind tonight.

Some other big muscle-bound nigga was trying to ease his way by one of the bouncers who was furthest from the door. The nigga was on some dope fiend, sneak shit. The bouncer was more concerned with watching the fight than doing his job and being on security, which could prove to be fatal considering the nigga had a chrome 45 in his hands.

When the nigga broke free of the crowd, he was only 10 feet from Linell and the bouncer still hadn't spotted him.

The fight, even if it could be remotely considered that, was clearly over a long time ago. Now Linell was just punishing the nigga. He slammed his head repeatedly against the wall. When the nigga fell, he picked him up and did it again, paying no attention to the amount of blood that was coming from his head.

Clark was gonna step in and prevent Linell from killing the nigga but if you knew Linell you knew not to grab him trying to break up a fight, that's when he really went berserk. That was the quickest way to be his next victim.

The nigga that got past the bouncer started to raise his 45 Magnum.

"Nigga I know you aint trynna turn dis bitch into a cemetery?" Neal challenged as he jammed the barrel of his .40 Cal into the side of the nigga's head.

The nigga stopped dead in his tracks the moment he felt the barrel touch his head. The sight of the long ass hockey stick (extended clip) hanging from the .40 quieted the crowed.

"Keith!" Neal called out to the bouncer, dude just walked by.

"Yeah Boss?" His voice was filled with nervousness when he answered.

"Nigga grab dat mothafuck'n Cannon out this bitch-ass niggaz hand." He told him as he rammed the barrel even harder into his temple.

Keith rushed to carry out the order. By now the new scene playing out had even gotten Linell's attention. The nigga he was beating was laid out bleeding profusely.

The nigga didn't hesitate to let go of the 45 when Keith reached for it.

"Now gone head and take that shit with you to the car", Neal further instructed Keith.

"Take it with me?" Keith looked so dumbfounded when he asked that.

"Nigga yo mothafuck'n job is security." In one quick motion Neal snatched his hand back then brought the bottom of the barrel crashing down on the nigga temple! Lights out! No questions.

He then turned and had it pointed at Keith. "Apparently you failed you job tonight Rogue. You fired nigga. Now is that a problem?"

Keith looked like he wanted to say something but then thought twice about it. "Naaw it aint no problem Rogue." He turned and walked off.

Keith didn't know how to respond; he and Neal grew up together. Neal didn't give a fuck though, all Neal cared about was the nigga almost let the mothafucka shoot Linell. Linell was his Ace-Boone-Coone.

Now that the excitement was over, the crowd began to disperse and head back to having a good time. The DJ came over the speakers and announced that the next couple of songs were dedicated to the solid niggaz who had gotten wrapped up in the Al-Qaeda sweep. He sent out prayers and wishes, then put on Dem Hoodstarz and the Young Fellons "Definition".

Back in the VIP lounge Clark saw Spiritual waiting patiently for him as he made his way back to her.

"Did you boys have your little excitement for the night?" She sarcastically asked him in good humor once he was seated.

"Shit I was making sure my folks was straight, but his people had him." Wasn't no need for Clark to front like he did something. "I'm ready for some excitement though", he told her as he grabbed one of the bottles of Crystal and drunk straight out the bottle.

"Then why we still sitting here?" She challenged.

He responded by grabbing her hand and standing up. He told Tut that he was getting ready to dip.

They made their way across the club headed for the door as Dem Hoodstarz "Move Mean" was playing.

Outside he took off his leather jacket and draped it across her shoulders. The sky looked like it would rain. The wind blew with a nice cold chill which made him drape his arm around her. Once they got inside the car he turned the heater up nice and good. Then he turned the music on low.

Spiritual sat quietly while a thousand thoughts ran through her mind.

This would be the first time that she cheated on her husband. Even though it had been years since he last touched her, her pride and dignity wouldn't allow her to cheat on him. She caught him cheating, it cut her deeply but eventually she forgave him because she still had love for him.

His love for her was not enough because he continued to cheat. Not only did he continue but he blatantly did it in the open. Finally, she got fed up and filed for divorce. He had the nerves to tell her to with-draw the papers, but she refused. He beat her so severely that she was in the hospital for two weeks and she still refused to withdraw the pa-pers, she was done.

One evening she got home from work and found a box with a note on top of it that said, "Play Me". When she opened the box, there was a DVD in it with another note. The note told her that if she didn't with-draw the divorce, he would upload the video to the internet. She played the video as tears rolled down her cheeks. It was the video that they made on their honeymoon. At that time, even though she was com-pletely against it, she did it for him. After all, he was her husband and it was their honeymoon. She sat in the living room crying all night. The next morning, tired, sad, scared and feeling defeated, she got up, took a shower and made her way down to the courthouse.

Spiritual was so confused. On one hand she was wondering if she could follow through with it and on the other, her pussy was on fire it felt like she was heating the seat. She glanced over at Clark and he was everything she fantasized about. A straight thug! Back in the day she had always heard the talk about that Thug Dick. She wondered if it really was what other females made it out to be. Her divorce wasn't final, but the marriage was over, she was just waiting for the judges stamp of approval. Spiritual made her decision, tonight she would find out if the rumors were true.

Clark pulled into the Four Seasons Hotel. He parked the car and they made their way inside. He requested the penthouse suite. He wasn't trying to floss when pulled out his knot of bills, shit just was the way it was. The inside of the Four Seasons was plush but neither one of them was paying attention to it. Their minds were on the debauchery that awaited.

While going up in the elevator, fear lost the raging war to lust! Spiritual's entire body was on fire and she needed Clark to put it out. Once they were inside the suite, she turned around and pushed him back up against the door, attacking him like a hungry puma. They kissed lustfully, eagerly anticipating what was to come next. They fumbled with each other's clothes while doing so.

Spiritual broke the kiss after biting him on his lip and got down on her knees. Her heart was pounding so loud she could hear it in her head. Her breathing was deep and heavy. She reached inside his zipper and pulled out his rock-hard cock. Her mouth watered at the sight of it as she thought to herself how it would feel. She circled the head with her tongue while stroking him.

Clark watched as Spiritual was playing with his dick and it was driving him crazy. She opened her mouth as wide as she could, then she swallowed him whole. He had neva seen anything like that. He was thinking to himself *how she was able to deep-throat all of that?* Spiritual suddenly began sucking his dick as if she was enjoying it more than him.

All Clark could do was hold on because she was clearly in control. Before he realized it, he was exploding in the back of her throat. It was over that quick. Clark couldn't believe that shit. It was that damn good. After she swallowed it all, Spiritual started sucking on the tip like there was more hidden in there waiting to come out.

He was still rocked up so now it was his turn. A magician didn't have shit on him, he had her out of her clothing so fast. Clark led Spiritual over to the dining area and gently pushed her down over the counter. The sight of her ungodly big, country, ass made his dick jump. He took his right hand and started rubbing circles on the side of that ass.

"You want me to fuck dis pussy, don't you?" He asked her while he rubbed her ass.

Slap!

When she didn't answer him, he smacked her ass so hard it left his hand print on her ass cheek.

"I said do you want me to fuck dis pussy?" Clark asked her again.

"Yes, I do", she moaned. Her pussy tingled every time he spanked her.

Smack!

Clark slapped her ass again. Spiritual was so turned on it felt like she was peeing on herself she was so wet.

"Please, Please, I said fuck me!" Spiritual cried out in pleasure. She was bouncing her ass while pleading. It bounced and clapped beautifully.

Clark slid the tip of his dick inside of her and wondered if her pussy could take it like her mouth had taken all of him. Then he slammed all of it deep within her with one thrust to find out.

"Aarrgh!" She cried out loud. She had neva had something so big in her. It hurt, but it was so damn good.

He pulled out slowly, rubbing her ass cheeks, then rammed into her again. This time he held himself in place deep inside her aching pussy.

Smack! Smack!

Clark spanked that ass and started thrashing that pussy. He was long-dicking her hard and fast, with every thrust he grunted and she made a sound that didn't sound human. Her ass cheeks were fiery red and sore from the slapping and pounding.

"Oh fuck! Oh fuck! Spiritual screamed over and over. The pain was gone and all she felt was pleasure. At that moment the only thing in the world that mattered was his dick.

"Ooh Clark! I'm about to cum fuck me harder, harder." By now she was throwing that big olé ass right back at him.

He leaned forward and grabbed a hand full of her long hair and yanked her head back. Then he repeatedly smacked her ass and fucked her.

"Aaaw shit! Shit! Shit! Yes! Yes!" She squirted all over him. The constriction of her pussy walls caused his nutts to swell and he erupted as well, letting out a victorious roar!

The night was just beginning!

The penthouse boasted two master bedrooms, a living room, a sitting lounge and three bathrooms. They sexed, fucked, and made love all night long in every room. Finally laying in one of the California King beds after they showered, Clark was drinking his third bottle of Figi water, Spiritual had two herself.

"God Damn! I might have misspoken last night at the club when I called you and Angel." Still breathing hard, he gulped down the remaining water in the bottle. "You might fuck around and be Jezebel, the Devil herself."

Spiritual snuggled closer to him, laying her head on his massively muscled chest. She draped her arm across his body.

"Umm, I told you he hadn't touched me in over two years. A sistah was backed up and then some." She kissed his nipple.

"I swear to God either the nigga was really gay the whole time and didn't want you to know or his dick broke on him, cause aint no way a nigga got all of this at home and not touch it." To Clark, that would be insanity.

While they talked, Clark let his hand caress her back and ample ass. He reached his other hand out and picked up the phone receiver. He could tell that he was going to need his energy. As he was ordering room service she kissed her way down his chest. When she got to his groin, she took him in her mouth and softly sucked on him until he was nice and hard again.

Instead of replacing the receiver on the phone when he was done, he just let it drop. Clark closed his eyes and put his hand in her hair, palming the back of her head. Just when it was starting to feel good she stopped. Spiritual stroked the length of his shaft a couple of times then climbed on him backwards. The sight of her massive ass sliding down his shaft was enough to make him bust. He held back though. She slid

De'Kari

up and down grinding slowly, moving her body like a snake. It was the most exotic shit he had ever seen. He was hypnotized.

Spiritual was cummin non-stop the entire time. With his massive size, he was touching places and scratching corners she had neva had touched before. As the high of the ecstasy took control of her she began sliding up and down faster. It got to the point, she was literally bouncing up and down. Her huge ass slamming down so hard on his pelvis it sounded like people were in the room clapping. He couldn't do shit but hold on.

"Pull my hair! Ooh Daddy pull my hair." She gasped out as she continued to bounce.

He quickly complied grabbing a fist full of hair and yanking her head back. She grabbed both of her breast and started pinching her own nipples, hard. Right then Clark started spanking her. She shook violently as a breath-taking orgasm shot thru her body. She leaned forward onto her elbows and kept bouncing that ass. Since it was winking at him, he rubbed his thumb around her asshole, driving her even crazier. He stuck his thumb into her asshole. She started making a sound like a wild animal. Not able to hold back any longer Clark shot another load of hot cum inside of her. A few more bounces and she exploded again as well.

Spiritual was so loud that the woman outside that had just arrived with their food was too embarrassed to knock on the door. Once she heard the loud, ear-shattering noise, she thought about turning around. After a minute, she worked up the courage to finally knock on the door. Spiritual go up and made her way to the door stark naked. Her skin glistening with sweat.

Spiritual opened the door and the woman just stood there shocked. Her eyes wide open and jaw dropped. She was frozen in place. Not only was she shocked but she was embarrassed. No one had ever just exposed themselves to her like that.

"Come on in Sugar", Spiritual invited as she stepped to the side.

Nervously, the woman wheeled the cart into the room. The scent of sex was thick in the air. She couldn't help but to look and admire Spirituals body.

Spiritual noticed the way the woman was staring at her even though she was trying to hide the looks. The attention was arousing her, so she walked over behind the woman who held her breath and stood motionless, she was in absolute fear. Spiritual stepped closer and pressed her pelvis into the woman's plump ass. She wrapped her arms around her and began fondling her breast and kissing on her neck. The little woman was powerless.

Gorillaz in the Bay 2

Desire had a grip on her body. She began rubbing her ass into Spiritual. Then Spiritual spun the woman around and invaded her mouth with her tongue. Her hand went under the woman's skirt, moved her panties and found her wet pussy and began to strum it.

"Aaah" she moaned as Spirituals thumb circled her throbbing clitoris and two fingers played with her G-spot. It didn't take long before she climaxed, spraying cum all over Spiritual's hand. No words were even spoken between the two. Spiritual showed her the door and wheeled the cart into the bedroom. Her carefree attitude was new, exciting and addicting.

She was licking her fingers and hand when she entered the room.

"Whatcha out there eating up all the food?" Clark joked when he saw her licking her fingers.

"Just tasting something"

"Just sampling a little of their goods?" He thought she was referring to the food.

The cart was covered with food, dinner and breakfast. They ate until their hearts were content and then washed everything down with glasses of mimosa's. Full, drained, exhausted and satisfied, they final fell asleep. It was already close to ten in the morning.

**** **N. D.** ****

Hours later, it was already dark when Clark woke up. He glanced at his lil sex demon and smiled. Hands down she was wifey material. Smart, sexy, perfect body, she was independent and already established. And her sex game was crazy. He couldn't figure out what was up. If the story she told him was true, then her husband was a complete fool.

As he was getting up, his cell phone began ringing. He answered it on his way to the bathroom. "What's up wit it Rogue?"

"Damn Dad was that Lil Shit that hot?" Tut laughed into the phone.

"Nigga I can't even begin to tell you. What's good though, is everything alright?" He asked as he started pissing.

"Shit everything's everything. I was just tapping to make sure the lil braud aint left you butt naked and tied up somewhere", he continued to joke.

"Nigga as good as that shit is I wouldn't give a fuck if I was tied up somewhere", Clark joked back but he was dead serious.

"I'mma let you go and get some more of that good shit. Oh! I almost forgot you aint gone believe this shit Dad, the buff nigga from the club pressed charges. They picked "L" up from his baby mama's spot in Hayward earlier."

"Nigga you serious?" Clark couldn't believe that shit.

"Serious Dad", Tut told him.

"Nigga keep me posted", Clark said as he flushed the toilet. "In Fact, get word to him and see if he need us on it."

"Aight nigga", Tut hung up.

Clark washed his hands and walked back into the room towards the bed.

"Damn you even sexier when you first wake up with no make-up on", he told her as he bent down and gave her a kiss.

He wasn't lying, she was the fucking truth. He asked her if she wanted to go out and eat or order room service. She chose room service. They talked until the food arrived. The server that brought the food was the same little lady from the night before. Her and spiritual eye-fucked each other until she left. For the remainder of the night, Clark and Spiritual talked and fucked like they were first time lovers.

**** **N. D.** ****

Tieka sat in her car waiting. Her entire back and ass was sore and stiff. They ached and begged to be freed and stretched. Her muscles were so cramped, they were numb. The car was hot and musty, even though it was a cold and damp night. But she had been sitting in her care since the night before.

Technically she had been in the same clothes since the day before. The only time she'd gotten out of the car was to take a pee behind the bushes.

She'd been following Clark since before he made it to the club. She saw everything. She watched as he made a couple of drop off's. She even saw the fight outside the club. Armed with two thermoses of coffee and a bunch of snacks. She was ready for him when he exited out of the club.

Upon seeing him exit with a woman that had a body that rivaled hers, Tieka was plagued with a bout of jealousy. She followed them while the jealousy continued brewing. Thoughts of the past raced through her mind of all his cheating ways. She thought of a time so long before, now it seemed like a dream or a fantasy. It was back when they were kids in love.

At least she was in love. Him, on the other hand, he didn't give a fuck about her love or her feelings. Clark dogged her like she was just some tramp. Breaking not just her heart, but her mind, will and spirit as well. After her nervous breakdown it took her years to recover. She became strong and determined. Her self-esteem grew as she began to love herself.

A new Tieka emerged from a cocoon of vengeance. A woman who had a plan and would carry it out. This was the woman who sat in that car in dire need of a shower. From where she was parked, she had a perfect view of his car while hers wasn't seen. She looked at her watch it read 11:45pm. No one was in the parking lot. All sane and reasonable people were in bed sleep. Tieka knew they were staying another night, so she decided to run home and take a shower and make it back before they left.

That was a good, solid plan. She reached for her keys and put them in the ignition. At the last minute she looked towards the lobby. What the hell! She took her keys out the ignition, grabbed her purse and went inside to get a room. She knew she looked like shit. She felt even worst as she walked through the glamorous lobby.

The desk clerk looked at her like she was covered in shit. Fuck if, she didn't care. When she pulled out her platinum Visa it changed the look on the hefer's face. Tieka thought about it and decided it would be better to pay in cash. So, she put her card away and pulled out a knot that Clark had given her. She peeled $1,000 off the knot and dropped it on the counter. Once she received her key card, she headed toward the elevator. Stanking and looking like shit, she walked away with her head held high.

"Olé Busted Bitch", she thought to herself.

**** N. D. ****
The following day

The Block was booming! It was a beautiful day out and people were taking advantage of that. Clark was sitting on the hood of his new Impala. The fellas stood surrounding him, chopping it up and kicking it. The fiends were coming steadily to get their fix.

"Blood I remember when yo ass got chased down the street by Shakeeta! Nigga you talking all that Rah-rah gangsta shit but nigga she had you ass running like a slave on the underground railroad!" Blood James teased the nigga Drew. Everybody was cracking up… "Nigga you was running round dis bitch talking bout Aaah! Quit playing Aaah!" He was running around flapping his arms.

Shakeeta was a bull-dyke, Tom Boy. She had hands like she was a real nigga. Niggaz all over the Town who she whooped on could attest to her hands.

De'Kari

"N-nigga I... I was only sixteen n-nigga and dat bitch was knocking out grown m-mothuafuck'n niggaz, you damn right I ran." Stuttering, Drew had to let it be known it wasn't 1980's or 90's. Niggaz aint fighting in dis bitch no more Niggaz bussin!

"Nigga I aint gone lie I would've ran from that bitch back then too!" Clark called out before he burst out laughing.

Everybody started laughing even harder cause they all knew they wasn't trynna fuck with Shakeeta. All while they kicked it they kept an eye on everything going on. Making sure the workers were working and security was on point.

"Aye Dad, on the real though, could you imagine getting yo ass whooped by dat chick and still have to walk around the hood. Knowing how embarrassing that would be?" Tut asked.

Clark didn't have to worry about that, for years he was hitting that on the low. She played that tough shit on the street but was Charmin soft behind closed doors.

""N-nigga dat b-bitch run up on me I'mma body her ass!" Drew was dead serious. "Fuck Fighting"

A black Trail Blazer came rolling down the block.

"Blood anybody know that Blazer?" James asked the group as he put his hand on his banger.

"No!"

"Nope"

"Hell naw!" Came choruses from everyone.

Tut made a loud whistle. Everybody on the block got on point and ready. If anything, or anybody moved wrong that entire truck was getting lit the fuck up.

As the truck got closer they could see it was some young niggaz in it. James wasn't playing he already pulled the .40 out from his waist. Ready!

The little Niggaz drove right on by. As they did so they had their mug on mean (staring hard). Clark was trying to see if he knew the faces, but he didn't'. The nigga in the back seat wearing a beanie sort of looked like that nigga Sutton. Which made him think about something.

"Aye Rogue, you heard anything about a funeral for that lil nigga Sutton?" He asked Tut while still looking at the truck.

"Naaw Dad. I aint heard shit bout that." Tut wasn't paying attention to Clark. He was focused on that truck.

After the truck passed without incident, they went back to just hanging out like nothing happened. Clark's phone started ringing so he checked his caller I.D.

"What's up with Sis?" He answered.

Gorillaz in the Bay 2

"Hey Brother! What you doing?" She asked in her cheery voice.

I'm out here on da Block just posted. Why what's good?" A nice little red-bone was walking by on the other side of the street as he was talking.

"Oh nothing. I just wanted to remind you about the show." She was so happy you could hear it in her voice.

"The 22nd. Trust me I wouldn't miss it for the world!" Clark had that date engraved in his head.

French Tip had been focusing her time on her project. She was having a Grand Fashion Show at the Paramount Theater, it was going to be a major televised event. Her clothing line, Satin Doll was for the curvaceous and voluptuous women. The show was going to have casual wear, fancy attire and sexy lingerie. Hell yeah! Clark was gone be there.

"Okay Brother, I'll talk to you later."

"Alright", he hung up the phone.

He was putting his phone up when a text message came through. He looked at the message. It was the message he had been waiting on.

"Aye Rogue it's time to bounce", he called out to Tut.

They both hopped into the Impala and pulled off. A little while back this cat Clark was locked up with in San Quentin reached out to him. Supposedly dude was doing his thang out there in San Jose. He was moving weight like a body builder back then. His bitch got on some jealous shit bout him and his side piece and the crazy-ass braud ended up getting him hit on a domestic violence charge. Some real bogus shit. While he was gone, he lost his connect.

Now he's home and ready to eat. Clark was gone see if he really knew what he was doing.

"You good Rogue?" Clark asked Tut as they drove.

"I'm good Dad. Just thinking bout what I'mma do for my daughter. Her birthday is coming up." He told him as he checked his bangers making sure they were fully loaded and good to go.

"Whatever you do I know it's gone be big." As he told him this his eyes were on the traffic.

"Yeah Dad, I might just fuck around and do something for all of them." Satisfied with the bangers, one went back on his hip and the other stayed on his lap.

"But check it out Dad. We're ready on that other thang we was waiting on." Tut told Clark getting back to business.

"Is that right?" Clark asked.

"Alright let's make it happen." The green light was just giving.

"Shit's been quiet since Sutton was killed. They didn't know if Y.N.M. was scared, done and over or what. Clark had been on some other shit. So, shit's been quiet. While it's been quiet, Tut's been planning. It was time to finish what was started.

They walked into the apartment complex each carrying a duffle bag full of dope without a care in the world, eyes scanning the apartment. There was some chick and a dude sat on the couch to the left of the room.

"Big Tree Top, what's up Rogue?"

"Young Money what's up?" Tree Top responds to Clark as the two embrace each other.

He sees Clark looking over at the couch. "Oh, brah don't worry bout them. That's my security."

Clark noticed that the braud had a nice lil blanket draped across her legs.

"Shit it's all good Rogue. So, nigga when you come home?" He asked the giant.

"Nigga two weeks ago. Nigga dats long enough to get it going and too long not to have started." Tree Top was a real hustla. Standing 6'9" you'd think he was a basketball player.

"Anyway, what you got for me?" Clark asked him.

Tree Top reached under the table and grabbed a black sports duffle bag a little bigger than the ones they had. Clark unzipped the bag, he was greeted with all big faces. Tree Top was true to his word. The bag contained two hundred and fifty thousand dollars. Payment for ten kilos.

"Since everything is good nigga, here's a welcome home gift for you." He sat his duffle bag on the table and Tut did the same. "The ten for the deal is in the first bag, the second is ten more on consignment. You can hit me when you done. But we gotta add two points on the other ten."

"No doubt, my nigga that's love! Nigga I got you. I'll be at you soon brah." Tree Top was hella excited. He was about to get back to his rightful spot as King of San Jose!

All while they were talking Tut and the two on the couch was doing nothing but watching each other. Out of the two he could sense that she was the problem. They'd been in there too long by Tut's calculation.

He was about to say something when somebody knocked on the door. Instantly Tut had one of his 40's out. Clark thought Tree Top was a good dude, but he didn't put nothing past anybody. His banger was out too. Little Mama was holding a baby AR in her hands. Dude answered the door. It ended up being some little old lady from the Catholic Church looking for donations. Everyone released their breath and relaxed. Tree Top gave her a hundred dollars and sent her on her way.

Gorillaz in the Bay 2

Clark and Tut got the fuck up out of there after that. The bag went in the trunk and they drove off.

De'Kari

CHAPTER XVIII
San Mateo

Voorheeze was just leaving the Hillsdale Shopping Center picking up a few things for Danika. He was high as hell, feeling good and ready to tear her sweet pussy up. As if she had ESP when it came to him being horny, Vieira called, she wanted him to meet her at the Four Seasons Hotel.

Now how in the hell was he supposed to turn that down. Plus, he was already heading that way. He would have to pass the Four Seasons in East Palo Alto on his way to the house. Shit, to him it was a sign, fate or destiny or some shit like that. He snorted some more coke and made his way to his little white addiction. He chuckled as he thought about the analogy.

"Snorting on that white chick, I'mma about to fuck dat white chick." Haha! Hahaha! He started laughing out loud.

Out of nowhere a vision of Jay being murdered by the police popped into his head. He saw his best friend being shot over seventeen times in the back by the police while running, after he jumped out of a stolen car.

The car swerved, he barely missed smacking into the back of a Suburban. Sweat running down his face Voorheeze realized that in what he thought was a split second he had actually traveled almost a mile down the freeway. Sweat was pouring down his face. He hit the button and rolled the window down.

"What the fuck was that?" He wondered out loud as he exited off the freeway onto University Ave. heading for the Four Seasons. As he was pulling up he received a text message "Room 428, your key card will be waiting for you. Hurry!"

Vieira was just getting out of the shower when she heard Voorheeze coming in the door. She stares at herself in the mirror as the droplets of water run down her body. She thinks of when she was twenty-five and men would fall head over heels for her. But that was years ago she tells herself with a frown on her face.

"Aint no way in hell you can be staring at all this beauty right here and be frowning. So, what's up?" Voorheeze says into her ear before nibbling on it. His huge arms wrapped around her body from behind.

"You talking about this big o'le fat ass?" She questions as she smacks her own ass cheek.

"Call it what you want but this big o'le mothafucka is sexy as hell." He tells her just before he grabs a handful exactly where she spanked herself.

De'Kari

Vieira feels his hardened dick pressing against her. She tilts her head back and presses back into him.

"Mmm." A moan escapes her mouth when his hands reach up and cup her breast. He pinches her nipple and bites down on her neck. The electric shock it causes races towards the tingling that was generated from him pinching her nipples.

When the two sensations collide, her pussy explodes!

"You want me to show you just how sexy you are?" He teases her.

"P-Please. Please show me." She begs, craving the feeling of him inside of her.

"Naaw you don't want me to show you." He pinches both of her nipples a little harder as he further teases her. He knows that pinching her nipples drives her completely crazy.

"I-I do! Right now, please LaMont give it to me give me that Big Black dick Babe." She seductively croons.

His dick jumps. He loves it when she talks dirty. He can't see the smile that spread on her face. She knows he loves her to talk dirty.

"Come on Daddy put that big black dick in this hot pussy. Spank this big fat white ass while you fuck me."

That did it! He roughly turns her away from the mirror and bends her over the sink. He doesn't check to see if she's wet or not. He doesn't have to, he could hear the lust in her voice. He rams all ten inches of his dick all the way in her.

"Aarrgh!" Vieira yells out more from the shock than the pain. She loves the feel of his rock-hard dick inside of her. Her favorite dildo isn't as hard as him.

Voorheeze is mesmerized at the sight of her big white ass bouncing back and forth off of him. That big o'le ass looks divine as the ripples flow across her flesh every time she bumps into him. When he smacks her ass, she really picks up speed.

"Yes! Yes! Oh, Give it to me! Give me that Black mothafucka!" She cries out. Her big o'le titties clap like two pair of hands their fucking so hard.

Smack!

He hits her ass even harder. Then he grabs a hand full of her hair and yanks her head back.

"Do it Baby! Do it! Fuck this puss! Fuck Mamaaaa!

Eeeee!" The dirty talk does it, he can't take it no more!

At the same time her walls vibrate as her pussy erupts again, spraying out a geyser as she cums.

"Oh fuck! Shit! God Damn! He calls out just before he pulls out of her and sprays that big white ass with about a thousand kids.

Gorillaz in the Bay 2

The shit was so powerful that his knees buckled, and he collapsed right there on the bathroom floor. Breathing deeply and sweating profusely. The cold tile on the floor was soothing to his body that feels more like a furnace than a body.

20 minutes later

They lay in bed, freshly showered and cleaned of all their earlier activity. Vieira rubs her hand across his muscled chest softly playing with his chest hair. They've been dealing with one another long enough for her to start developing some serious feelings.

Every time they're together he treats her like she is the only woman on earth. He gives her his utmost, heartfelt attention. Voorheeze always seems to say the right thing at the right time to make her feel special. When he looks at her it's with so much desire that she feels like she is the most beautiful woman in the world. She snuggles closer to him trying to absorb as much of his body heat as she can.

Voorheeze on the other hand is miles away lost in his own mind. Haunted by his memories. Memories he tries desperately to bury in the back of his mind forever. He's not that lucky though.

He's back in San Quentin Reception. The filth tier back bar inside of West Block. They just released for dinner. As he walks by Big Country's cell, Voorheeze sees that Country's back is against the bars. He slides the make-shift knife out his waistline and stabs the huge mothafucka over and over.

Next, he's in Berkley. This is his first time ever being in this city. It took him a year to track down Oscar Piggy, but he finally did. Pleasure intoxicates him as he stands over the lifeless body.

He got Mondo eight months before that, leaving some bitch's apartment on 59th in East Oakland. He sees the blood flying out of Dawoo as he stabs him over and over, fourteen times inside the cell in Tracy.

The bodies start to swarm through his mind. He doesn't realize he's starting to sweat all over again. His heart rate accelerates, and he begins to yell. It's really a cry that just sounds like a yell.

"LaMont! LaMont! Baby wake up! LaMont!" Vieira knows the signs she's been thru this before with her brother.

"Come on Baby it's okay wake up." She's cradling him in her arms now.

When LaMont finally wakes up he doesn't know what just happened. He remembers all the dead mothafuckas but he doesn't remember ever closing his eyes. He thinks it was a nightmare, he doesn't realize he suffers from PTSD, Post Traumatic Stress Disorder. He doesn't know about the yelling and had no idea about the crying he did. He senses something aint right.

First, he feels embarrassed, then he realizes there is nothing to be embarrassed about cause he doesn't know shit!

He frees himself from her and goes to take another shower.

**** N. D. ****
A week later

It was a bright and shiny day. Nice and warm with a slight breeze. The type of day you would have a picnic or a bar-b-q. It should've been a day of laughter and fun. Instead it was one of loss and hurt as they gathered at the Church preparing to bury one of their own. Naturally the entire family came out to say farewell to their sister.

Anne was the last member of rank to join the Family. It wasn't that long ago but with all the shit they've been through their bond was unbreakable. She wasn't just a She-Wolf, she was a Chiba! French Tip couldn't believe it when she heard the news. None of them could.

All the She-Wolves stood wearing pink instead of black.

Voorheeze was there but he wasn't. His physical body may have been at the Church, but his mind was elsewhere. He felt bad for ever questioning Anne's gangsta. Something had snapped in Voorheeze. The only thing on his mind was actually written on the T-Shirts that everybody was wearing, R.I.P. Revenge Is Promised! He didn't want to step on his brothers toes with this shit. But fuck it! It was time to do what should've been done. Send in the Wolves! All of them!

The picture of her in the frame sitting on top of the closed casket was a beautiful one. Anne's smile was so beautiful. A smile that will neva be seen again. Jenn sat in the front row with a face full of tears. She was holding a little baby in her arms.

The preacher was doing his thing. He was a young minister yet the message that he shared was always powerful. Right now, he was speaking of the ills of the violence connected with the street life. He was a soldier in the streets. He was sharing with the crowd how he used to be in the streets but changed thanks to God.

His name is Pastor Juan. Now he was a soldier for God. Though he doesn't know it, because it will be a while before it surfaced, his message touched the hearts of a couple of people. It was that heart-warming.

When the preacher was finished, it was over, and people began saying their good bye's and leaving. Voorheeze needed some air. He hated funerals. He was trying to hurry up but the people in front of him were moving too damn slow. Finally, he was at the door. He heard Jenn call him, but he ignored her. Shit he needed some fucking air. He opened the door and stepped out into the blinding sunlight.

BOCCA! BOCCA! BOCCA!

Taat! Taat! Taat! Taat! Boom! Boom!

Shots were coming from everywhere. Unfortunately, most of the people outside were friends and relatives of Anne's, they were civilians who got mowed down. But those that were Dragon Gang got off wit them thangs.

BOCCA! BOCCA! BOCCA! BOCCA! BOCCA! BOCCA!

Voorheeze didn't hesitate he let that .40 sing a tune.

There were two niggaz to his right side standing in the middle of the street next to a minivan. About four or five little mothafuckas were in the front of him across the street ducked off behind cars and shit. He couldn't see to the left, but he knew somebody was there. He could feel them. He needed to get to the parked cars and use them for cover. The relatives were squirming on the ground trying desperately to find somewhere to hide. Some were screaming, others crying and calling out for help.

BOOM!

The door to the Church came busting open. Unfortunately for the niggaz that came to shoot up the funeral a platoon of killaz came thru that door.

BOOM! BOOM! BOOM!

BOCA! BOCCA!

BOOM! BOCCA! BOOM!

Neva Die came storming out of the Church getting off.

Voorheeze used that distraction to his advantage and raced to the parked cars. Now that the tables were turned, he figured niggaz would try to run. He wasn't having that!

He ran, crouching down past two cars.

Gunfire was still going off everywhere. He rose, both bangers ready.

BOCCA! BOCCA! BOCCA! BOCA! One of the niggaz standing to the right in the street spun around from first slug from one of Voorheeze's 40's. The second nigga got hit in the chest.

The nigga on his left started to lift his hand and return fire but stopped midway. He couldn't lift his arm, something was wrong. He didn't realize a slug ripped through his head.

It's over, kleets! His body collapsed right there.

As soon as French Tip heard the shots she rushed to the door. By the time she got there her 40 was in her hand. First thing she saw was a nigga in the street aiming his gun at her brother.

BOC! BOC! BOC! BOC! BOC!

When he hit the ground his body just started convulsing, she looked for another target.

During the commotion and chaos Drew made it to his car.

Taata! Taata! Taata! Taata! Taat!

He had the AR-15 in his hands lighting shit up.

Two little niggaz dropped as soon as Drew opened fire.

A shot came from the left and caught DJ in the shoulder spinning him around. But his finger was on the trigger, when he got shot his finger squeezed the trigger and the bullet smacked Drew in the back of the head, killing him instantly.

Voorheeze ran to Drew, picked up the AR and prepared himself. He looked at French Tip, she already knew. She nodded her head to let him know she understood. She raised her arm and sent as many shots as she could for cover. Voorheeze used that time to run across the street. He ducked down behind a car and peeked around it. He could see them.

He raised up.

Taata! Taata! Taata! Taata! Taata! Taata! Taata! Taata!
BOC! BOC! BOC!

Every last one of them lay dead on the ground, bodies riddled the fuck up. Voorheeze turned and started to cross the street. Suddenly, his legs felt like they weighed one hundred pounds each, he couldn't take another step. He looked across the street at French Tip, he tried to say something to her, but he couldn't. He felt helpless. The helplessness scared him. The AR-15 fell out of his hands. Then he stumbled forward and fell on his face.

**** N. D. ****

Officer Hedgecock knew that his instincts were right. He caught up with Voorheeze the other day and had been tailing him ever since. This morning when he followed him he was shocked to see him going to church. *Not this guy*, Hedgecock thought.

Hedgecock realized it was a funeral. Looking at the type of people he was seeing he knew it was trouble.

"Fucking niggers always make trouble". He was sitting low in the seat almost falling asleep when he saw the two vans pull up and a bunch of teenagers jumping out with all types of guns and rifles in their hands. These were damn kids for Christ sake! He wanted to radio in and call for back-up because from what he saw there was going to be a massacre. He couldn't call-in because he was not supposed to be there.

Gorillaz in the Bay 2

Hedgecock wrestled over what he should do when before he knew it, all hell broke loose. One-minute people were walking out of the church and suddenly, the little kids started shooting at the people leaving.

He couldn't believe he was witnessing multiple murders and he couldn't do anything about it. If he tried to stop them, he would have been killed. He watched as one, big bald guy was taking on all of them by himself. Hedgecock saw him kill the first two. When the church door flew open it was complete pandemonium.

These weren't your average criminals. These were monsters! They were having an all-out war in the middle of the street. A stray bullet busted the back window of his car. Hedgecock was so fucking scared. He tried to scoot and crouch down under the steering wheel as far as he could.

This wasn't police work. This was begging for death. Hedgecock couldn't remember the last time he prayed but he prayed right then. Another bullet slammed into the car and he screamed. After a while he didn't hear any more gunshots so he waited a little longer and checked. He didn't' see anything but bodies. He got the fuck outta there!

**** N. D. ****

The thought of moving literally terrified him. He was in that much pain. Every time he took a breath it felt like he was being stabbed in the chest by hella knives at the same time.

The days and nights ran into each other. He didn't know how long he had been here because he constantly faded in and out. The sweat pouring off his body by the buckets was proof of his high fever.

Only God knew how many of his ribs were broken. But, it felt like all of the were to him. Mothafuckas were going to pay in the worst motha-fucking way imaginable. Once he got back on his feet.

All he could do is smile about what he had in store for the mothafuckas who were responsible for his fucking pain!

4 days later

There was nervous tension in the air so thick you could cut it with a butter knife. The waiting room was packed tighter than a fat broad in a pair of Seven jeans. The look on the faces of everybody spoke volumes. There had been two altercations and stand-offs with the police already. Both times it nearly erupted into violence. The authorities wanted the waiting area cleared out.

189

De'Kari

That's what caused the second altercation because the visitors in the waiting area made it clear that they weren't leaving. When the police tried to force the issue, they wouldn't back down. Hospital security had to get between them and the police. The first incident came when police detectives came into the room while Clarkola, French Tip and their mother sat watching over Voorheeze. He'd lost a lot of blood from the gunshot wounds and there were complications with the surgery, resulting in the coma that he was in.

One of the bullets hit an artery which accounted for a lot of blood loss. They were grateful that the doctors were able to remove the bullets from his chest and repair the damaged artery. Due to the amount of damage, he would possibly need a ventilator for the rest of his life, if he came out of the coma. That was the doctor's prediction at least.

His mother took the news very hard. For years Voorheeze didn't think his mother loved him because of the way she treated him. But if he could see how she was now, he would know that she did. She refused to leave his bedside at all not even to eat. French Tip had to finally bring her some food.

When the police detectives came with the handcuffs and a warrant stating that he was under arrest for murder, it was his mom that got Gangsta! She got all up in one detectives face, cursing and ranting that her name was Bernice and he better recognize. Just as he was getting ready to put the handcuffs on her, Clark stepped in and pulled her back.

Word of the interaction between his mom and the detective got out to the family and immediately the Wolf-Pack and She-Wolves stormed into Stanford Hospital ready to get it popping. Murda, Styles and Double G came as well. If the police thought shit was going to be sweet, they had another thing coming. Matters only worsened the next day when A.J. showed up ready to show out.

Though they hated to admit it, there was nothing any of them could do about the murder charge. He couldn't just say that he was a bystander that got shot because the police had found gun powder residue on his hands.

Clark was lost. He wanted to ride down on Y.N.M. and make mothafuckas pay. But he didn't want any more shit that could lead back to them and make things worse for his brother. He wanted them mothafuckas so bad. Standing there looking at his little brother with all those fuckin tubes sticking out of him, hanging onto life by a limb, made Clark want to turn it up. Deep down his anger stemmed from regret and guilt. He was wishing he had of spent more time with his baby brother, but he was busy running the streets, chasing females and making money. Neither of which could bring his little brother back.

Gorillaz in the Bay 2

French Tip sat in the corner by the window silently crying. The doctors said that there wasn't a guarantee that her brother would come out of the comma. She prayed and prayed. She didn't' just want her big brother to pull through, she needed him to. Tip would be lost without her big brother. He was her protector. Voorheeze was the one that came to the school when the bullies used to mess with her. He's the one that always made sure her birthday was special. Like the time when they were kids, he was a teenager on the run from the Feds and even though their apartment was under surveillance, he still managed to get inside to wake her up and sneak her out. They ended up at the taco truck, then played video games and shot some pool. She needed her brother.

Somebody knocked on the door, "Umm some young Hispanic dude is out here, he claims he's a Pastor and that you know him Frenchie", Nina stated in a hostile manner. Nina was one of the twins, she was on fire and ready to pop off.

"Yeah that's Pastor Juan, I called him". French Tip was wondering how Nina didn't recognize Pastor Juan from the funeral, but it really didn't matter.

Pastor Juan came into the room. Nina closed the door behind him. The atmosphere in the room was too gloomy. He knew he needed to give them some hope.

"Hello Everybody", he spoke.

The two women spoke, Clark just nodded his head.

Father Juan walked over to Bernice. "Ma'am I've come today not just for your son, but for all of you". As he talked to her, he took both of her hands into his and got down on his knees.

He looked her directly in her eyes. "I promise you that God can make miracles! You just must believe. I know you hear that a lot but I'm telling you the truth of what I know from experience. Two years ago, I was in a street gang, banging and killing people. Today, not only do I no longer gang bang, but I'm a Pastor!" This revelation shocked all of them.

"Pastor I believe in God. I just don't know if he wanna help". The truth of her feelings bringing more tears to her eyes. "I'm tired! I'm so tired! These kids are driving me crazy. They out there trynna be like their uncles and it's just killing me!" The tears just poured down her face.

"I know, I know. You just got to give it to God. Let go and let God. He's waiting to do something here. You just got to let Him." He patted her hand and stood up.

As he turned away from Bernice, he looked at Clark. "Brotha God is telling me to tell you that vengeance is his and that going tit for tat is not the answer". Clark wasn't trynna hear nothin this Mexican mothafucka was talking about. If God had something to tell him then He better come tell him Himself, that's the way Clark felt.

He continued toward French Tip, giving her a hug. "How are you holding up, sister?" He asked her with a voice full of concern.

"Pastor I'm not ready to break down. I'm just trying to be strong for my mother", she spoke truthfully.

"Just hang on in there sister, God is God!" He squeezed her hands gently and let them go.

Next, he walked over to Voorheeze. He looked down at a lost soul. He mumbled some words in Spanish. Every one of them was watching him intently. Whatever he was chanting, he started mumbling a little louder.

Suddenly Voorheeze body jerked. Pastor Juan switched over to English then. It was clear now that he was mumbling a prayer. He spoke softly, yet with conviction. He was telling God if Voorheeze soul was indeed bought by Him, then he was indeed His child. And if he was His child, then to help His child. He was telling God that saving Voorheeze would ultimately save many lives.

Pastor Juan was speaking like he knew things that God didn't, about Voorheeze changing and saving lives himself. What they didn't know was Pastor Juan only knew this because God told him. Pastor Juan knew sometimes we had to remind God, so He would know, but more importantly so he would know we remembered.

"Heavenly Father in Luke 7:14 you told the widow's dead son to get up! And he did! You told Lazarus in John 11:43 to come out! And he woke form the dead and came out. Father in John 14:13 You tell us that You will do whatever is asked in Your name so that the Father may be glorified in the Son. Well Heavenly Father, Lord Jehovah, I ask you in Jesus' name, be glorified and show your Love, your Mercy and your Strength and awaken this man!" At that moment, he reached out and took Voorheeze's hand.

**** **N. D.** ****
Milpitas

"*Uuunnch!*" *Clink*!
"*Uuuurgh!*" *Clink*!
"*Uuuurgh*! *Aaaaw*!"

Clink! After his twelfth rep. Batman let the dumbbells fall onto the rubber mat. That was his fifth set of dumbbell presses. He stood up and checked himself out in the mirror. Batman was nowhere near being a big muscle-bound nigga, but he had size to him. He stayed in the gym.

Gorillaz in the Bay 2

Batman didn't work out to be huge and buffed up. He worked out to stay strong and fit.

"Say man I've been watching you. Man, you drive pretty hard! Are you training for something?" The guy who was on the next bench over walked up to him and asked.

"Oh! Thank you. Uh no guy, sorry no training. I uh just normally workout with my pal and this is how we workout". Batman responded trying to sound as preppy as possible.

"Wow! I wish I had a partner. The guys at the station always want to use the station gym but it just doesn't do it for me." The white guy told him.

"I know what you mean. It just isn't the same without a partner". Batman paused and looked around. "I tell you what guy. I'm barely halfway through. If you're not done how about we finish together?"

"That'll be swell. I'm Benjamin by the way", as he extended his hand for a shake.

"Robert, Benjamin nice to meet you". Batman took his hand and shook it.

They were at 24 Hour Fitness at the Great Mall in Milpitas. It was one of the gyms that usually had a big crowd. Batman has a membership, but he didn't swipe in tonight. The white guy was just a tad bit shorter than Batman, but he was just as fit. He had a lot more muscle than Batman but surprisingly he wasn't as strong as him. He drove just as hard on the weights. They ended up driving for two more hours, they were so into it.

At the end Benjamin was worn out, "Whew! Now that was a good workout".

"Yeah, I'm beat, thanks for the push. I hope I don't pass out at the wheel." Batman began gathering his things.

"You're not going to hit the shower?" Benjamin asked him.

"Oh no, I soak in the tub at home".

"Oh, okay." They shook hands and Batman headed out.

When he got to his car, he drove around the building, parking by a door that was slightly ajar. He took his time putting some gloves on. Next, he grabbed the brass knuckles and a plastic bag. He got out the car and walked in the door. He headed to the locker room, which was empty thankfully, except for Benjamin.

He was singing in the shower. Batman slipped on the pair of brass knuckles and made his way towards the back toward the showers. He stopped at the stall Benjamin was in and opened the door. Benjamin's back was turned, he was soaping and singing away. Batman stepped inside the shower.

De'Kari

"How you doing Sgt. Costa?" Costa turned around alarmed. Whap! A right hook from Batman with those knuckles, knocked Costa on his ass!

Batman pulled out the plastic bag taking his time to enjoy it. He didn't give a fuck if anyone came in or not. He'd kill them too. He placed the bag around the sergeant's head and tied it. Being unconscious, he would die soon. With the water running, he wouldn't be found for a while. Satisfied with his work, he left out, made it to his stolen car and drove off.

"That's for you Robin." He mumbled as he pulled off.

He didn't know how to deal with what was happening with Voorheeze. He hadn't been to see him because he was scared to lose his brother and he was angry because he was scared. At least that's what they say. For now, he'd just keep up with what his brother asked him to do. Shit, Batman & Robin was for real! Neva mind that they both were a little crazy!

**** N. D. ****
Stanford Hospital

Everything was pitch black. A darkness like no darkness he had ever known. His movements were fluid, he felt weightless. The weirdest thing of all is he could feel his thoughts. Almost as if his thoughts were actually real actions. Like he could be or was his thoughts. What the fuck was this he wondered. Where am I? Why is it so fucking dark? He tried to open his mouth to tell somebody to turn on the lights, but he couldn't figure out how to work his mouth. Shit he couldn't feel his mouth or the rest of his body for that matter! Now he began to worry, what the fuck was really up!

"It's okay Baby." That was Aunt Pat's voice He knew it. He knew her voice, but he couldn't see her.

"Auntie where you at?" How did he do that? He didn't speak he just thought it and it was.

"It's okay nephew, I'm here with you, we all are", Aunt Pat told him.

"Who's we all? And what's here?" He needed to know.

"Hey

Since I lost you... I can't explain it. You were the only one who knew what happened to me."

"It's okay cousin, I've always been there", Trisha tells him.

But I've let yall down. I've messed up so much in life, this time I'm scared. I think it's over". He knows that he is crying but he can't feel any tears.

"It's going to be okay son. Church! Sunday School!" Grandma says.

"I love you! Grandma." Voorheeze feels so much love and warmth right now.

"Grandma, I need you. I know a piece of my mind was lost, when I lost you." When he hears his comments, it's not his voice. He sounds like a little kid.

"You're lost cause you aint in the Church", a man's voice says.

"Who are you?" He asked the strange voice.

"I'm your grandfather son.

"Hey!... Hey"! Voorheeze calls out.

"He doesn't know how, but he can sense that they are gone. He doesn't know how he knows, but he does. It's starting to get lighter.

Somehow, he could see. He was visioning his thoughts. His thoughts were his dreams. His dreams were real.

She was real. She was the most beautiful woman he had ever laid eyes on. Her chocolate brownie skin and alluring eyes. She was smiling so beautifully. Her body was banging so hard, she could start her own gang.

She was the woman in his dreams. The one he compared all other women to. She was the one he wanted but couldn't have. The one he'd been in love with since childhood. She was a good girl and he was all fucked up. She was dedicated to helping those in need and supporting the community.

He did dope, guns, violence and murder.

But look at her, fuck! Doesn't she understand I didn't ask for this shit? Can't she see the good in me? If only I could talk to her, get her to understand. "Hey Li. . .!"

"I know what I did was wrong, but you didn't have to kill me Voorheeze." Who was that? Where did she go?

"Yeah! I didn't even do anything to you. That shit was between me and Tasha blood. Who the fuck was you to kill me? Nigga you killed me over a broad!"

I'm tired of these damn voices all in a nigga head. In my dreams.

"Voorheeze you bitch ass nigga, I wish I was alive bitch ass nigga, I'd do it again, fuck you! And you had to sneak up on me to do it. Yo little bitch ass couldn't even face me! Nigga fuck you and Belinda."

"Fuck! Make it stop! Every last one of them sick fucks got what they deserve!

De'Kari

"Aye youngsta, man I was just playing with you in the cell. Man, I wasn't really gonna rape you. I was just testing yo gangsta. You didn't have to stab me up like that Cuz. Aye Cuz, you hear me? Say Cuz! Alright fuck you then, O' Bitch ass nigga! You lucky Cuz, I was gonna have yo chocolate ass sucking my dick bitch!"

"I miss you granny! It's lonely here. I'm scared. Voorheeze you tried to help, but you messed up. He didn't die and when he got out the hospital, he said it was all my fault for telling you what he did to me. He told me he was gonna teach me a lesson for running my mouth. I've been here ever since." Damn little Lamar I'm sorry brah. When you told me what he did I just wanted to end your pain, but you can't even hear me."*

Voorheeze didn't realize he was in a coma. He's been hearing the voices for so long in his sleep that he didn't know that the voices are really his conscience fucking with him. He justifies everyone he's ever killed. That's how he copes. But his conscious doesn't buy his justifications. So, his thoughts and dreams are haunted!

Now he can hear his mom but doesn't know why he can hear her.

"Pastor I believe in God. I just don't know if he wanna help."

What? What the fuck is she talking about? God help for what? Who is she talking to?

"Mama! Mama!" She can't hear him cause he's not talking but he doesn't realize that. "Chocolate what's wrong?"

Who the fuck is that talking to her? What's the fuck wrong with me? Voorheeze can hear everything that everybody is saying but he can't say shit. He can't move his body. He hears the guy saying something in Spanish. Who the fuck is that nigga?

"He's my vessel and now isn't your time my son." The voice sounded like nothing he had ever heard. Like thunder or something.

"LaMont, wake up!"

**** N. D. ****

Pastor Juan was praying.

"Well Heavenly Father, Lord Jehovah. I ask you Jesus. In the name of the Heavenly Father! Be glorified and show your Love and Mercy and your Strength. And awaken this Man!" At that moment, he reached out and took Voorheeze's hand.

The moment he touched him, Voorheeze's body jerked like he had been electrocuted. He raised his torso off the hospital bed sitting straight up. At the same time, he opened his eyes and took a deep breath.

Gorillaz in the Bay 2

His mother jumped out of the chair. She ran over and hugged Pastor Juan thanking him. He told her it wasn't him, that it was God. But she didn't hear anything he said.

"I need some water", Voorheeze whispered.

French Tip was crying. She was glad her brother was okay. Clark wasn't feeling that God shit or whatever little magic trick the Migo cooked up.

Voorheeze's chest was on fire. The pain was a bitch. The last thing he remembered was the shootout at the funeral. He asked them what happened. French and his Mama filled him in on everything, even his charges.

**** N. D. ****
Price Barber Shop

The entire town heard about what happened to Voorheeze. Most were wondering what the outcome would be. They knew retaliation was a given. They just wanted to know how far Clark was about to take it!

Clark's entire team was there. He'd also called the Wolf-Pack. He was done playing games with these niggaz.

"Check it out! Yall already know I aint wit all that talking so I'mma make this shit real quick and easy like. And then Stone got something to say." He looked around the room at this niggaz, all of the ones he knew would ride for him and would die for him. Clark looked at his brother's niggaz, he didn't know if they would go the distance but the looks on their faces told him they would.

"Aint no hustling, not a single pack is to be sold. I want everyone's attention on making them mothafucka's disappear. They touched my brother, they touched us! Aint nothing spared; mama, sister, auntie, grandma! Kill everybody who gets in the way!" He looked at his watch, it read 6:50am." By 1 o'clock nigga I better hear the body count rising!" Then he thought about it and said, "I was tripping. Stick to the script. We don't do women and children. But any nigga over 14 can get it!

Stone Cold had assumed the leadership of the Wolf-Pack after Marlon got killed in the shootout with faggot Lynch. The same shootout that T'Rida got shot up with the A.K.

Stone stood up, "Look! The shit I'mma bout to say aint up for discussion. When safety and security is breached. I assume command over the entire Family. My leadership aint to be questioned! Don't test me!" Stone looked at each and every person to make sure they understood that meant, Everybody. "Clark's team, you will handle every city but

197

P.A. You niggaz are from here and mothafuckas expect yall to be coming. So, hit them niggaz in Hayward and Halfmoon Bay, then we'll meet in Oakland. I'll let big brah divide yall."

"Naa Stone we mashing as a unit. Straight annihilation." Clark told him.

"Aaight. Wolf-Pack! We hunt solo. Keak, Stunna, J. Spitz, yall knock down Menlo and the Mid. Mike Vegas, hit the G and work your way to the Vill. Africa hit the Vill. I want everything in P.A. knocked down by 11am if possible. I'm going to Oakland, yall meet me there. Thanks to the Beast and the rest of them Northerners, we know where they lay, let's make it permanent."

**** N. D. ****
1300 Block of Windermere

The niggaz sat on the porch talking shit and smoking some grapes. He could just bounce out now. This shit was too easy. But Keak always wanted to test himself. He drove around the corner and parked in front of the house behind little Gary's house. He went thru the backyard and hopped the gate into little Gary's backyard.

Fuck being cautious. He pulled out an AR pistol, known in the hood as a baby AR. He opened the sliding door and walked in. There was a bitch moaning like she was getting fucked in the front room.

He checked the back of the house. There was a nigga with his back towards him counting money. Keak sat the choppa down and pulled out his knife. He walked up to the nigga from behind and slit his throat. Mothafucka didn't utter a peep. That's why all the Wolf-Pack carried a knife for the *Silent Kills*. He walked out and headed for the front room.

Sure, enough there was a Puerta Rican chick with big ass titties riding a nigga on the couch. His back was to Keak and she was facing him. *Damn this easy* he thought, her eyes were closed. He figured he would wait until she opened them. He didn't mind watching her bounce them big ass titties. She was really riding that dick, talking in Spanish and shit. Her tits were flapping all over the place.

When she opened her eyes, she was staring down the barrel of the AR. He had his finger over his lips telling the hoe to be quiet. She stopped riding the nigga. He asked her what was up, but neva heard a reply. Keak smacked him in the back of the head with the barrel, knocking him out.

"God damn you badder than a mothafucka, girl! I'm only gonna say this once, if you wanna live, stay quiet and go into the bathroom." When she got up to run, she had an ass like a Straight Stuntin model.

Gorillaz in the Bay 2

He waited to hear the door close, once it did, he walked out on the porch like it was his house.

Taat! Taat! Taat! Taat! Taat! Taat! Taat!

That took care of that shit. No hesitation! No problems! He stepped back into the house. The nigga on the couch didn't stand a chance. Three shots to his head killed him. He went to the bathroom and opened the door. She was scared shitless.

"What I look like?" She didn't understand. She stood there frozen in fright.

"Let me make it easy for you. It was a skinny, light-skinned nigga with long dreadlocks that did this." He spoke slowly.

She finally understood. "Si Papi, crème colored negro with the long things." She had thought he was gonna kill her. Now she was beyond happy.

"Papi Tu want some Pinocha?" She was that happy.

The offer was tempting as fuck! She was that bad.

"Naa Mami, Tu mucho bonita, mucho! But I aint bout to get it cause you terrified." He could neva be that kind of nigga nor would he kill a woman. Keak left the house headed for the next destination.

**** N. D. ****

Young Sav might have been young but he was far from a dummy. His gunplay was already known and respected, this is why he was Sutton's second in command. Sav had the mind of a nigga whose been to war and came out on top.

He was giving Pinky that good long dick when the motion detectors started going off. She was yelling and screaming so loud that he almost didn't hear the faint beeps. He liked to see that big, yellow booty bounce as she rode him backwards. So, the lights were on in the room. Without alarming her, Sav got her attention. Their bodies were covered with sweat and the entire room smelled like sex. Pinky continued moaning and yelling like she was still riding him.

Sav instructed her to hide behind a recliner that he had on the East side of the room. She was to continue making sounds like they were having sex, he told her. Next, he turned off the bedroom lights and crouched down by the closet with a baby Draco in his hands. After a few moments he could hear voices mumbling outside the door. His heart was racing in his chest. Mothafuckas came in his house intending to bring him harm. Pinky was on the other side of the room going at it like she was really being fucked. The room door slowly creaked open, two figures stood in the doorway. Sav wanted to start shooting right then but he knew he had the element of surprise and he couldn't fuck that up. He had to remain still. As the seconds ticked away his heart beat pounded.

The two figures stepped into the room. Black Rob motioned for D-Roc to hit the light switch. They both had their guns cocked and loaded aimed at the bed. Just as D-Roc reached for the light, Black Rob realized something was wrong. The sounds that he was hearing weren't coming from the direction of the bed, they were coming from the right side of the room. D-Roc hit the switch, the lights came on in the room. Black Rob and D-Roc were both looking at an empty bed. The moaning was coming from behind the leather chair, but instincts told Black Rob there was danger to the left.

Blaaad! Blaaad! Blaaad!

Sav squeezed the trigger from his crouched position.

Blaaad! Blaaad! Blaaad! As he tapped the trigger the loud sound of the mini Draco echoed throughout the room.

Pinky was scared to death. The sound of the gun going off was the loudest thing she'd ever heard. She was so scared that she didn't stop making the sex sounds.

Blaaad! Blaaad! Blaaad!

The sounds went off again, terrifying her even more. Her eyes were closed from fear. So, when a hand grabbed her shoulders she jumped and screamed.

"Pinky, Pinky, it's me! Babe it's me!" Young Sav called out as he wrapped his arm around her.

Feeling his familiar embrace brought her out of her shocked state. Sav was standing there butt ass naked holding a big ass gun with a smile on his face. Pinky looked over his should and saw two dead bodies laying on the floor by the door, bleeding onto the carpet.

"Come on ma, get dressed. We gotta get outta here!" Sav told Pinky. While she got dressed, he checked the rest of the house. After seeing everything was secure, Sav threw some clothes on and they got out of there.

**** N. D. ****

"So, what do you think?" Hedgecock asked Sheriff Deputy Laiens.

Laiens was a twelve-year veteran out of San Mateo County. He knew the ropes. He was by the book and still fair. Always understanding and non-judgmental, yet stern when needed.

Hedgecock just asked Laiens his advice on what he should do. La-Mont Simpson was checked into San Jose Main Jail on murder charges. No one as of yet knew that Hedgecock was there. If he spoke up, he

Gorillaz in the Bay 2

will get into trouble, but the fact is he knows what happened was self-defense. Simpson will walk.

From what he observed, Hedgecock knew Simpson was guilty of something.

"Well, it's like this. At the end of the day the decision is yours to make. So, I won't say what I think you should do. What I will do, and I think you will agree it's the right thing to do. And that is to ask you did you take an oath to protect and serve and uphold the law? Or to uphold the law when you see fit?" Laiens made a face like, "think on that and took a swig of his beer.

He knew Laiens was right, he just didn't want him to be.

Laiens saw him getting down about the decision he needed to make, so he figured he'd throw him a line out there.

"Look at it like this, sure he could go down today for the murders, but you wouldn't be able to live with yourself because you'll know that it wasn't just. If he truly is dirty, you will eventually catch him, and it will be a good collar. Then you'll celebrate. Shit I'll buy the booze!"

"So, what did we do to get one of Milpitas finest over on our side? Deputy Myers asked as he pulled up to the table with a Blue Moon in his hand.

"Hey Myers, I'm just picking the old guys brain on something", Hedgecock responded.

"Must be mighty important to get you to drive all the way over here on a weekday." Myers was fishing for some information.

"You know that shooting at the funeral a while back?" Hedgecock asked Myers.

"Shit, who doesn't! They said it was the Korean War out there." Myers grabbed a handful of peanuts out of the bowl.

Laiens signaled for another round.

"Yeah, well I was out there. I saw the whole thing personally."

"Get out of here."

"Serious, even got my car shot up!" Hedgecock loved telling a story. "I was tailing this guy that I suspected to be dirty and he goes to the funeral. So, I'm out in my car, damn near asleep. Then these two vans stop in the middle of the street." He's fully animated now.

"All of a sudden, they open up on the funeral-goers as they're coming out of the church. I'm telling you bullets were flying all over the place. For a minute I actually thought I was going to get shot."

"Now, that there was something you don't see every day. I bet my black ass you don't." Myers was loving the information and the conversation.

The new round of drinks made it to the table. Hedgecock was so eager to finish talking since he had Myer's full attention. He didn't even take a swig." Let me tell you the most important part. The guy Simpson, it was actually self-defense, not murder.

"Fuck no!" Myers couldn't believe it. "It always happens that way. Just when you think you got the asshole in your hands, whoops, he wiggles out." With damn near twenty years in, Myers had seen it all.

"Look at the ass on that waitress! I think I'm having a heart attack.

"Oh yeah brother, that's nice." Hedgecock chimed in.

"Deputy 6844, what's your 20?" Laiens radio interrupted the good time.

"Dispatch 6844 I'm two blocks away from the jail." Deputy Laiens responded.

"6844 be advised Menlo Park PD and East Palo Alto PD is 10-32 requesting assistance. The situation is 10-18. You are advised to head to the East Palo Alto Police Department and see a sergeant Norris.

"10-4 dispatch. Do we know the nature of the request?"

"That's affirmative 6844. So far there's been 15 homicides this morning they know of."

"Good Lord!" Laiens spoke out. 15 murders yeah it was 10-18 or urgent.

"Okay dispatch I'm 10-17."

"Uh Myers tell your buddy he's assigned over there as well." She was referring to Laiens, his partner in crime.

"10-4 dispatch we are both 10-17." Myers looked at Laiens waiting for it. It didn't take long.

"Well it would appear someone is very happy about our boy being shot up." Laiens had a knack for putting together what happened even before he got on the scene.

This really got Hedgecock attention. "You really think so?"

"Absolutely! They didn't do the funeral to prove a point or send a message that was pure retaliation. Simpson must be somebody very important. Fifteen murders and it is 11:00 o'clock. This isn't retaliation. This is clearly annihilation." He just didn't realize how close to the truth he really was.

"Come on we better get going." Myers said as he grabbed another hand full of peanuts and stood up, Laiens stood up as well.

"Hey, you guys mind if I tag along?" Something was telling Hedgecock to tag along. Somehow, he knew it was all connected.

**** N. D. ****
(East Palo Alto)

Sergeant Norton couldn't believe what kind of day it turned out to be. He started off working a double the night before and then all the killings started. Being Senior officer, it was a given that he would be called to stay and help get to the bottom of what's going on, or at least try to make some sense of it all. 22 homicides in one day was fucking ludicrous. This must be some type of gang war because all the victims were kids and young adults. It seems like just when you thought it was all over another call would go out at one time. East Palo Alto's homicide division only consisted of four detectives and two officers. They were not prepared for this.

And if that wasn't bad enough this was turning out to be one of the hottest summers the Bay Area has seen this decade. Today it was 105 degrees. A fucking furnace. Sgt. Norton was finishing up his last report and was getting ready to head home to a hot bath and some much-needed sleep, but something just kept nagging at him at one of the crime scenes, it was at the house of a kid named Radolpho Jenkins. He was known in the streets as Roscoe. Norton knew that if he didn't satisfy the curious itch then it would tug on him all night. Hungry, overworked and tired he got into his car and drove to the location.

Past the caution tape, through the front door Sgt. Norton went. The smell of blood was overwhelmingly strong. In total four people were found dead in the house. There was so much blood in the house. The mother was found first. She was on the living room couch with her head blown off.

The girlfriend must have been alarmed by the gun shot and came out of the shower to investigate. Her naked body lay in the threshold of the bathroom still wet. There six bullet holes in the bathroom door indicating Roscoe laid in wait for an ambush. One that apparently failed he was shot twenty-five times. Next to his body was a six-year-old boy. One shot through the face.

Norton looked over the room Roscoe was found in for the tenth time. Whistling "*My Girl*" by the Temptations while he processed everything. Whistling helped him think, helped him tap into his analytical mind. He let his eyes slowly drift over every inch of the room. He didn't see anything yet.

His instincts were screaming. He scanned the room a second time. Again nothing. Wait. There it is; the dresser top. It's a different shade than the rest of the dresser. The difference is barely noticeable. Hell, Norton missed it along with the rest of the detectives. He put on a pair of gloves and tested the top; it moved. He carefully lifted the top of the long dresser and flipped it over.

On the bottom side of the top was some type of plans, a list, what looked to be a map and a bunch of other stuff. The problem is it was all written in some weird language or code. There was only one thing that was legible out of everything. In red marker, all capital letters were written NEVA DIE! It had a black bull's-eye drawn over it. Who or what was Neva Die? Was it some type of rival gang or a group of drug dealers? Could Neva Die be responsible for all the killings today?

Norton had to find out what Neva Die was. He was getting ready to flip the top back over when he saw something. He bent down to look closer. There was a faint line. He followed it. There was another one. He followed that one. Four perfectly straight lines with 90-degree angles. It was some type of trap door. He pressed until he got it open. It was a stack of polaroid's. A couple of buildings, a nice house, a woman, two kinds, then there was one of the murder suspect LaMont Simpson. A few more of him and some other people. This had to be Neva Die.

The photos had to be some sort of surveillance. Then Norton flipped another photo and hit the jackpot. It was taken in front of the popular club Carsjanae's. There were perhaps fifty or sixty people. Simpson was in the center standing next to the cop killer, Thomas Smith, and embracing him. This was big. This was very big! He bagged the photos in a plastic evidence bag and headed towards the front door. He was so excited he didn't even notice that something was out of place. Someone was sitting on the couch in the same exact spot as Mama Jenkins dead body was.

"You know cop. I'm willing to bet this is one time you wish you would've said excuse me." 9mm with silencer in hand, Batman had his hand in his lap, gun pointed at Norton.

It took Norton a few moments before he realized who the man on the couch was. But three bullets crash landed into his chest before he could speak. His body fell into the wall before sliding down to the ground. He was dead. Batman shot him twice in the head anyway.

Earlier that day Batman just happened to be in P.A. seeing his mother-in-law. After he left her job on Pulgas, he decided to go to Three Brothers Tacos. It just so happened Detective Norton hadn't had time to get anything to eat much less take a break that morning. So, he rushed over to Three Brothers Tacos for a quick bite on the run. To say that he was pissed was an understatement. Also, he was going on thirty-six hours straight working. He grabbed his food and rushed to get to the next call. Not paying attention to where he was going caused he was trying to get his keys out of his pocket. He ran right into this middle-aged brother who was coming into the restaurant.

"You could say excuse me brother", was all Batman said after Norton kept going.

Norton was already having a shitty day and he didn't like the authoritative way the guy said it. Hell, he was the authority in this fucking city.! "Nigga, fuck you punk" he called over his shoulder.

Gorillaz in the Bay 2

Three Brothers smelled so good a vegetarian mothafucka would slide thru and snatch up some tacos. But the smell of food now made him sick. He was craving one thing only now, that cop's soul!

He followed and waited patiently all the while telling himself he tried to be nice. After, he shot him twice in the head, he walked out. A pig was a pig; not just Milpitas police. Batman took it upon himself to declare war on all cops.

**** N. D. ****
(The Next Day)

Tieka walked out of the office with a smile on her face. She'd just finished giving her presentation to her supervisor and he was highly pleased with her work. He was ready to tell her to pack it in, but she was able to convince him to extend the deadline. She felt deep down that she could do more and make it better.

She walked out of the big building downtown thankful to God for the strength he gave her not to give up or give in. As a gentle breeze blew a feeling of calm overcame her and a single tear of joy rolled down her face. She remembered all too well when her only tears were tears of grief, heartbreak and agony. Clark needed her to run a few errands for him but that could wait. Right now, she felt she deserved a celebration. Hell, a girl deserved to get her nails done then she could take care of his needs.

**** N. D. ****
(Milpitas, CA)

Now was the time, Lt. Urena had been waiting on this day for the last three years. He made his mind up back then on what he wanted to do. He had been waiting on a way in and he just found it. He picked up his phone and dialed the number. While it rang, his eagerness built.

"Hello?" The caller finally picked up.

"Me and you are about to become very close." Urena practiced time and time again exactly just what he would say and how he would say it.

"Who da fuck is this? Man are you playing on my phone?" He didn't recognize the number or the voice.

"I assure you this isn't a game. Everything and everybody you love is in danger." Urena paused to make sure he had his attention. He was smiling and stroking his mustache, a habit he has. "I'm going to send you something right now to look over. After you look over it give me a call, we need to talk. Oh, and this is Lieutenant Urena of the San

Mateo Sherriff's Department currently working out of Milpitas." There was no response. The call was terminated.

Urena knew he would call back. He had no choice. Urena would be willing to assist him in solving the problem. But it was going to be expensive. His gambling debt had gotten so high he knew he could neva pay it off. The threats had already started. His other addiction, high priced prostitutes, was only putting him further in the hole. He needed a payday, and this was going to be it.

This would no doubt cover all his debt problems and vices and still he'll have some left over. But he wasn't trying to make this a onetime payday. He wanted this to open the door and be the beginning of a continued working relationship. Then he'd be able to finally live life the way he wanted.

Who knows maybe Amber would stop hooking and be with him. Sure, he would leave Esmeralda. He's been tired of her for the longest. She disgusts him with her fat ass. All she does is eat and complain. She is driving him crazy.

As he exits the freeway, he thinks back to the time he thought about killing her. He thought, planned, thought and planned some more but ended up chickening out. He'd neva killed anyone before. He didn't think he could do it. His ringing phone brought him out of his thoughts.

"Hello?" He answered so cheesy.

"I'll be at the Milpitas Public library tomorrow at 1:00 o'clock in the afternoon. Look for the Urban Street literature section. I'll be reading Backstreet Life by Dekari." Again, he didn't wait for a response. He just disconnected. The line.

Urena pulled up to the apartment complex just as the conversation was ended. Of course, he was at Amber's place. Tomorrow, he was going to be filthy rich so there was nothing wrong with spending a little money that he didn't have for a little taste of heaven. He popped a Viagra then dialed her number.

(San Jose Main Jail)

There was concrete and brick walls, a two foot by seven-foot concrete slab for a bed, a metal make-shift desk and shelf plus a stainless-steel sink and toilet combination. Voorheeze was used to being locked up; he had been doing time since age eleven.

He knew how to do time, but he still hated it. The fucking air was always stale. It was a mixture of piss, funky ass and garbage. A smell that has accumulated over years of neglected cleanliness. They threw him in the hole when he arrived. Double red jumpsuit to signify he was fighting a murder. He wasn't nothing special though, everybody on his floor was fighting a murder. He just happened to be charged with the most.

Voorheeze had been transferred here almost a month ago. He'd lost so much weight due to not eating the bullshit they call chow. Even though he didn't let it show, the prospect of him doing life in prison stressed him the fuck out. To pass the time he often reflected on what he'd experienced when he was in the coma. Not the dead people. Fuck them niggaz, they got what they deserved; except little Lamar. That will always hurt his soul. But he reflected on the visions of his lost angels Patricia, LaTrisha and Emma. Damn he really missed them. Just hearing them gave a boost to his spirit.

What about the visions of her? She'd always been his one true love; all his life, no matter who he was with. Could seeing her have been a sign? Lisa don't you know I would give all this shit up for you? But it wouldn't matter cause I'm all fucked up anyway. I'll just end up fucking it up somehow. Luckily the guard walked by doing a security check and distracted him. Her name was Officer Presley. She was a cool down to earth sistah. One of the few guards that still treated people like they were human and one of a select few who still remembered that they were Black. She was cute too. Most of the cats on the floor tried to holla at her. She even checked niggaz in a respectful manner. Voorheeze wouldn't play himself trynna holla. Shit it wasn't nothing she could do for him but get him a roll of toilet paper and pop his cell door for a shower.

Presley had doubled backed. He could tell by the way her keys dangled. That's what happens when someone becomes institutionalized. You develop senses that are unheard of such as waking up from a deep sleep merely from someone standing in front of your door. Or sleeping and still being aware of and hearing everything going on around you. But the best thing is being able to tell whose approaching your cell by the sound of their steps.

"Simpson, you got an attorney visit." She tells him when she gets back to his cell door.

"How you doing today, sistah?" He asked her as he stepped out of his cell.

"I'm doing good how about yourself?" This is the first time he has ever actually looked at her. She looks so much like her.

"I'm beautiful cuz life is good." He truly means it. Every word.

Inside the attorney visiting room, Patience is sitting with a big ass smile on her face.

De'Kari

"Do you remember what I told you when you said you would give me whatever I wanted if I was able to get you out of here?" She asked him as soon as he sat down.

"Patience don't be in here fucking with me." He learned back when he was a kid, neva to get his hopes up in regard to the system.

"I want you to know that I will be importing the entire living room and sitting room furniture." When he told her, he would give her anything money could buy, she told him to refurnish her house.

"Look, I'm telling you ma. If these feet touch pavement again, you can import the whole fucking house." Except for the occasional basketball court, prison was concrete.

She looked at him and smiled some more. LaMont was a good guy. He'd made some terrible decisions, but he was a good guy.

"Well it seems that there was an officer following you while he was off duty, in fact he followed you out of the church for the funeral. He saw them open fire on everyone as you all were exiting the church. He also saw you when you returned fire." Now that she had his attention. She continued, "By right you should be walking out of here but it's the system, so we got to fight."

So, what are you saying?" Fuck the principal he thought.

"All of the murder charges have been dropped. They're still charging you with manslaughter. There's a weapons charge and discharging a fire arm in a public area. You've been given a bail. It's $500,000 of which I've already had the bondsman start the paperwork. You'll be out of here in a few hours." Patience was telling him everything, but her mind was really on the new furniture she was going to order.

Voorheeze was thinking of all the shit that he had to do. Mothafuckas done took his kindness for weakness for the last time. He respected what Clark had done to the fullest but niggaz ain't seen nothing yet. Walking back to his cell looking at officer Presley, he made his mind up. He was going to approach the woman that he loved. The worst thing she could say was no, fuck it! Oh! And how could he forget about Danika! He was going to break both of his feet off in her ass! Punk bitch ain't answer not one call. She ain't wrote or came to visit. The bitch had left him for dead. He had something for her.

Real talk!

CHAPTER XIX
(East Palo Alto)

It's been a couple of months since the shooting at the funeral home caused Clark to go on one. The losses that were dished out were crippling. However, Neva Die took losses as well. Each loss was a blow personally felt. That was the rules of the game, give and take.

Clark walked out of the McDonalds into the Home Depot lot with a bag of Chicken McNuggets and fries in his hand and an extra-large coke in the other. He juggled his cell phone between his shoulders and ear.

"Look I'm serious I'mma come by early tonight. I'mma take care of everything I gotta take care of, then I'mma be at you." He said into the phone as he walked to his car.

"Don't be trying to fill my head up with a bunch of bullshit Clark. I'm tired of sitting here waiting for you at night while you run to the next bitch!" She was yelling so loud in the phone it hurt his ears.

"Tieka I'm serious! I'mma be over there! Look I'll tell you what. I give you my word I'll be there before 8pm." Hell he sounded so convincing he almost believed himself.

He was so caught up in the conversation he didn't see the blue Chevy Malibu driving up on him or the two niggaz who hopped out.

"Clark I'm serious, if you don't come tonight then…"

BOCCA! BOCCA! BOCCA!

Taaat! taaat! taat! taat! taaat! taat!

They opened fire. Clark felt bullets hit his body, the sharp pain causing him to drop what was in his hand. Some of the bullets went into the car. Some shattered the windows. One of the shooters had a hand gun and the other had an AK-47. People were screaming and scrambling to make sure they didn't become a target or a casualty of a stray bullets.

"Clark is that gunfire?" Tieka asked. She knew the sound of gunfire really well. "Clark! Clark! Answer me God admit!" Genuine concern was now in her voice. God this can't be happening, not to him, not now!

"Clarence answer this damn phone!" Her fear and frustration made her use his government name.

He was bent over holding his stomach. The pain was fucking unbelievable! The blood running out of the bullet wounds felt like hot, liquid lava coming out of his body. He was still desperately grabbing for his banger but couldn't get. It didn't matter anyway because the shooters had already left. He was on the phone with Tieka but his

De'Kari

thoughts were of Spiritual. Bystanders felt it safe enough now to come and gawk at him. They couldn't believe the sight. By now he was on the ground. The charges literally looked like a prop at one of those active shooting ranges. Once people recognized who it was the phones came out. Some took pictures other made phone calls.

The police arrived on the scene and began pushing back the spectators. There was no use asking if anybody saw anything. This was E.P.A a.k.a. Lil Bhag Dhag, nobody going to say shit. The ambulance arrived on the scene and quickly picked him up and put him inside of the bus. The siren came on and the ambulance sped away. There was some type of construction or something going on. The detour made the ambulance drive through the parking garage of IKEA.

It exited the parking structure after a while and made its way to University Avenue. With the sirens blaring the ambulance traveled through traffic and finally turned left unto University speeding up the over-ramp. Suddenly the right rear tire blew out and the driver lost control. First the ambulance swerved, then the rear fishtailed and swerved back. The ambulance jumped up onto the curb and crashed through the chain-link fence.

Drivers of the cars that witnessed it, gawked in disbelief as the ambulance tumbled off of the over pass and lands on the 101 South-bound Freeway lanes. Shockingly it didn't hit any other vehicles. The ambulance exploded and erupted into flames. The explosion was so loud it was heard in the Gardens almost one mile away.

The police, another ambulance and the Fire department arrived on the scene quickly but there was nothing that could be done. The blaze was too intense to try to get into the ambulance and attempt to save anyone. Everyone watched in terror as the fire refused to be extinguished. By the time the fire was completely out, and it was deemed safe to approach, three bodies were pulled out, barely recognizable as human bodies, they were so charred.

**** N. D. ****

(Milpitas)

Hedgecock was on a two-week suspension for his off-duty surveillance of Simpson. The penalty wasn't that bad considering. On the one hand the murder charges were dropped to manslaughter, which Simpson would most likely beat. Hedgecock was taking Laiens advice and was looking at the brighter side of things.

Seeing the destruction that was caused out the day he accompanied them to East Palo Alto. If Laiens was right with his assumption, and it

210

looked like he was, the shooting at the funeral home sparked the slaughter that occurred that day, then he was onto something big.

He had a buddy pull him all the murders in East Palo Alto just on a whim. Though in actuality the cop killings were what he was working on. He believed in his gut, somehow it was all connected.

He still had a few days left to carry out on his suspension. However, the Chief wanted everyone assembled for an addressment. He didn't have a problem with the Chief, but he was on suspension, so he figured he shouldn't have to be here for any type of meeting. Hedgecock wanted to keep thinking and going over everything that he had formulating in his head.

He ignored the idle chatter that was going on around him. All of it some way revolved around the officers who were missing and presumed dead. He looked over to his right at the empty seat. Sergeant Costa usually sat in that seat. He thought it was a fucked-up day when a man couldn't even wash his ass without having to worry about being fucked with.

The Chief walked into the room and all chatter ceased. Everyone gave her their undivided attention. Chief Vieira was naturally a warm kind-hearted woman but years on the force had toughened her up and thickened her skin. She walked to the podium with her ample ass swaying as she passed. Chief Vieira was a middle-aged white woman with a body like a sistah. Rumor in the department was she liked brothas. God only knew brothas loved all that ass she had.

"Let me have your attention please." Everyone was paying full attention, but she still paused. It was a display of her authority.

"As you all should know by now, a number of our colleagues have either gone missing or have been murdered. Truthfully the consensus now is that they all have been murdered.

Unfortunately, we have yet to capture the party or parties involved. From what I'm told by captain Sweeney, we don't even have a lead. Now, I didn't call this meeting to tell all of you stuff that you already know so don't think that." Chief Vieira was fuming with anger. It was taking all of her will power to keep control.

"As of 7:35 this morning the FBI has been notified and made aware of what's going on. Now as you all know I fucking hate the FBI. So naturally this was done without my consent which has only added insult to injury. Now the decision that was made by the assholes who are above me is that we have been given a time table to gain some lead way on this issue, if not those fuckers are coming in here. If another officer is killed or comes up missing they are coming in. Now I don't want those assholes in my city or my department. Those are our comrades out there lost and gone. We need to be the ones to bring their murders to justice. Thank God this has still somehow managed to stay out of the media. Let's find these assholes before they strike again." She turned to look at the Captain. "Captain Sweeney find me the sons of bitches who are responsible or find yourself another job!" That was how she ended her briefing.

All the officers were beyond stunned. There was no sugar coating, no diplomacy or courtesy whatsoever in how she said all that. The message was clear. Captain Sweeney ran the ship. If he couldn't navigate it correctly she would find a new Captain. After all she owned the ship!

After being put on the spot like that, all Sweeney could do is tell everybody to get to work and be safe. Red faced and embarrassed, he stormed out of the room. Nobody wanted the Feds to come in. The chief was right, it was their responsibility to solve this. They owed it to their fallen comrades.

**** N. D. ****
(San Jose Main Jail)

Voorheeze just posted bail through Zig Zag Bail Bonds and was released from the main jail. Air ever smelled so good There was just something about the way the air smelled when a nigga was just released from lock up. The air was purer and sweeter. It was a little after 10:00pm by the time the cab dropped him off at his house. You could tell summer had come and gone form the night chill.

The entire ride home he thought about the ass kicking he was about to give her mothafuck'n ass. Voorheeze didn't condone hitting on women. Neva in his life has he laid a hand on a woman, but she had to get it! How was she gone leave him stranded like that after all the shit he did for her in such a short time? All the shit he opened up to her about? The deep, personal, embarrassing shit about his childhood. The more he thought about it the more pissed off he got. He was gone knock her mothafuck'n head off!

He opened the front door and gagged. He thought he would throw up from the stench. It was that strong.

"God Damn!" was the only thing he could say in response to the fucking odor. It smelt like death, ass and spoiled food.

Where was this trifling heifer at? Mothafucka could have at least taken care of the house, he thought as he entered. All the lights were off in the house. He didn't bother turning any on. He just made his way to the back room in the dark. As he got close he could hear muffled sounds.

Gorillaz in the Bay 2

"If she got a nigga in my shit I'mma kill both dem mothafuckas," he mumbled as he approached the door.

He opened the door and turned on the light. Danika lay balled up on the bed crying like a little baby into the pillows. Her hair was all disheveled. Her clothes looked like they hadn't been changed in days. The room was a mess but the worst of all was the body odor.

The smell was so strong he could taste the sourness. Instantly all his anger dissolved. Seeing her in such a weakened and helpless state pulled at his heart and crushed him. Here he was being selfish as fuck! Only thinking about what she didn't do and hadn't done to help him. Neva once did he stop to think how his being locked up was affecting her. Danika still hadn't noticed that he was standing there. He walked over to the bed and sat down.

"Shh… don't cry thickems it's okay." He said as he caressed her hair.

Danika looked at him and immediately jumped into his arms. She was so happy she couldn't talk. She just cried more.

"Shh..Shh.. Baby I got you." He hugged her as tight as he could hating himself for ever doubting her to begin with.

"Daddy I thought that I lost you. I didn't know that I was going to do without you." She sniffled and lifted breaking their embrace.

She looked at herself for the first time and noticed her appearance, "Oh my God, baby look at me. Ooh I probably smell too." She said sniffing under her arms.

"Ain't no probably about it, you need to take about six or seven baths while I burn them clothes." He told her jokingly.

She gently punched him in the shoulder and then placed him in a headlock. He couldn't believe it. She smelled just as bad as one of them old winos who slept under the bridge. He hurried up and got up out of that hold.

"Woman you aint right! Don't ever do that again" he stood up and picked her up. "Now come on and get in the tub."

While she was in the tub he emptied all the spoiled food out of the fridge and then threw the garbage away. It was the same garbage that was in the can from the day before the funeral. He had eaten Boston Market but had gotten full and threw half of it away. Next, he opened some windows and lit a few incents. The final thing was to straighten the room up. She talked to him while he cleaned up. As they talked, and she confessed her love to him he realized he couldn't approach Lisa. Danika needed him just as bad as he needed Lisa. Here he was talking about how she left him for dead and he was getting ready to leave her, what kind of hypocritical shit was that?

De'Kari

By the time he finished cleaning the room she was finished with her third bath and was starting her shower water. The entire room was smelling like her pomegranate mango body wash.

Voorheeze decided to pick up the phone, he hit Batman first.

"Aw shit! They done let my mothafuck'n nigga out!" Batman yelled into the receiver recognizing the number on his caller I.D.

"Yeah and I had to hit you and let you know. We need to meet up." Voorheeze didn't need to say no more. They were Batman and Robin, Left and right arm.

"No doubt same Bat time." Batman told him.

"Same Bat channel" with that response he hung up the phone. Whenever they needed to discuss some shit it was always at Texas Roadhouse. Always at the same time.

He knew it was late, but he still felt he should call his mom and leave a message to let her know that he was home, so she could stop worrying. He waited while it rang. Danika just stepped out of the shower. Just when he thought the voicemail was going to pick up his mom answered.

"Hello?" she barely managed to say through the tears.

"Mom, what's wrong?" Immediately he was on alarm.

"LaMont! Oh my God! My baby! Nooo Nooo! She was hysterical. Now he was really ready to go. "Mama what's wrong?!"

"My baby LaMont! They took my baby! They took him" She shouted and started crying some more.

What the fuck did she mean they took her baby. Who took her baby? A flame ignited in his mind as revelation of what she was saying hit him. Somebody had the fucking audacity to touch his brother! His big brother!

"What? Who? When?" He was irate and yelling at her now. He only got more pissed off. When she didn't answer him. "Mama! Mama! What you mean they took him? Mama! Where the hell is my brother!" He yelled at the top of his lungs trynna get through to her over all her crying.

"Dead! Your brother is dead!" She cried out.

Voorheeze dropped the phone as if it had burnt him. He was stunned silent. He couldn't have heard her correctly. His breath got caught in his throat. His chest felt like it was caving in. Danika was saying something, but he couldn't hear her. His older brother, the nigga he looked up to and always competed with, only cause secretly he always wanted to be just like him, was gone.

He picked the phone back up off the floor. The sweet smell of the body wash Danika used was now making him nauseous. When he put the phone back to his ear, Mama was still crying.

Gorillaz in the Bay 2

"Mama?" Hearing the pain in her voice was crushing his heart.

"Why God why..?" She cried over and over.

"Mama I'm on my way!" He couldn't stay on the phone no more, he had to hang up.

For a minute he just sat there trying to wrap his head around it. Did his brother really get killed? He reached for the bottled of Don Julio that he kept by the bed and took a long drink. Danika sat down next to him and put her arm around him.

"What's wrong baby? She asked him in her angelic voice.

"Somebody killed my brother." Hearing the words come out of his own mouth made something snap inside of him.

He broke her embrace, walked to the walk-in closet and removed the bullet proof vest. The streets were about to rain blood. He wasn't about to shed tears, he was about to shed blood! After he got dressed and put his vest on, he kissed Danika and sped to San Jose.

When he arrived, he could hear his mother's cries through the door. The night chill giving him goose bumps felt like an omen. His little sister answered the door. When she saw her protector, she fell into his arms. Her tears were knife slashes in his armor of toughness, she was his everything. To know she felt pain made everything else obsolete.

"I love you Brother." She whispered as they walked into the apartment. Voorheeze sat on one side of his mother. French Tip sat on the other.

"It's going to be okay Mama." He put his arms around her.

SMACK!

She slapped the living shit out of him. Voorheeze was shocked like a mothafucka.

"It's your fault! You got my baby into this mess!" while screaming she continued slapping him. He just sat there. "You and your big shot fucking dreams. You got my son killed! I fucking hate you! LaMont I hate you! Get the fuck out of my house!" She was beyond hysterical.

"Mama, I'm…" He tried to get out some words of sorrow.

"Get out! Get out of my fucking house!" The way she was shaking he thought she would have some type of breakdown. French Tip was starting to get angry. She couldn't believe her mom. LaMont was always the black sheep and outcast of the family. Their mom always treated LaMont like shit. It wasn't his fault though. They all knew what they were doing. Shit she used to be in the streets herself so how could her mom blame her brother. Just when French Tip was about to say something, Voorheeze stood up. With a heavy heart, he walked to the door.

"I'm sorry Brother" French told him as he opened the door.

De'Kari

"It's ok, Booger." He gave her a hug and a kiss and walked out. Voorheeze neva in his life felt so much like shit. He was fucking hurt too. Shit, his big brother was gone. At that moment he felt like the little lost boy who just wanted his mother's love but didn't get it.

**** **N. D.** ****

(A week later)

No one had heard from Voorheeze in days. The way their mom talked to him that night didn't sit right with French Tip. She understood his pain because she witnessed the abuse and neglect he constantly received all while they were growing up. No one understood her brother like her. He may have played the tough role, but French Tip remembered too well how not feeling a mother's love affected her She remembered the violent cries and outbursts her brother displayed when he would feel rejected by his mother and when he would see a mother loving her son in public.

All of this was why French Tip was parked outside of her brother's house. She had just pulled up. She sat debating on whether or not she was making the right choice being here. Clearly, he didn't want to be bothered. Her brother prided himself on safety and security. He thought no one knew where he lived, but he had taught her. She knew all the tricks because she knew how he thought. She loved her brother unconditionally. No one else may have known but she knew he had a drug problem. She already lost one brother she couldn't lose the other. She wiped her tears away and finally climbed out of her car.

She knew that he neva parked a car in the driveway so not seeing one now didn't alarm her. Her brother always told her that if you parked your car in the driveway, niggaz could tell when you were home. She walked up to the porch and rang the doorbell. She could hear the doorbell ring through the door. Moments passed with no answer. She rang it again. Out of respect for the lady of the house, she rang the doorbell a third time. When no one answered this time, she said, "Fuck privacy," went to her purse, and pulled out the key she had made.

French Tip walked into the house as if it were hers. The alarm control panel didn't even make her flinch. That was how well she knew her brother. She punched in the four numbers on the keypad. 02,11,04,28. Alarm disabled read across the screen. He always used his birthday 02-11 as well as someone else's birthday 04-28. She just neva knew who that person was. But it was always his passcode.

Gorillaz in the Bay 2

The air inside the house was too stale for anyone to be here. But she would check anyway. She had to know that her brother was okay. She turned on the light in the front room. From what she could tell everything was in order. The only weird thing she noticed, there were a few empty picture frames spread out along the family room. She made her way to the master bedroom. The bed was untouched. Again, she noticed the empty frames. One in particular caught her attention. It was a selfie taken of her brother. In the picture he had his arm out like it was wrapped around someone and his face was turned like he was kissing that person. But no one was in the picture with him. There was stenciling across the picture "Me and Danika".

"What the fuck is going on?" French tip wondered as she continued to look around.

Inside the walk-in closet his stuff was on the left. The right was full of women's clothes. She took a closer look at the clothes and noticed that everything was brand new with the tags still on. Not one piece of clothing had been worn. She was puzzled. Inside the bathroom was a his and hers sink. Once again French Tip noticed that all of her stuff was brand new, Not even the toothbrush had been used.

She made her way back to the room. Something on the bed caught her attention. She got closer and noticed there was a polaroid on the pillow. She picked up the polaroid and read the words "DANIKA" sewn into the pillows. When she looked at the photo she gasped. It was a picture of Lisa, she was in the parking lot of her job. The picture was taken from across the street with a high-resolution camera. She was smiling while talking on her cell phone as she appeared to be getting into her car.

French sat on the bed confused, why would a picture of Lisa be laid out on Danika's pillow. Then she thought about all the empty picture frames. The picture of Voorheeze acting like he was holding and kissing somebody who wasn't there. As a light began to go off in her head, she tried desperately to erase the thought. But the facts were there all around her. Then she thought how no one had ever met Danika. Every time there was a function or something, Danika just happened to be sick or had something else to do.

"God damn!" French Tip said out loud to herself. "She doesn't exist. Could Danika be Lisa?" She asked herself.

Voorheeze had been in love with Lisa for so long and loved her so hard that he had to have her anyway he could. He knew that as long as he lived the life that he lived, that he could neva have her. He was in too deep to leave the life that he led.

Something inside of him snapped. He was delusional. His mind created Danika out of what he always envisioned Lisa to be like. That night at Texas Roadhouse with Batman, the hostess was the spitting image of Lisa and with the added stress that he was under, that was the straw that broke the camel's back.

French Tip placed the picture back where it was and with tears rolling down her cheeks she stood up and walked out. She had to find her brother before something happened. He needed help. All this time her brother had been there for everybody. He has always been the back bone of the family; the glue to hold everyone together. But he was being eaten from the inside out. He needed help, and no one was there to help him. No one ever knew he needed help.

LaMont was always the smart one, the strong one. She made it to the car and called her brother, but he didn't answer. The overcast clouds and cold gloomy night matched her mood. He had always been there for her whenever she needed him. Now he needed her, and she was going to be there for her brother!

**** N. D. ****

Special Agent Greer has been with the Drug Enforcement Agency for nearly ten years now. She'd busted her ass for countless hours sacrificing any hopes of a personal life or a sense of peace. She was a woman driven. A woman with a purpose. Honor and pride were not her motivation. Revenge and vendetta were the fuel that drove her closer and closer to her goal.

As Agent Greer rode the elevator down to the lobby. She thought back to the years she'd lost. The countless nights of pain and agony from a broken heart. Many of those nights she cried out to God to heal her from her severe pain and take it all away. But God didn't answer. The answers to her prayers were determination and vengeance.

She couldn't believe the cruel joke that life just played on her. It was like a scene out of Macbeth. For nearly a year now she had been building not only the biggest case of her career, but the most important fight of her life. She compiled the necessary evidence after having to literally beg her supervisor to allow her to pursue the case. Since no one had heard of this particular group at the time, that task was very difficult. In the end, her supervisor gave in and said ok to a brief surveillance detail which quickly paid off.

Within a couple months of work, Agent Greer was ready to bring down her target with ease. But she didn't want to just stop there. She wanted the entire organization and felt she could get enough evidence on the entire group with the same relative ease as she compiled the evidence against her initial target. It was going slower than her initial investigation, but she was gathering what she needed. Diligently she worked, pushing herself to the limit and taking necessary risks.

Then life's cruel joke!

Finally, Agent Greer had gathered enough evidence on her target and his top lieutenants. From experience she knew that she would be able to flip some of them and use that as a leverage to bring down the rest. Greer knew his little brother was involved, that much she was sure of. She was shocked to learn that somehow, they had gotten their little sister involved as well. She would go down with the rest. She refused to allow anyone to see any of her evidence. She only gave her Boss enough to give him reason to grant all her request.

This was going to be big! Huge! Bigger than those Nutt Case guys or that A-Team! This organization was larger than those and far more dangerous and she brought them down single-handedly.

"Then this asshole up and gets himself killed!" She thought to herself.

This brought a halt to all of her hard work. She wasn't a quitter though. She had learned a lot over the years. Once she learned of his death, she rounded up some of his associates and affiliates and executed search and seizure warrants on all of his dope houses and stash spots. She did not want to be denied, but she was. His boys were rounded up with relative ease. However, one by one teams executed warrants on empty houses. Nine houses and eighty-five agents later and they didn't find a single gram of narcotics and not one solitary bullet! Not even so much as a food stamp. She was humiliated. All of her hard work down the drain.

How in the hell was it possible she wondered as she stepped off of the elevator into the lobby? A tear slowly fell down her cheek. She was placed on unpaid leave for four weeks while the department assessed what happened.

As Agent Tieka Greer walked through the doors of the downtown federal building, she couldn't help but to notice how gloomy the weather was. For days now, the Bay Area skies were dark and gloomy. Signs that it was going to be a very ugly winter. A reflection of her mood. To make matters worse, a construction crew prevented parking anywhere near the building, so she was forced to park inside of a high-priced parking garage a few blocks over. Lost in her thoughts the tears fell effortlessly.

About fifteen minutes later Special Agent Tieka Greer finally made it to her car. Inside she finally lost all resolve and cried like a baby. All of her emotions; pain, heartache, frustration, despair, they all came rushing to the surface at once. So, lost in her sorrow, she didn't see the lone dark figure arise from her back seat.

De'Kari

"What's up Tieka?" The sound of the voice startled her. She looked in the rearview mirror just as the piano wire was pulled around her throat.

It couldn't be! Tieka opened her mouth to scream but the piano wire biting into her throat was preventing it.

"You's a mothafuck'n Fed! Fucking D.E.A." He growled into her ear as he pulled the wire tighter slicing into her skin.

Tieka fought desperately to get free. Panic and fear seized her little body. Her lungs burned and smoldered as they screamed for oxygen. She looked back into the face of her assailant. How could it be possible. She thought maybe the fright had her seeing things, but that wasn't the case. She knew those devilish eyes intimately; eyes she once loved and adored. He knew the thoughts going on in her mind, but he refused to give her the pleasure of answering any of the questions. Instead, he continued to squeeze and pull the wire with all his might. Her struggles became more frantic and more desperate as life began to leave her. Her hands clawed at the wire urgently trying to free herself; her nails tearing her skin. All to no avail. The vein on the side of her forehead popped out. Tieka knew that it was over. She knew that her fears were becoming reality. She would die at his hands. "*Love was a mothafucka!*" Her last thought before death snatched her.

Even after she stopped fighting and her body went limp, he continued to hold the wire tightly wrapped around her neck.

"Fucking cockroach tried to fuck him over." He thought.

After he was satisfied that she was truly dead, he stepped out of the car and walked off blending into the murky day.

**** **N. D.** ****
(A Week later)

Voorheeze sat in his car reflecting on everything. The past year had been one hell of a year. Jr., Sauce, J. Spitz, Drew and T'Rida, had all been taken. That was way too many losses. While he was away he did a lot of thinking. He believed he figured out what was going on. There was unfinished business and there was a score to settle.

No-one had seen Voorheeze since that night at his mother's. But they knew he would show up, that's why everyone sat in the church waiting for him.

Voorheeze zeroed-in on Scoot's verse:

/ *This morning the judge gave my nigga 20 / and yesterday we buried my little nigga a few months before he turned 20 / I could cry but I done see plenty / I lost my mama and grandma in less than sixty days / Thangs shity /*

220

Gorillaz in the Bay 2

He opened his bottle of Remy to take another gulp out of the bottle. It was time to get shit over with. He had a score to settle. While he was away, he did a lot of thinking. He believed he figured out what was going on. No one double-checked, there was still unfinished business.

BOCCA! As he bent own to pick up the top to the bottle of Remy Martin the passenger window exploded.

BOOM! BOOM! BOOM! He let his Dragon speak.

He quickly opened the door and dove out of the car. He didn't want to be boxed in the fuck'n car! As he made his way around the car, he didn't see anyone. All of a sudden…

BOC! BOC!

A bullet flew by his head!

BOOM! BOOM!

Guaranteed he's dead.

BOOM! BOOM! BOOM! Voorheeze let both Dragons breathe.

"You can't kill me Bitch! Bitch I knock shit down! I don't get knocked down!" Voorheeze was fuming. He was ready to kill the devil. Mothafuckas tried to steal him on the day he was burying his brother! Fuck that!

Everything happened so fast. Both bodies were laying on the ground. Voorheeze was panting heavy like a rabid dog as he stood over the bodies. His senses were on high alert as the blood and adrenaline raced through his veins.

Suddenly he felt the hairs on the back of his neck stand up. He'd been in the game too long to ignore his instincts. Even as he turned around he could sense that it was too late; this time he had got caught slipping. Time stood still. Even the wind had ceased blowing. The image in front of him made him laugh. Unfortunately, his hunch about unfinished business was correct, Sutton wasn't dead!

All of the shots Sutton took from Keak that night in Oakland, he took in the chest all except one that grazed his cheek. The blood that Keak saw wasn't from a shot to the face like he had thought, all the shots went to his chest. Or at least into the vest he was wearing. As a result of the gunshots, Sutton suffered a cracked sternum and four broken ribs, but he was alive.

Taata! Taaat! Taaat! Taaat! Taaat! Taaat!

The force of the bullets slamming into Voorheeze, knocked him off of his feet!

The door to the Church flew open! Batman came storming out of the Church just as Sutton let the Mack II sing. Rage engulfed him as he saw the bullets drill their way into his brother.

BOOM! BOOM!

De'Kari

The first missile ripped through Sutton's shoulder causing him to stumble sideways. The second found its mark in his upper torso.

Batman wasn't done, he continued squeezing without remorse. Batman stood over Sutton's bullet riddled body.

Sutton coughed up some blood and spit. He looked up at Batman, "Young Nigga Mafia Bitch!"

BOOM! Batman shot one straight to the head.

Batman looked over at his brother. He was coughing on the ground. Blood coming out of his mouth. Batman couldn't believe it. His brother had needed him, but he was too late. Mama B was screaming her head off. French Tip had made her way over and was on the ground holding her brother's head in her lap. Tears cascading down her face and falling onto him.

"Ssh! Ssh! It's okay brother." She was telling him, but she knew it wasn't. Her words were only words of comfort.

"I.. I... I..." Voorheeze kept trying to tell her something but every time he tried, he coughed up blood.

The onlookers thought to themselves, "Such a tragedy for a mother to lose both sons in one week." Those who had the courage mumbled words about the expectations of Street Life. Something about living by the gun and dying by the gun. They wouldn't dare say it loud enough for Mama B to hear it.

The distant ambulance sirens were getting closer now. French Tip was singing a soft song to her brother trying to soothe his pain. Hoping, against all, that God wouldn't take her brother away from her. She thought about the revelations she just discovered at her brother's house.

"He needed help, Father he didn't need this!" She cried with her head to the sky.

His whole body felt hot, like fire. He didn't know how many times he had been shot but this time was different from the first time. It burned, and it was hard for him to breathe. It felt like his lungs were full of water. He kept coughing and choking. Voorheeze could hear his mom's cries and screams. He could hear his sister singing to him. Damn he loved his little sister! He was gonna miss her.

Then she appeared! She was looking so heavenly, smiling with her angelic face. He wanted to tell her how he felt and how much he loved her, but he couldn't. He tried to say her name. He needed his last words to be her name. The name of his one and only true love...

"Lisa!"

But he didn't have to, she knew. She has always known. She assured him that she loved him too. Now he could let go. He was tired anyway, so tired. Jason Voorheeze needed to rest so he closed his eyes.

Gorillaz in the Bay 2

The Saga Continues…
Gorillas in the Bay 3
Coming Soon

De'Kari

Submission Guideline

Submit the first three chapters of your completed manuscript to ldpsubmissions@gmail.com, subject line: Your book's title. The manuscript must be in a .doc file and sent as an attachment. Document should be in Times New Roman, double spaced and in size 12 font. Also, provide your synopsis and full contact information. If sending multiple submissions, they must each be in a separate email.

Have a story but no way to send it electronically? You can still submit to LDP/Ca$h Presents. Send in the first three chapters, written or typed, of your completed manuscript to:

LDP: Submissions Dept
Po Box 870494
Mesquite, Tx 75187

DO NOT send original manuscript. Must be a duplicate.

Provide your synopsis and a cover letter containing your full contact information.

Thanks for considering LDP and Ca$h Presents.

Gorillaz in the Bay 2

Coming Soon from Lock Down Publications/Ca$h Presents

BOW DOWN TO MY GANGSTA

By **Ca$h**

TORN BETWEEN TWO

By **Coffee**

BLOOD STAINS OF A SHOTTA **III**

By **Jamaica**

STEADY MOBBIN **III**

By **Marcellus Allen**

BLOOD OF A BOSS **V**

By **Askari**

LOYAL TO THE GAME **IV**

LIFE OF SIN II

By **T.J. & Jelissa**

A DOPEBOY'S PRAYER **II**

By **Eddie "Wolf" Lee**

IF LOVING YOU IS WRONG... **III**

LOVE ME EVEN WHEN IT HURTS **II**

By **Jelissa**

TRUE SAVAGE **VII**

By **Chris Green**

BLAST FOR ME **III**

A BRONX TALE III

DUFFLE BAG CARTEL III

By **Ghost**

ADDICTIED TO THE DRAMA **III**

By **Jamila Mathis**

LIPSTICK KILLAH **III**

Mimi

WHAT BAD BITCHES DO **III**

De'Kari

A HUSTLER'S DECEIT 3

KILL ZONE **II**

By **Aryanna**

THE COST OF LOYALTY **II**

By **Kweli**

SHE FELL IN LOVE WITH A REAL ONE **II**

By **Tamara Butler**

RENEGADE BOYS **III**

By **Meesha**

CORRUPTED BY A GANGSTA **IV**

By **Destiny Skai**

A GANGSTER'S CODE **III**

By **J-Blunt**

KING OF NEW YORK IV

RISE TO POWER III

By **T.J. Edwards**

GORILLAZ IN THE BAY III

De'Kari

THE STREETS ARE CALLING II

Duquie Wilson

KINGPIN KILLAZ III

STREET KINGS 2

Hood Rich

STEADY MOBBIN' **III**

Marcellus Allen

SINS OF A HUSTLA II

ASAD

TRIGGADALE II

Elijah R. Freeman

MARRIED TO A BOSS II

By Destiny Skai & Chris Green

KINGS OF THE GAME II

Gorillaz in the Bay 2
Playa Ray

227

De'Kari

WHEN THE STREETS CLAP BACK I & II III

By **Jibril Williams**

A DISTINGUISHED THUG STOLE MY HEART I II & III

LOVE SHOULDN'T HURT I II III

RENEGADE BOYS I & II

By **Meesha**

A GANGSTER'S CODE I &, II III

By J-Blunt

PUSH IT TO THE LIMIT

By **Bre' Hayes**

BLOOD OF A BOSS **I, II, III & IV**

By **Askari**

THE STREETS BLEED MURDER **I, II & III**

THE HEART OF A GANGSTA I II& III

By **Jerry Jackson**

CUM FOR ME

CUM FOR ME 2

CUM FOR ME 3

CUM FOR ME 4

An **LDP Erotica Collaboration**

BRIDE OF A HUSTLA **I II & II**

THE FETTI GIRLS **I, II& III**

CORRUPTED BY A GANGSTA I, II & III

By **Destiny Skai**

WHEN A GOOD GIRL GOES BAD

By **Adrienne**

A GANGSTER'S REVENGE **I II III & IV**

THE BOSS MAN'S DAUGHTERS

THE BOSS MAN'S DAUGHTERS II

THE BOSSMAN'S DAUGHTERS III

THE BOSSMAN'S DAUGHTERS IV

THE BOSS MAN'S DAUGHTERS **V**

Gorillaz in the Bay 2

A SAVAGE LOVE **I & II**

BAE BELONGS TO ME

A HUSTLER'S DECEIT I, II, III

WHAT BAD BITCHES DO I, II

By **Aryanna**

A KINGPIN'S AMBITON

A KINGPIN'S AMBITION **II**

I MURDER FOR THE DOUGH

By **Ambitious**

TRUE SAVAGE

TRUE SAVAGE II

TRUE SAVAGE **III**

TRUE SAVAGE **IV**

TRUE SAVAGE **V**

TRUE SAVAGE **VI**

By **Chris Green**

A DOPEBOY'S PRAYER

By **Eddie "Wolf" Lee**

THE KING CARTEL **I, II & III**

By **Frank Gresham**

THESE NIGGAS AIN'T LOYAL **I, II & III**

By **Nikki Tee**

GANGSTA SHYT **I II &III**

By **CATO**

THE ULTIMATE BETRAYAL

By **Phoenix**

BOSS'N UP **I , II & III**

By **Royal Nicole**

I LOVE YOU TO DEATH

By **Destiny J**

I RIDE FOR MY HITTA

I STILL RIDE FOR MY HITTA

De'Kari
By **Misty Holt**

LOVE & CHASIN' PAPER

By **Qay Crockett**

TO DIE IN VAIN

SINS OF A HUSTLA

By **ASAD**

BROOKLYN HUSTLAZ

By **Boogsy Morina**

BROOKLYN ON LOCK I & II

By **Sonovia**

GANGSTA CITY

By **Teddy Duke**

A DRUG KING AND HIS DIAMOND I & II III

A DOPEMAN'S RICHES

HER MAN, MINE'S TOO I, II

CASH MONEY HO'S

By Nicole Goosby

TRAPHOUSE KING **I II & III**

KINGPIN KILLAZ

STREET KINGS

By **Hood Rich**

LIPSTICK KILLAH **I, II**

CRIME OF PASSION I & II

By **Mimi**

STEADY MOBBN' **I, II**

By **Marcellus Allen**

WHO SHOT YA **I, II**

Renta

GORILLAZ IN THE BAY **I II**

DE'KARI

TRIGGADALE

Elijah R. Freeman

230

Gorillaz in the Bay 2

GOD BLESS THE TRAPPERS I, II, III

THESE SCANDALOUS STREETS I, II, III

FEAR MY GANGSTA I, II, III

THESE STREETS DON'T LOVE NOBODY I, II

BURY ME A G I, II, III, IV, V

A GANGSTA'S EMPIRE I, II, III

Tranay Adams

THE STREETS ARE CALLING

Duquie Wilson

MARRIED TO A BOSS…

By Destiny Skai & Chris Green

KINGS OF THE GAME II

Playa Ray

De'Kari

Gorillaz in the Bay 2

www.ingramcontent.com/pod-product-compliance
Lightning Source LLC
Chambersburg PA
CBHW071324250626
47159CB00004B/1455